# Full Steam Ahead

Tom couldn't get Sophie out of his mind. He thought of her arse as she'd stretched out over the green baize of the card table. And the rude words she'd said. Forget haunted houses, a pair of gorgeous thighs was spooking him. Sophie wanted him to do her. That's what she had said. Jesus H Christ! And now he was on his way to her cabin. He knew it was a bad idea; he knew it in his head, his gut, his very soul, but his balls ached and his cock was shouting, 'Why not? You deserve it!' There was no way back.

# Full Steam Ahead

## TABITHA FLYTE

Black Lace novels contain sexual fantasies.
In real life, make sure you practise safe sex.

First published in 2001 by
Black Lace
Thames Wharf Studios,
Rainville Road, London W6 9HA

Copyright © Tabitha Flyte 2001

The right of Tabitha Flyte to be identified as the Author
of this Work has been asserted by her in accordance
with the Copyright, Designs and Patents Act 1988.

Typeset by SetSystems Ltd, Saffron Walden, Essex
Printed and bound by Mackays of Chatham PLC

ISBN 0 352 33637 4

# Prologue

*T*he Captain studied the computer screen. The ship was quiet and would stay that way for the next couple of hours. People do not rush to get out of bed on a cruise. Out through the portholes, the turquoise Caribbean was lapping peaceably as far the horizon. The sky was a promising light blue and the weather forecast did not predict any trouble.

He wished he could see his reflection in the computer screen. But he knew what extraordinary vision would shine back at him. Men of a certain age tend to trade off looks for power – with the Captain, however, there had been no such trade-off; he had retained both and more. He looked proudly at his shiny boots. He doubted that he had ever in his whole life seen boots as perfectly shiny as his were then, under the table in the internet café on the illustrious *Prince Albert* – a ship named after his own heart. Or thereabouts.

His priority that morning was to sort out the latest staff crisis: a female croupier had run off with a newly-wed passenger. One of his crew had blushingly reported that the pair had been 'shagging like bunnies' in the boiler room. Her legs were wrapped around his back and she was, as the sailor put it, 'squealing like a stuck pig'. Apparently, the newly-wed's trousers were down by his knees, he had a mole on his left buttock and he was still licking the woman's ears as the valiant sailor tried to separate them.

He had made the request for a replacement at 20.00 hours and it was now 05.00 hours. Staff at the ship's HQ had emailed the photo and CV of the candidate as quickly as they could.

To his amazement, it was someone the Captain already knew. Well, OK, he didn't know her exactly, but he knew of her. Everyone did. Sophie Hemingway was one of the best croupiers in the Caribbean; a woman with more balls than the average sailor. Just the name, Sophie Hemingway, was enough to send shivers down his body, his spine and up his cock. Sophie Hemingway – the woman who gave promiscuity a good name. Surely it wasn't pure chance that she wanted to work aboard his beloved *Prince Albert*?

She was a handful, old Sophie, and not just temperamentally. She had lovely round satsuma-like breasts that put him in mind of a belly dancer he used to know when he cruised around the Aegean. She had the most exquisite skin. It looked like she rubbed baby oil into it every few minutes. The Captain allowed himself the liberty of imagining himself doing the same, and then told himself, not now, you can fantasise about this later. He didn't get to be a Captain of a cruise ship by falling for anyone.

What reason could she possibly have for applying? The *Prince Albert* was the first boat to combine hardcore gambling and luxury holidays in the Caribbean, and from the start it was the target of Gamblers Anonymous. Before the *Prince Albert*, the only alternative for the risk-inclined was the tired day-trip casino boats that operated 150 metres out in international waters. But, after a review in the travel supplement of a Sunday broadsheet called the *Albert* 'a fantasy fulfiller', and 'the perfect start to married life', the honeymooners began to arrive. Now only about half of the passengers were gamblers – the other half were newly-weds – which meant that while one set of passengers spent the week in a daze of blissful

2

contentment, the other half (the honeymooners) rowed and fought over the expense.

The Captain considered long and hard why a woman like Sophie Hemingway wanted to board the *Prince Albert*. Only one answer seemed to fit; only one idea came back ringing relentless and true.

He emailed a quick message back to base saying that he was delighted with the new appointment. Then, back in the privacy of his quarters, he rubbed his hands together. He always looked forward to breaking the new girls in.

# Chapter One

*T*hey say women go for different men at different times of the month: at ovulation, the more feminine type and during other times, the more macho guys. Well, thought Sophie, this guy was so gorgeous, so universally perfect, that he could have had anyone, anywhere, at any time of the cycle.

This was her first time on the *Prince Albert* but it was her twelfth year working on the Caribbean cruise ships. And Sophie had also decided that this was going to be the last. After this she was going to be free, forever. No more noisy casinos, no more putting up with gamblers who asked her to 'be lucky' or to give them a smile – 'Cheer up, it may never happen' – or to fetch a manager or to show them the way to the restrooms. They would ask her to wipe their stupid arses, if they thought they could get away with it. This would be the last time she would have to face off dumb players who didn't know their dice from their craps; who didn't know their maths from their English; who didn't think she was better than a glorified waitress, a glorified hostess – better than all of them.

And in front of her stood the guy who was going to help her bring that about.

He was tall with tousled blond hair, just like her

connection had told her – but her connection hadn't told her how handsome he was. His eyes were twinkling. He had that sort of face – that embarrassing sort of face – that makes you red just to look at it. He had pleasant features, a nice but not overfull mouth, and his teeth were (unusual for a Brit) white and even.

'Hemingway, I presume,' he said, stepping out from the shadows of the top deck.

'Please, call me Sophie.'

Even out there, on the deck with only the stars to illuminate them, she saw that his eyes were black, too dark for his fair hair, really, but then it wasn't so much that the pupils were dark, but that the area around them was shadowed. This made him look troubled, as though not only had he *seen* the dark side but he regularly made excursions there.

'You must be Mick Salem,' she said. And they shook hands with the sea breeze whistling through their clothes and caressing their faces. He had big hands. Sophie was pleased – forget big feet or big noses, hand-span is the place to look for those kinds of clues.

'I thought you were going to be a man,' he said.

'Are you disappointed?'

He grinned. 'Makes no odds as long as you keep your cool.'

'Of course I can. You can trust me.'

'I never usually trust people who say that.'

He lit a cigarette, and the flame bathed his face in a warm orange glow. It was a lovely face. Sophie wanted to cup his cheeks in her hands and give him a kiss, so relieved was she that this was to be her partner – the Clyde to her Bonnie. If she was really going to be a Robin Hood of the high seas then this was the perfect Maid Marion.

'So, you are on for it then?' she asked.

'No problem.'

'Have you done anything like this before?'

'Like this?'

'You know . . .' (Did she have to spell it out for him?)

'This kind of scam,' she whispered urgently. Then she realised that not only were his eyes a bizarre coffee colour, but they were fringed with spiky black lashes – more fitting a young girl than a man in his (at a guess) early thirties.

'Yes. But never on a ship, never for this amount of money, and never –' he met her gaze with a quizzical smile '– with strangers. We need two other people, right? The inspector and the cashier?'

'I'm working on it,' said Sophie, with more bravado than was appropriate, although she had picked out the candidates who were most likely to assist.

'I'll leave it to you then.' The casual yet hopeful way he said it made Sophie melt.

Maybe she could kill two birds with one stone on this trip after all. Just because she was here for money didn't mean she couldn't have a bit of fun as well. There was no reason she couldn't have her scam and eat it. All work and no play makes Sophie a very pissed-off girl. And he was gorgeous. She moved towards him, lips slightly open, eyes slightly shut.

'I'll be off, then,' he said abruptly.

'Oh. Aren't you free now?'

'No.'

'You're very expensive?' she said, and then when she saw his face, she added, 'That was a joke by the way.'

'Oh,' he said.

She felt put out by his manner. 'I think we should discuss things.'

'What's the hurry?' he said, and she resented him for making her look over-zealous.

She touched his sleeve. She ran her fingers up the Indian cotton. She was well practised in the art of seduction. She found the tender spot of the inside of his wrist. 'Since we are working together, we might as well be friends.'

'I would like that,' he said, but his tone belied the words. 'I really would ... but ... you know it's best we are not seen together. As far as everyone else is

7

concerned, you are just another croupier and I'm just another passenger.'

'We will just have to meet privately.' Persistence was Sophie's middle name. Not that she usually *had* to be persistent. Most people succumbed as soon as they knew what she was offering. 'How can I put this? It's a custom of mine to break rule seventeen on my first night aboard.'

'Rule seventeen?' He grinned again.

'The one about not fraternising with the passengers.'

'You're quite the rebel, aren't you?'

She raised her eyebrows. 'Maybe . . . it depends on the cause.'

'Not tonight,' he said simply, 'I don't want to . . . to chat tonight.'

'How about tomorrow?'

'How about the day after?'

'What's wrong with tomorrow?'

'Nothing. Just . . . all right, tomorrow it is.'

'I look forward to it.'

'Hmm,' he responded, ambiguously. He backed against the sides. It was so dark that when he was more than a foot from her, he almost ceased to exist. Below them, the lifeboats flapped gently against the ship's hull. It was a romantic setting – better than romantic, even. Sophie leaned forward again, but this time she kissed the side of his mouth, that sensitive space where the upper and the lower lip met and curved. She let her mouth linger over there for a time, just long enough for her breath to join with his, and for the ache in her loins to grow strong.

He pulled back.

'We're here for the money,' he persisted, 'that's all.'

'That's all,' she agreed, but she felt a pinch of disappointment as she looked out on to the black horizon.

# Chapter Two

$A$lthough it was past midnight by the time they had finished their meeting, Mick went to the outdoor pool. On every cruise, there are the people who take advantage of the wealth of sports activities and there are the people who take advantage of the heaving buffet tables and six-course meals. Mick, however, tried to do both.

Swimming was another of the many things he was good at. He liked diving best; he loved soaring off the board, and the way he hit the water like a knife. Yet, for a man so at ease in the water, it was remarkable how ill at ease he was aboard the *Prince Albert*. It was his first time on a cruise and Mick, a landlubber on the quiet, did not like ship life one bit. He had nightmares about sinking and drowning, and he couldn't wait until this job was over. Of course, his role was the easy one; he knew that. He just had to gamble and keep quiet. It was Sophie who had the hard job, not only cheating the house, but also convincing the others to cheat as well.

Mick was surprised at Sophie. For a start she was as cute as a button, which was *definitely* not what he had expected. In his experience, the kind of people who usually went in for cheating the house (well, what other word for it was there?) were slimy, greasy con men with oiled moustaches and flint eyes. She was very different. Plus, she had nice breasts. Gorgeous things, poking at him, capped with those little erect nipples. He remembered her breath as she kissed him and her faint natural scent. She was certainly not the usual scam-merchant; she was head and shoulders (tits and thighs) above the rest.

He had to think of something else, otherwise he would get a hard-on. As he thrust through the water, he resolved that he wouldn't get involved with her, no way. Women always wanted more, more than he was prepared to give. That's why he focused his attention on the married women. They were just looking for fun, 'a laugh', and there was never any heavy stuff. You would be surprised at the amount of honeymooners who were, as he put it, 'in two minds'. And Mick had only to work on one of those minds and, hey presto, they were his. There was always someone wanting to make the 'Romantic Tour' that little bit more memorable. And then, in the three weeks he had been on board, he had also discovered there was the other kind of passenger – the valiant jilted. Women who ended up on their honeymoon alone, whether it was because the wedding had been cancelled – the altar-victims – or new hubby was too busy to come. These were the other women who came on to Mick regularly. They would pair up with anyone and, although Mick was not proud of it, he had been known to take advantage of their vulnerability.

A woman slipped out of her towel and slid gracefully into the deep end. She was watching him. Mick continued swimming but he lost count of the lengths. The woman swam up close to him. Sometimes, after Mick met women in the pool, he found he couldn't help going off them when he saw them with their clothes on. He imagined it would be like that on a nudist colony. You might fancy them – until you saw them dressed in tennis shorts and stupid T-shirts. (Not that Mick would dream of going to a nudist colony.)

'You swim wonderfully,' she said as they both clung

10

to the end of the pool, breathing heavily. He knew that often women compliment you because they want to be complimented themselves.

'Thank you. You do, too. Fantastic breast . . . stroke.'

He wondered what it would be like to stroke those breasts. What it would be like to free them from their functional costume and to run his hands over them. She gazed at him and it was almost like she knew what he was thinking. Mick wondered what it would be like to suck on her wet nipples.

'Do you like . . . swimming?' she asked, and he knew that she was desperately trying to make conversation, but the words were slipping through her like the water.

He worked his feet off the ground. From the surface he bobbed gracefully, like a swan. But underneath he was paddling like a mad thing.

'Yes.'

'I'm a water sign – Pisces, Scorpio rising,' she murmured. He could see the 'available' sign flashing from her forehead.

He smiled enigmatically, still pulling his legs up. It was good exercise.

'What are you?'

'I'm the ram.' Before he registered her reaction, he ducked down under the surface and held his breath for as long as he could. When he re-emerged she was still there. He slicked back his hair. She thought he was the best-looking man she had ever seen.

'You can hold your breath for a long time,' she said.

He nodded. 'Uh huh.'

'How did you get so good?' she asked.

'Practice.'

'Where?' She was gazing at him so eagerly that he was tempted to shock her, *'between women's legs'*. Instead he said, 'Nowhere special,' and ploughed off. He did butterfly stroke, his weakest, but even so, he could still manage ten lengths with ease and style. He imagined he was a butterfly, a beautiful creature in balance and harmony. Mick did a few more lengths. He loved the way the water suspended his body. He loved the sensation of weight-lessness. In the water, his body was powerful, graceful, and he could almost forget the concerns he had when on dry land. Maybe he was some kind of sea creature. Maybe he hadn't fully evolved.

He felt uneasy thinking about Sophie. They couldn't get involved because involvement was what it would be: entanglement, a woolly mess.

The woman imagined he was doing the butterfly stroke over her, in her bed, his arms strong and sinewy and his legs kicking powerfully. She pictured him coming up for air, the strong neck held high, the concentration etched on his features. Her goggles steamed up.

He stood and nodded at her. She rose out of the water, knowing that she would follow him.

He used to think swimming didn't do much for women. He didn't like the way it broadened their shoulders and thickened their arms. But she was excep-tional. Every part of her seemed to have been skimmed down to a perfect minimum. Later, he discovered that she had a tattoo on her belly. And that she was an unnatural blonde.

# Chapter Three

On the way back from her meeting with Mick, Sophie decided to further explore the *Prince Albert*. Some parts of the ship were out of bounds to entertainment staff but if anyone stopped her, she would pretend to be lost. After all, everyone got lost. The ship was like a rabbit warren, albeit a high-class one. There were six floors, each floor with its own bar and restaurant, but it was easy to mistake the lower second with the upper first. And, as a member of the entertainment staff, Sophie should have been wearing her name badge at all times – three times caught without and you would get thrown off the ship. That was rule number fifteen. Sophie had memorised them all – and broken at least half of them – but she didn't want anyone to know her name yet.

She too thought about the scam. And the money. Especially the money. Money may not buy you love, but then poverty doesn't buy it either. And of course it can buy some serious lovemaking. Sophie thought about Mick. She wondered what it would be like to make love with him. She had a feeling that they were destined to; in fact, she was certain they would.

The guest corridors were thickly carpeted, and the lights were low and flattering. Every few yards there were elaborate fake plants, and even Sophie, who hated anything that artificial, had to admit that these were good. There was a noise coming from one of the rooms, a cooing, craving noise. Sophie hesitated, she knew she should get back, should go to safety, but the sound compelled her to continue almost as strongly as if she were being tugged along by a rope. It was a loud breathing, groaning even, a man's voice and a woman's. She crept forward to have a peep. Surely, she justified, if the door was left that brazenly wide open, so carelessly ajar, then they were virtually inviting passers-by to take a look.

Pink silk Chinese robes adorned with dragons lay discarded on the floor. She took in a silver tray, a bucket of champagne, glasses toppled over, a settee, armchairs and a stereo. But the only thing she really noticed was the couple on the bed: the honeymooners in all their glory. A woman was sitting on top of a man, straddling him with her back towards the door, and he was stretched back. His arms were behind his head, victorious in his defeat.

This was what Sophie loved best about the honeymoon cruises – there was so much love in the air. It made her shiver with longing. Every morning, every evening, she could sense them; she could feel how they made the ship toss about. The cry of the honeymooners was louder than the seagulls. The thought of all those cabins rocking with unbridled lust, swinging to one god, pumping, humping in motion – well, it was too much to take in. She wondered what was behind that next door, and that one, and that.

She was glad to be on board.

She watched as the woman bounced exuberantly on top of the man with the certainty of the just-married. They had signed up to the club, done their duty and now they were enjoying the fruits. Sophie could see the man's balls as they begged higher and higher, the base of his cock taking off. The woman's smooth back was slippery with lotion and there were faint white lines from where a bikini strap had been. The woman bounced harder and harder on the cock. Their sighs were increasing in volume and colour and, as they began reaching a happy crescendo, Sophie could feel her own arousal mounting. Mick had made a deep impression on her – but she wanted him to go deeper.

Imagine if that were her and Mick, yes, her and Mick fucking cheerfully, carelessly, on a bed of dollar notes. She saw herself slipping her fingers down his jeans – he wore them so well – and introducing herself to his cock. He would envelop her in those big arms of his, and then ... let the celebrations begin! No inhibitions, no restraints, and nothing to worry about, only, money, money, money. Throwing their future up in the air, and then rolling on it, rolling in it, happy as two pigs in ... Sophie gasped as she felt a heavy hand come round and cover her mouth. She spun round and found herself face to face, or rather face to chest, with the Captain.

'In my quarters, now,' he hissed, his face thunderous.

The Captain's luxurious quarters made even the best passengers' rooms look squalid. Sophie was jealous. This was exactly how she wanted to live – and she would one day – that was a promise.

'All staff, and that includes entertainment staff, are expected to behave in an exemplary fashion – and that doesn't involve spying on passengers. Do I make myself clear?' He looked her up and down, the way you would look at something in a shop while considering whether to buy it.

'Yes, sir.'

'Did it excite you?'

'Sorry?' Sophie wasn't sure that she had heard right.

'Seeing them, did it arouse you?'

'No, sir,' she said vehemently. 'Of course not.'

'And there are to be no sexual –' he spat the word out '– relations with passengers, either.' He looked like he had decided not to buy.

'Yes, sir. I mean no, sir.'

She kept her head bowed. Spying on the passengers

could get her thrown off the ship. Thrown out before she had even begun to realise her plans. She could only imagine what Mick would say – 'Trust her? Trust a woman? Don't make me laugh!'

'Some members of the crew may take it upon themselves to test the durability of a passenger's marriage. Your predecessor was one of those, but I will not tolerate it. Do you understand?'

'Yes, sir,' said Sophie, wondering if a 'no, sir' was expected in this case.

How did the Captain keep so white and smooth looking? Sophie couldn't help recalling that moment in *An Officer and a Gentleman* when Richard Gere came to the factory and whisked Debra Winger away. Only the Captain was considerably taller than Richard Gere.

He lit a fat cigar. The sermon was over.

'I'll be watching you, Sophie Hemingway. You do understand that you are here on a trial period?'

'I do.'

'And if you do not live up to my very high expectations, I will see to it that you are removed.'

'I understand.'

'What did you come here for, Sophie?'

'The *Prince Albert* has a . . . good reputation.'

'But you were offered a promotion on the *Princess Virginia*. They wanted you to work as an inspector. I looked up your file. There must have been another reason.'

'What do you mean?'

'You could have gone anywhere. What made you choose our . . .' the Captain paused dramatically '. . . humble vessel?'

'I prefer working the floor, where the action is.'

'Is that the only reason?'

Sophie looked at her hands.

'Don't worry. I'll find out.'

The Captain blew smoke into her eyes. He was an ugly-handsome man. Big nosed and shaggy, plain but with a certain something. Maybe it was the definitely real

16

'I've been there' suntan, or maybe it was the uniform, stretching just a little too tight over the chest. He was an arrogant man; the kind of man who irritated her. Nevertheless, Sophie had to act carefully and play the game. She couldn't afford enemies in high places.

'If you give me cause to reprimand you again, I won't be so lenient,' he finished.

'There won't be cause, sir,' she said meekly.

As she hurried back to the door, she noticed a whip hanging on the wall, over a pair of black boots. Turning back, for a last look, she saw a hint of a smile nestle on the Captain's face but, before she could be certain, it had vanished.

# Chapter Four

*T*here was a scurry of last-minute action before Tom turned the wheel. The players' tardiness annoyed him. He thought they were greedy – greedy for money, greedy for shortcuts. And they stuffed themselves with sandwiches, delighted at the free food. Didn't they realise that management knew that a full gambler gambles much more than a hungry one? That the whole place was designed to make them lose? Fools. He felt the same way about the people who gambled as the cook did about the cockroaches, or the crew did about storms. He used to love the challenge, but now he alternately dreaded them or scorned them. Mind you, everything annoyed him recently.

His Jennifer was the most beautiful girl on the ship, in the whole fucking Caribbean probably, and what's more she was all his. She was devoted to him, even if he was as poor as a church mouse. She didn't mind, so she said, but he had a complaint of his own. Christ, couldn't she just let herself go?

Last night, in bed, he had begged her to speak dirty. 'What do you want me to say?' she had asked and, immediately, he knew it was going to turn out badly. 'I don't know,' he had said airily, as though he had only just thought about it, when in fact he was burning with

18

it, desperate for her to say, 'Feel my clit, rub me, take me, fuck me hard.' Jesus, she was so shy. He couldn't even tell if she came or not. He knew he shouldn't get too wound up by these issues, but he couldn't even tell if she liked it or not. When she lay beneath him, his flanks, and he dug his hands squeezing her buttocks, she sighed very slowly and lovingly, but he didn't want to be loved sensibly. He wanted to be fucked senseless. At least give him a sign that he was welcome.

Perhaps if their living quarters were a bit more romantic, a bit more sexual, then she might liven up. It wasn't easy having sex in a room that was below the water line. Maybe, in a different environment, she might be less of a dead fish. She was fantastic, no doubts about it; all the same, it was enough to make a man less confident than he was, have some doubts about himself, and maybe enough to make a man less committed than he was, have wandering thoughts.

The last croupier had left the casino high and dry. He should have been inspecting but then he had been roped in to deal, and now, tonight, they had thrown this new girl at him; so now he was a babysitter as well! At least she was prettier than the last one. Not stunning like his Jennifer, but wide-eyed and eager. Then again, all the girls became prettier once they had spent a few hours abroad; it was like they became reconstituted.

'Shall I?'

Tom let Sophie take his place at the card table. She slid past him and her bottom brushed against his crotch. Wow. He wondered if she had done that on purpose. It was so hard to tell with women. They seemed to give out signs that pointed in all directions. He hoped she might do it again, come close to him and send shivers down his pelvis – just so that he could tell if it was deliberate or not.

He watched as she adeptly dealt the cards. A gaggle of admirers was flocking around. He had heard of Sophie Hemingway. She was known as an accomplished, popular dealer, but probably that was more because of her smooth black hair and her revealing black dresses than the lay of her cards.

All the female croupiers were paid a clothing allowance. The last time Tom heard, it was the sort of allowance you would expect a Hollywood starlet to have, not a card dealer. Sophie's dress looked as if it was worth a few bob. It was a floor-length midnight-blue creation – not that you noticed the dress; you couldn't see the dress for the body. It wasn't just the chips that were well stacked. Tom had to wear a tuxedo and, although the cummerbund was uncomfortable, he couldn't really complain; Jennifer said that it made him look even more handsome.

After the casino closed, Tom asked Sophie to stay behind, to check that everything was all right. Since she had already dealt that evening, the check was little more than a formality. However, Tom was in no hurry to go back to his cabin, and nor was she.

Tom wasn't as interesting as Mick, but to Sophie he was even more attractive, in a 'regular guy' kind of way. As he leaned over the tables his buttocks pushed at his trousers. She wondered what it would be like to take one cheek in each hand and to squeeze. That's all she would do, just squeeze those peaches as he leaned over the table. She knew she was staring and told herself to concentrate. She had worked it out: Tom was the inspector most likely to help them in the scam. One, because he was hard up and, two, because he was hard up *and* engaged to Jennifer, the ship's beautician and a world-class snob.

'Do you see what I'm doing?' he asked earnestly.

'I do; I'm watching very closely.'

'Good.'

His arse was a handful. And if his backside was that beautiful, what did it say about the front? Surely they were two sides of the same coin. Surely his cock would be equally mesmerising. Concentrate, she told herself.

20

'Do you get it?' Tom asked, sweeping his hair back like a sodding movie star.

'I think so; can you show me one more time?' She had been playing and dealing cards since she was knee-high to a grasshopper. She knew every move, every trick in the book and then some, but . . .

He leaned over, and she could feel her pussy moisten just from looking at him, but then he abruptly turned back.

'I thought you had been working on boats for years.'

'I have. Just refresh my memory . . .'

'OK, this is poker,' he said.

Poke me, Sophie thought dreamily. Press me down on this table and poke me. Let me wrap my legs around you, and I'll come all over you.

It was time to go for the kill.

'I bet it's possible to make a lot of money from this.'

'Not really. The idiots plough it all back in. They win one night and then lose the next three. That's how the house always ends up on top.'

Sophie hesitated. 'I don't mean by playing.'

'What do you mean?' He squinted at her, laughing. 'Like the man who broke the bank at Monte Carlo?'

'I mean, syndicates, you know . . . cheating the house.'

He laughed again. It riled her – she wanted to burst his stupid arrogant bubble.

'Don't you think it would work?'

'I don't know anyone who would be foolish enough to try.'

'So, you would never do anything like that?'

'No way!'

'Not even if it were foolproof?'

'It's never foolproof,' he said knowledgeably.

Sophie realised that she wasn't going to get him to change his mind, not this way at least. The scam was proving to be harder than she had thought.

# Chapter Five

The Captain had enjoyed giving his little scolding immensely. As he went through the day's duties, he found it hard to keep his mind on his work. Instead he replayed the events of the afternoon over and over again. He had given Sophie a right dressing down. A right dressing down! He would like to give her a soaping down. He pictured him and her frolicking in the shower. He would be handy with the sponge. Diving in and out all her nooks and crannies. He pictured the foam flying, bubbles bouncing and her legs opening to welcome him in.

The Captain had to search to fill his days, now that the computers did most of the navigation and sailing work. Increasingly his tasks could be reduced to high-class customer relations: one passenger's dog had had to be put down and they had to make arrangements for a burial at sea. Another's husband had inconveniently passed away – the old folk always had heart attacks on the third day – and he had to arrange the helicopter transportation. It was all quite mundane. He preferred to think about the lovely ladies. Sophie fancied him; he was sure of it. He knew what the flush that came up from her neck, the mottled aroused skin on her throat, meant.

She reminded him of a stripper he knew in Casablanca;

all curves and sweet smells. And she looked a little like his fourth wife, an aeroplane walker, who had walked off with a Turkish pilot. Sophie was a naughty girl, a bad girl. He could see it written all over her. He wanted to hold her head to his cock and make her suck, suck, suck for ever. She was a femme fatale, the sort who would bring a man to his knees – if you didn't bring her to hers first. He would anchor her down, have her on every surface imaginable – the desk in his office, the chairs in the hall, the piano in the music room. There would be no place for moderation, for apathy. Instead they would fuck and buck and suck as though their lives depended on it. She might beg for mercy, but deep down she would be desperate for his thick cock. He would fill her up to the gills. Pump up her tight crack. Escape is impossible, he would tell her if she gasped for restraint; resistance is futile!

'What did you say?' said his second-in-command.

The Captain found it difficult to think without mouthing the words as well.

'Nothing,' he murmured. He continued to dream of Sophie; that lithe, sexy woman who couldn't possibly be as self-assured as she pretended.

Moira slipped off her clothes, folded them carefully – creases were not in her vocabulary – and put them in the lockers, then padded over to the sunbed. She didn't bother with a towel.

The tubes were so generously warm, she could feel the heat soak through her body, and she knew it was making her even more beautiful. I look wonderful, she told herself; the only shame was how few people saw it. If only she were invited to film premieres and parties, then she too would have an audience for her firm cleavage, the slim thighs – not an ounce of cottage cheese or even chives on her.

Dancing was how Moira coped. She had no interest in being a cashier – her mind was on far more important things than exchanging cash for chips. Every night, after the casino count, Moira liked to dance. She liked shocking the passengers with an eyeful of outrageous moves. Sometimes, she teamed up with another exhibitionist, drunk, or high, or both. Anyone would do; all they had to do was stand there and let Moira shimmy up and down their body. This she would do in the centre of the dance floor and, before long, the crowds would gather round, clapping her on, encouraging her. It was funny how the indignities of her work evaporated if the night was spent dancing, flaunting her body. It was funnier still how even the straightest of women would dance like a whore if the music were right.

Moira moved her fingers to her bikini bottoms – well, it was silly to have white bits – and she moved them down her legs. She let her hands rest on her pubic bone, but then that also was silly, really, to have white bits there, so she should really tuck her fingers out the way. Moira let her legs widen and she touched herself. She began to whisk her fingers around; before long, she had felt her way to her clit and she started dancing there.

'Oh, hello, I didn't know anyone was in here,' lied Sophie as she went over to the second machine. She raised the lid and popped herself inside. She didn't much believe in artificial tanning – couldn't understand the fascination with looking orange – but she knew this was the place to catch Moira.

She had anticipated that Moira would be harder to work on than Tom. Women are. It's more difficult making new girlfriends than it is meeting new boyfriends. With women it's more ambiguous, more embarrassing. In Sophie's experience it takes months, years even, to build up a relationship with another woman, but she had a time limit; she wanted to get the scam over and done with within the week. Then she and Mick could disembark, with the money in their hot, little hands.

She eyed her nervously. The cashier's skin was treacle coloured and smooth, except for the shock of pubic bush. She had pre-Raphaelite looks, galloping hair and sensual heavy features. She reminded Sophie of a picture she had

24

seen in a gallery (with a man whose idea of foreplay was to look at Botticelli). In the picture, the woman was pouring water from a jug over a man's feet, but rather than look as though she was subjugating herself to him, it made you think that he was her servant. Moira had a similar look. Her beauty was classic, timeless, the sort that drives men wild. Sophie, by contrast, always had to work hard for her lovers. They really were conquests. She chased them, persuaded them, made them believe that they couldn't live without her. Moira didn't look like she would have to lift a finger, never mind open her legs. But then, Sophie consoled herself, she didn't look any happier for it.

'You've got such a lovely tan.'

Moira grunted a thanks.

'I wonder how often I would have to use these machines to get a tan like yours,' Sophie mused.

Moira rolled on to her side and looked at Sophie with cow-eyed disdain.

'You're the new croupier, aren't you? I saw you with Tom last night. You looked very cosy.'

'Not really.' Sophie laughed defensively. 'I like to get on with everyone.' Was the cashier jealous of her and Tom? Tom was good looking but he was not that good looking.

'The new croupiers always try to get on the good side with the inspectors and the cashiers.'

Oh shit. She seemed to have Sophie sussed.

'Do they? Why's that then?'

'You tell me,' Moira said languidly. She let her legs drop apart and felt the heat cascade over her body. Sophie wondered if this was the time to ask if she wanted in. It was more premature than Sophie would have liked, but then Moira seemed to be inviting her to say something.

'I guess they think that if they all work together they could ... get away with something ...'

Moira merely shrugged her shoulders.

Sophie persisted.

25

'You've never thought of doing that?'

Suddenly Moira's sunbed stopped whirring and the machine clicked into darkness. Moira raised the lid abruptly, stood up and walked round the small room. Sophie wished she hadn't said anything. The room felt like a cell, and now Sophie felt as though she were under interrogation. At the same time, she couldn't help but feel a surge of awareness, awareness of her neighbour's long and silky thighs as she paced round. Moira leaned right down. Sophie wished she could get up, but with the machine still blasting out the heat, it would look strange if she did so. Moira's face was right next to hers, and she thought it odd how a face can invade your space as effectively as a knife or a gun.

'Are you asking me if I ever cheat?'

She stared boldly at Sophie, who tried to avert her eyes from her face, but the only thing that stood out were the red nipples, long and inviting that seemed to press against the air.

'Of course not!'

'Because if you are . . .'

'Don't be silly. I hardly know you!'

'Yes. You hardly know me!' the cashier repeated self-importantly and danced off to the changing rooms.

Well, thought Sophie, that was that. Game over.

# Chapter Six

The deck was moving ever so slightly. Sophie fancied that, rather than being caused by the waves, it was with the resolute sway of the honeymooners all around them, locked away in their cabins, making love. It was a lovely thought; one that propelled her along the corridors of the fourth level to Mick's cabin. Ever since they met, she had been thinking about him.

His door was open, so Sophie wandered in, thinking he would be there – but the cleaners must have left it open. Once she'd decided to wait for him, it wasn't difficult to have a nose around. His bed was smooth and his clothes were folded in a pile on an armchair. She didn't know what she was hoping to find, maybe a letter or a photo, perhaps – a clue to who he was. She wandered over to his desk but found only the ship's brochure, some magazines about investment and, more bizarrely, a magazine on cosmetic surgery.

She crept into his bathroom, guilty as sin. I'm only looking, she told herself, what's wrong with that? Deep down, she knew he would be angry. All the same, it was satisfying to explore – to see the products he used, his shampoos, his razors, his aftershaves. It made her feel closer to him. These were the things that touched his hair, his skin, that grazed his cheeks, his chin. These were the things that he rubbed against him. There were blond hairs trapped in the drain of the shower. She wanted to pick up one. She left the cubicle but felt compelled to return. It was silly, but she bent down and retrieved one. Yes, she had one of his pubic hairs. She put it to her lips and poked her tongue at it. It tasted soapy, of course, stringy wet. Then she wound it round her finger, all the while feeling terrifically foolish but, at the same time, triumphant. She would put a spell on him.

She returned to the bedroom, sat on his bed and placed her feet in his slippers. Mmm, they felt warm. Other people's shoes have a unique feel, a special flavour and usually they weren't too inviting – but this felt intimate and safe. Her feet were content wrapped like that. She stroked her calves, wondering about him.

Then she heard footsteps. She jumped up and nervously watched the door open.

'What are you doing here?' he asked, but he didn't seem particularly annoyed or even surprised. He didn't shut the door, though. It was as though he wanted to stay attached to the world outside.

Usually, the second time you see a man you like is a disappointment. You build them up, up, up in your head and they can only fail to fit the image. But Mick was even better than she had remembered. Beautiful, serious, but with a humour bubbling underneath; and he was on her side. They were a team; they should act like a team.

She was compelled to touch him. She did. She reached out and stroked his cheek. It was smooth but had the faint promise of stubble. He took her hand and patiently, as you would to a child, put it down her side.

'I like you,' she burst out. This time, she pushed her lips on to his and felt the shock of his kiss. It was like kissing for the first time ever. She felt herself swoon, whoosh into his arms. Her lips were pressing on his. And yes, he was kissing back. He tasted perfect. But just as she trailed her tongue into his mouth, he stepped back.

'I like you too but . . . I don't want to get involved.'

How could he say that when she felt like she had been launched into orbit?

'Umm, can I ask why?'

'Oh, you know,' he said vaguely, 'plenty of fish in the sea and all that.'

'People say that when they've been dumped, not at the start of a relationship,' she said. She felt stupid, really stupid, but she was certain he liked her. This wasn't some teenage thing – by the time you get to her age, you get the instinct, the feel for whether someone is into you or not.

'Start of a relationship?' he echoed. She couldn't tell if he was sneering or trying to suppress a smile.

Is that what they had been doing? No, of course not. She was silly to overestimate what they had between them.

'Actually, there was another reason I came. I seem to have run into a problem.'

'What?'

'They are not interested – neither the inspector nor the cashier will have anything to do with it.'

Why she had thought they would jump at the chance, she didn't know, but she had expected them to purr and roll over, and of course they hadn't.

'Of course, what did you expect? You have to persuade them that they are.'

'Yeah right, and how do I do that?'

'You'll manage.'

'Can't you help?'

'All you have to do is get them on your side. How difficult can that be for a woman with your charms?'

His words didn't reassure her at all. He turned away and walked to his desk. He seemed intent on ordering his magazines into a neat pile.

'But maybe you're not as gutsy as you like people to think. I should have known,' he added. His tone was almost vicious.

'What?' Her temper was stirring.

'The sexy woman-in-control persona is all just an act,

29

isn't it? Deep down, you're just a timid little girl. I knew I couldn't trust you.'

'You can,' she said weakly, all anger dissolved. But she wasn't so sure herself this time.

'Close the door behind you,' he added.

Twenty minutes later, and Mick felt even more guilty than he had immediately after she departed. But he had been so shocked to see her in his cabin. He had reacted badly because he was confused; it was as though she had invaded his world. Maybe she had found out parts of him that he didn't want to reveal just yet.

Also, he had been to see the ship's doctor only that morning about his seasickness and his constant feeling of dread, but the doctor had merely laughed and asked why he had decided to come on a cruise in the first place?

He decided to find her. He would apologise, make friends; maybe he would be able to talk, really talk, to her. He loved her power, her aggression. That kiss was unbelievable. Usually, a first kiss is tentative, questioning even, but she had thrown herself into him. She wanted him; it was obvious. She wanted him fucking badly.

He never thought a woman could want him like that.

She was so beautiful, so honest and yet so sexy. When she looked up at him, half mystified, half overwhelmed, he could barely stop himself from grabbing her in his arms. And he had wanted her so much, more than she would ever know, but he just couldn't go through with it. He couldn't bring himself to do it then – perhaps he could now.

Chasing down the corridors, he spotted her from behind. And what a gorgeous behind it was. The word suggests an end, an aftermath, and it didn't do justice to hers; there was nothing backwards about her behind. Her arse stuck out like two balloons, like an Italian beach babe. Imagine burying your face in that! One leg was wrapped around the other, legs like the curved calves of a screen starlet.

He sneaked up behind her, heart pumping. She was on

the phone. He might even kiss her neck as she stood there. Whisper hot words into her ear, nibble on the lobe. She would lean back into his arms and let him touch her. He is up close; he will do it, he will. The explanations, the excuses could come later.

'It's all right, Josh, I promise. I love you more than anyone in the world – just you remember that. Everything will be OK soon, I promise.'

Mick edged away. His whole world was coming apart at the seams. He should never have listened to her. He crept away, back to the sanity of his cabin, but one hour later he was still shaking and he knew he couldn't trust her.

# Chapter Seven

Sophie disembarked at the next port. She needed to step back from events, and to decide how to proceed. Clearly, neither Tom nor Moira were as desperate for money as she had been led to believe, and Mick? Well, Mick was just going to let her get on with it.

She deliberately went a different way from most of the passengers and ended up, by chance, at a quiet side of the island in a beach bar full of locals. The owner was a huge gregarious man who insisted that Sophie, as the honorary foreigner, have free drinks. He was wearing an apron with a woman's naked body printed on it and even though she didn't understand his stories, she found herself laughing at him along with everyone else. She had felt unhappy when she left the *Prince Albert* but before long, her spirits had revived. She decided that it was Mick's loss if he didn't want to sleep with her; and he probably had his reasons.

Soon she was chatting to the barman in pidgin English and to a couple sat at the bar, and then to a man on his own who came over to offer her a drink. He was pretty rather than handsome. He had white teeth and dark skin, the stuff boy bands are made of, and Sophie measured that he would be the perfect medicine to take her mind off her lovesickness.

A crackling wireless in the corner was playing calypso tunes and soon the couple began to dance. She watched as they whirled round, and she waited for the man next to her to ask her to dance. When he didn't and she ran out of patience, she asked him and, looking surprised but eager, he agreed. He held her by the small of the back and bumped his thigh between her legs. They swayed to the slow songs and bopped to the fast ones. She could feel his cock rubbing at her leg. Yes, he was the perfect antidote to her love-Mick-ness.

He called her Snow White but added that he had never seen snow, except on TV. He said that he liked white skin. She offered to show him some more. He asked her if she would like to go out for dinner with him that evening.

'I've only got a few hours,' she said. 'The ship is leaving tonight.' (Sophie had long before decided that 'Does not mess around' would be her epitaph.)

He raised his eyebrows.

'But I'm not doing anything this afternoon.'

He looked at her closely, then he hesitantly suggested that they could explore the island.

'I would prefer to explore an islander,' she insinuated.

Finally, he asked her to come back to his room.

'What took you so long?' She grinned.

As they walked hand in hand, giggling with anticipation, she saw some of the ship's passengers and they smiled at her indulgently. Newly-weds like to see everyone in pairs. Single people threaten those in the state of coupledom. Sophie felt conscious of their attentions and she smooched up to her new friend perhaps even more keenly than she would have done if there hadn't been an audience.

A few people were playing gin rummy on his porch. Usually Sophie loved to watch a game in motion, but they were in a hurry. A man on a hammock blew her a kiss. Someone yelled out, 'Hey, Simon.' Sophie wished she hadn't heard his name. He still didn't ask hers and she didn't want him to. It was exhilarating to fuck as strangers – to find out everything about each other's body and yet to have no access to their mind. Inside the shack, two men, both in loud shorts, were talking heatedly. Her man, Simon, greeted them with a kiss and a shoulder rub and then said something that made them laugh and look at Sophie knowingly. They moved over to the shuttered window and began discussing again.

'Don't worry about them,' he said cheerfully. He pulled a curtain across, dividing the room in half, but she could hear the whispering and the shuffling of the men nearby and all the other people outside. He sat on the bed and held out his hand longingly. He had a quaint smile. His fingers curled into hers. She couldn't stop looking around the room, but he had eyes only for her. Amazing eyes, full of desire and longing, so fucking beautiful, she didn't know what to do. Yes, she did.

She sat down beside him, but as she did so, laughter broke out from the other side of the curtain. It didn't put her off though. In fact, the proximity of the men excited her. Simon's fingers were on her wrist. When she worked in the casino, hundreds of people saw her wrists, but no one looked at her there or touched her there like he did. She almost swooned when he put three fingers against her pulse. Her heart doctor.

'Am I still alive?' she joked. He didn't get it.

Sophie thought it was funny how, back at home, the lonely hearts columns were full of requests for GSOH. As if that was important when it came to fucking! (Unless they didn't mean good sense of humour, but something else, like Good Sex, Oh!)

He brought her arm up to his lips and ever so slightly bit the frail white skin there. Sophie reached out, put her hand behind his neck and grabbed him to her.

Occasionally, you hear women talk about men who do everything for them, and they usually say it incredulously, with their eyes wide and meaningful. Sophie had never properly known what that meant until she met him. It was as if he had been born to serve her. She didn't have to do a thing – of course she wanted to, she loved

34

responding to him, showing him what she liked – but she didn't have to. He damn near picked it all up perfectly.

He kissed her arms and then put a finger under her arm, in that soft tender spot, that no one else had noticed, no one knew existed. She was wet, he knew it, but he didn't rush. He was a thorough lover. He left no stone unturned, no part unkissed. Yet, he didn't know her at all. There was security, freedom in the anonymity. She allowed herself to be fondled, to be played with. She was groaning and sighing for more. She started thrusting her pelvis up at him, rocking back and forth on that narrow bed.

But he took his time. She grabbed at his crotch but he said, 'Slow down, wait.' She was glad he made her wait, because when he eventually did pull himself out of those jeans, he was harder than iron and beautiful, oh so beautiful. His cock was gigantic, smooth and well shaped. He pulled her pussy open and inserted himself very gently at first and then, when he was sure that she could take it, he pushed himself in. And then out. And then in again. He was magnificent. She could feel the shape of his cock – the swollen head as it pressed against her again and again – and she knew he could feel her, all of her.

And the men behind the curtain continued talking, so casually, that Sophie wanted to yelp and let them know: 'Look, we are actually fucking in here! What do you think about that?' But he put his hand over her mouth and all she could do was sigh around the palm of his hand, and at the same time she squirmed with his prick thundering inside her. She watched his fervent face, his tender concern, and she bit into those caressing fingers gratefully as he worked back and forth. Coming, coming, come.

He lay on his side, one long brown leg draped over hers. She didn't bother pulling up the covers but flopped naked on the mattress. It annoyed her that in the movies, the women are always shown naked while having sex,

35

but then they are all covered up, clinging to the blankets afterwards. He traced her mouth with his fingers, then his lips. She loved his accent and the easy way he talked.

'I've an offer for you, if you're interested.'

'What is it?'

'This.' He walked over to the cupboard. She couldn't take her eyes off his hard buttocks. He had a light sprinkling of downy hair on the back of his legs. He turned round and she was treated to that beautiful view of cock. He was semi-erect and the folds of skin looked tender and inviting. He was completely unaware of the wonderful sight he was, completely unselfconscious. He was holding a bag full of powder.

'It's worth a few million.'

Sophie tore her eyes from his prick and tried to concentrate on what was going on. The contents of the bag were worth a few million! Think what she could do with that!

You would imagine you would clutch it to you, cradle the potential money like it were a precious thing, but he merely dangled it in front of him carelessly. God, if he dropped it though, there would be the equivalent of thousands of dollars' worth disappearing through the wooden floorboards. He studied his package. He didn't like drugs himself – but you have to make a living somehow. If it weren't for the changing appetites of the people in rich countries, they would still be quite happily growing cocoa.

'What's the deal?'

'Take it into Florida.'

'That's all?'

'That's all.'

It would mean abandoning her plans. And why not? Tom and Moira were so far proving non-starters, intransient, and Mick, her co-conspirator, was about as friendly as an alligator in a Florida swamp. It certainly wasn't smooth sailing – this could be the lifeboat she needed. But still, Sophie considered, it was her own thing; it was her baby. Plus, Mick didn't think she could do it. He really was a sceptical bastard and she wanted to prove him wrong. However awkward the key players were proving, the operation was going full steam ahead.

Simon was stroking her again. First her breasts, and then moving down southward across the mound of her tummy, down, down. Yes, she knew what was coming – and she knew she would be too. Round two commenced. He said he wanted to taste her again. Laughter bubbled alongside arousal. She wondered if this was part of his plot to persuade her, but hey, who cared? He parted her knees expertly and slicked back his hair so it wouldn't fall in his eyes and obscure the view. Ready. He was an obedient, willing slave. She felt a slap of guilt. He was so sweet to her. And yet she was going to turn him down. While he worked at her pussy with his fingers, his tongue was making his way up her leg, alternately making small shivery nibbles on her inner thighs. She put one arm behind her head and another lightly on his. She loved to see the back of a man's head there. Simon licked and nibbled. When he came up for air, she murmured, 'Sophie's choice.'

Then she said, 'It's really good of you to give me this chance. I appreciate it, truly, but I'm going to do it my own way.'

She was almost there now. He was worshipping her skin, inhaling the scent of her pussy. His eyes were locked on hers. The intensity of it was killing her.

'You don't mind, do you? If I don't do it?'

'Suit yourself,' he said.

Simon was cool; he wouldn't press her. Then his face was between her legs, pressing her all over, and she forgot all about the scam, the money, the drugs. She even, for a moment, forgot about Mick.

# Chapter Eight

'You're a very attractive man,' Sophie told Tom later that night as he stacked the counters away. It was time to put Plan B into action. If Tom and Moira weren't going to join the scam when she asked them nicely then she would bloody well have to persuade them. Tom smelled as gorgeous as he looked; she could sniff the eager scent of his aftershave and knew that she must be making progress, even if it was not as speedy as she would have liked.

'Mmm, you smell very fresh,' she added for good measure. Sophie edged nearer him, like a fox prowling the chicken coop. She stood so close that she could see the faint lines circling his neck and the wrinkles at the outside of his eyes. The afternoon spent with Simon had filled her with a renewed determination. And the seduction of Tom was the first task. When she had won him over, she would convince him to help in their scheme.

Tom blushed and pulled at his collar. The new lotion was making his neck itch. When Jennifer found the bottle (impossible to hide anything from her) she had said, 'Aren't we supposed to be saving money?'

Jennifer hated life on the boats. She wanted to leave, but he had insisted they did one final round. The guilt he had from dragging her along had overshadowed all

38

the last dregs of pleasure. But this was their last chance to save some readies before they went back to Berkshire, he got a job in her father's company and they had their wedding. Her plans for their wedding were so elaborate, so expensive, that Tom longed to cover his ears when she brought them up. But how could he say no? 'It's once in a lifetime,' she kept saying (as if everyday there didn't occur something that only happens once in a lifetime).

Sophie's attentions were weird. It wasn't that he didn't have much luck with women. Women did like him; they always had. Before Jennifer, there had been plenty of affairs, liaisons, and even since Jennifer there had been enough flirtations to keep the wolf of adultery from his door. But there had never been anything like this, like Sophie. Never had he been the attention of an attraction cluster campaign. Never had he been singled out, so doggedly pursued as he was now. He felt a fizz of excitement in his gut. It was thrilling, like getting an invitation to some great event, or feeling the wrapped presents under a Christmas tree. Relax, he told himself, it was just some silly game, that was all.

He watched her sashay down the corridors before work. She wore incredible clothes: hot pants and halter-tops, knee-high boots and low-slung skirts. Clothes that sang to him – songs of jazz and blues – and at the same time taunted him. On the other hand, Jennifer's clothes sang whatever was No. 1 at the time. Jennifer had the more fashionable figure; she was slim-hipped, yet with the round, almost robust bosom, but Sophie looked as though she was good in bed. He couldn't help wondering – wondering about everything. When Sophie wore tight trousers that outlined her arse, he couldn't help speculating what colour her bush was. When she wore that white vest top, which skimmed her erect nipples to perfection, he couldn't help thinking how they would feel between his fingers. He just wanted to get in there, to submerge himself in that body. To fill her up, pump her up and make her come. Jennifer, of course, hated her. Snap, just like that; the instant she saw her, she had judged her.

Jennifer wasn't stupid then. She knew him inside out, and she would know if he strayed, even an inch, from the path of fidelity.

His relationship with Jennifer wasn't worth jeopardising for a five-minute screw. Or even a ten-minute one. For a man who worked in the risk industry (perhaps a consequence of working in the risk industry), Tom wasn't much of a daredevil. He wasn't interested in playing away. Before meeting Sophie, he had been largely immune to the attractions of other women. But something about her gave him the horn. Big time.

He loved Jennifer in a way that made his heart ache and he thought she was the most beautiful thing in the world. Trouble was, he didn't fancy her; not really. She just was so remote, so distant. And she never questioned their relationship; their future together was as clear as a bell. He too hoped they would always be together, but he sometimes had his doubts.

Their sex life used to be good. Very good even. Actually, for a long time, nothing had happened. They had a very proper courtship, befitting Jennifer's very proper nature, and at first they kept it a secret – not because it was against the rules to have relationships with other staff members, it wasn't, but because they didn't want to be the target of the gossip. He didn't tell his friends what was going on, but gradually they found out – as you do on a ship like the *Albert*. The funny thing was that his mates, the musicians and the entertainment staff, assumed that they were at it like bunnies, even before they had kissed. That made him feel funny, deceitful even, and he wanted to do it even more perhaps because of that.

He had booked a hotel for that weekend they had free in Cuba. He was very coy, very embarrassed about telling her but she seemed to like him for his shyness and so, astonishingly, it happened then, before they even got to Havana. What happened was that, when he told her, she was so pleased that they had started kissing. And then some. And before he knew it, he was lying on top of her,

her knickers were tangled on the floor and he was euphorically inside her.

That night, as he had walked back to his cabin, he thought, can this be true? I have just fucked the most beautiful girl on the ship. And it sounded crude when he phrased it like that, to put them in a little box, but it wasn't at all. It was amazing; she was amazing. The others, his mates, did not know the history that stood between him and Jennifer, and he didn't mean the history of their few short weeks at the Oak Grill and the Coconut Bar, but the thousands of years of shared history that he was certain they had. His mates asked what was going on and he gave them the usual flannel. What did they know about love? The other staff members had flings and trysts with anyone who would part their legs. Maybe the cruise ship was a sexual odyssey for some of the staff, and indeed for some of the passengers, but for him it was the end of the line. He and Jennifer put in an application for a shared cabin. They were physically and emotionally compatible. They shared the same goals and interests. He cut out the old friends. He didn't need them; she didn't like them. She wanted him in their cabin, keeping the bed warm. They never repeated the extravagances of their first coupling but still Tom was happy. (Well, he was not unhappy.)

It was flattering to be fancied, after all. And Tom was as susceptible to being fancied as the next man.

Women liked Mick; they always had. And the women on the *Prince Albert*, although they were mostly of the honeymooning variety, liked him a lot. Mick had always known that, before they married, some men have their stag piece, or their strippers, or their oral sex in the toilets, but what he hadn't known was that women have their extra-curricular fun too. Often after the wedding – it was a kind of pre-emptive strike against forty years of boredom.

In the Coconut Bar he had caught the eye of a mature redhead with pleasing freckles on her shoulders. All day he had been sweating about Sophie – stupid, when he couldn't give her what she wanted, but it seemed she didn't really want him anyway. He knew that the best way through cold turkey is distraction, and so the redhead and he trod the usual path: eye contact, a drink offered, a drink accepted, chatting, the sudden and inexplicable need for some air. Mick knew what she wanted him to do, so he did it. He took her hand and steered her to the upper deck. The moon was a suitably shiny sliver, perched over the Caribbean.

Mick liked slightly older women. They were less sentimental, less idealistic – and they fucked with enthusiasm. Even so, this lady displayed an agreeable amount of guilt. Her husband had got food poisoning from a bad fish dish. Mick had heard everything, from the prawn starter to the head-down-the-toilet dessert. The women carried the heavy scent of disappointment. They came on the *Prince Albert* with all these romantic ideas about honeymoons, but whereas the ship didn't let them down, the men, being human, invariably did.

Mick, however, could pick up the pieces as easily as if they had been dropped into his outstretched hands. He had his own story, an explanation about why he was travelling alone, that he had refined. Some women liked the hospital bed wedding tale, where his new wife succumbed to her (unspecified) illness; others were given the 'she ran off with my best friend' story. Either way, the ladies yearned to console him. He rarely got round to telling it these days, he had become so adept at his 'Let's talk about you' lines.

'I should go back,' she suggested, after they had walked the perimeter of the ship three times. Apart from her words, however, she showed no inclination to disappear.

Like an animal, Mick sniffed fear. Excellent. It was the ideal evening – the sort film-makers labour over long and hard to reproduce with special effects. The wind swept through their hair. The breeze was cardigan cool, but no colder. Mick believed himself to be a city-boy, but nights like this were exceptional.

'Let's stop here.'

He led her up to the very front of the ship, his favourite hunting ground. He brushed his hand across the woman's skinny thigh. Not a murmur. Boldly, he left his fingers there – the first test.

'Look at the stars,' he said.

A piece of luck: another cruise liner passed by, illuminating the ocean with fairy lights and faint party cries. His seduction was almost complete, and he had barely had to do a thing.

She gave a few sorry excuses. Her husband didn't understand her. Her parents had wanted them to marry. Once all the arrangements were made – the church booked, a dress chosen – it had seemed impossible to stop.

'Like a runaway train?' he suggested. He had heard all this before. Oh God, were there no original excuses to be had among any of these sorry souls?

'Yes, exactly!' She looked up at him, wide-eyed, as though she had at last found someone who understood her.

He hugged her, and from a hug it was easy to turn into a friendly kiss, and then from the friendlies he was rolling into the tongues – mouth open, writhing stuff. The woman responded heartily, aggressively even. Soon her hands were round his neck, pulling him towards her.

He didn't waste his time. He stroked her back, stroke, stroke, stroke, and then he was down among her buttocks, squeezing and clasping her arse like his life depended on it. She covered his lips with deep, wet, grateful kisses.

'Thank you for understanding me,' she was saying. 'This isn't wrong, is it?'

'Of course it's not wrong,' reassured Mick. Why ask me? he thought. Of course I'm going to say that!

'He makes love to me every night,' the woman continued. 'And I just lie there, thinking of ways to escape.'

'Oh dear,' he said.

'But I love him. What shall I do?'

43

'Let go,' Mick said. 'Forget him for a few minutes.'

The woman compliantly kissed him back. Mick went for a cursory fumble of her tits. He liked them, the nipples were erect, but he had a higher plan. Mick climbed up her skirt. There was no obstacle, not yet. Higher, higher, he searched. There was still no slap, no pulling away; it was a case of easy access. He was a gambler by nature, and he gambled that she would not stop him. Yes, he was straight in. He did not have to pass go.

'I shouldn't, but I can't help myself.'

Mick felt his way into her knickers. He pressed against the thin material with soft, searching fingers. He was such an accomplished player. Christ, she was wet, wetter even than the sea itself. He felt the wool of pubic hair, went down further, stroked the slippery wetness lovingly.

And still the woman wouldn't stop talking.

'He just doesn't listen to me. All he wants is to fuck me.'

'Oh, that's a shame,' he murmured. For a brief moment he felt guilty but then, when he felt the incredible moistness in his fingers, he knew he wasn't going to stop. She was letting him dip his fingers in the till.

'He doesn't know how to touch me,' she whispered. 'He just climbs on and off me, as though I am an animal or something. Oh, sweet Jesus, that feels nice. I shouldn't be telling this. Oh, don't stop, please. I shouldn't be telling you this, but he doesn't make me come. I just pretend to have orgasms, because if I don't he gets angry. Oh yes, fuck, that's good.'

He pushed her against the railings and his finger was pressing on her clit. What were the odds of her letting him have a quick nibble, out there, out where they could be caught?

The woman (damn, he'd forgotten her name; was it Jane or Rebecca?) was now talking non-stop, the gibberish of the pre-orgasmic.

'I need someone more responsive. Someone who understands my needs.'

He understood them. Oh yes. Two to one that she would let him. Evens. Better than that. Yes he would, yes he would. He pushed himself down.

'I wish he would do this. I wish he was more like you.'

Mick nodded, his mouth full of this woman. She smelled gorgeous; she tasted even better. He loved doing it on the deck.

'We mustn't,' she murmured weakly, but by then it was too late.

He was teasing her lips with his tongue, little by little – softly, softly, catchy monkey – and he was playing with her, down there, with his middle finger. The woman shivered, trembled, then she clutched Mick against her, still talking and moving faster and faster, until Mick felt the hot liquid pour over his fingers. He had won again.

'I'm knackered,' he said. 'I think I'll have an early night. Look, I'll catch you tomorrow, Rebecca.'

'Don't you want me to touch you?' Jane pushed her hair out her eyes, bewildered at her rapid change in fortune. One moment she was winning, the next she didn't know what game they were playing.

'No, thanks but . . . I'll catch you around . . .'

The worse thing was, though, that it meant nothing. Mick couldn't stop thinking about Sophie. Fucking hell, he thought, I'm really falling for her. He smoked a cigarette, but it left a sour taste in his mouth. He chucked the butt over the side and watched it wash away into the open sea.

# Chapter Nine

*S*ophie was pleased to find that Tom was her inspector for the evening. The pressure on him had to be maintained, like the drip, drip, drip of Chinese water torture. Soon he would give in. She was more determined than ever that she would succeed. It wasn't just for the money, or even for the kicks; she wanted to prove to Mick that she could do it. She could pull this off (and in the doing of that, she would pull him).

The first player arrived. He was one of a crowd of salesmen from Texas. He looked ridiculously out of place in his ten-gallon and boots. He wanted blue chips, his lucky colour. Told her that he never lost when he played blue.

'Really, sir?' she said. She couldn't give a toss what colour he wanted but he played seriously, gambling fuck-off amounts of money and she enjoyed that. A couple of bored wanderers sat up on the high stools and handed over some big money, wanting to be part of the scene. The players smoked and howled at their hands, rubbing their heads frantically, and Sophie raised her eyes and looked over at Tom. Tom stared away and thought of Jennifer.

Then the observers came over, couples, singles, all watching the big chief play. Sophie didn't much like onlookers but she preferred them to the drunken groups that pretended to be familiar with her. The cowboy was doing well, and then he had two bits of bad luck. The chips tumbled back to her side and he scowled at the injustice of the game.

'You're obviously lucky in love, sir,' she said smoothly. His winning streak over, the crowd started to disperse. They melted over towards the dice and the blackjack. Soon the table was empty of players.

Sophie had to work quickly if she was going to catch Tom in her web. She leaned forwards, over the table, arse up, so that Tom could get a full view of her backside. Wouldn't he be picturing having her doggy-style over the board? Wouldn't he imagine nailing her here, having her like this? Could he see that she wasn't wearing any knickers? That it was a freeway?

'Roulette is a great game, isn't it? I like to see the balls . . . any balls.'

Tom was saying nothing.

'As they tumble around. I want to touch them, before they go into the hole.'

Tom was resistant. He had a strong immune system, which he topped up with regular doses of his girlfriend. Still Sophie was determined that she would slip in there. If there were any cracks in their relationship (and of course, a relationship being two people inevitably meant there were cracks), she could exploit them and get in there.

'Balls are great, aren't they?'

Sophie's voice trailed away. She couldn't tell if he was listening or not. The casino was animated with the clanging of bells from the arcade machines and the chat of the crowds. Perhaps all her insinuations were falling on deaf ears.

'So cute somehow. I want to lick them and suck them and blow them . . .'

Tom had closed his eyes. He looked pained.

Time to make it obvious. Sophie started the low-voice

murmuring, the sweet pillow talk. Saying his name like it was a dirty word, whispering it, breathing it.

'Tom, Tom, I'll show you something. Do you want to watch me? Do you?'

A couple more gamblers showed up. Chinese Americans. They stared at the tables with no humour, no patience and, fortunately for Sophie, very little English.

'She's my favourite girl,' one said, while the other laughed a little too hysterically. He wasn't lucky though. However thoroughly he covered the numbers, the balls refused to land on them. They wandered off to try their hand somewhere else.

She and Tom were alone again, alone in the crowded room.

'I want to feel you,' she said. And then, finally, she went straight to the point, 'Look at me.'

She was sat up high on a stool. She opened her legs, knowing he was looking. Yes, he could see. His eyes widened. How could they not? Anyone would look. He realised that she was not wearing any knickers. Through the tunnel of her legs was a vision of pink invitation, the bitch goddess.

Sophie cleared her throat before whispering, 'Do you want to help me?'

Oh yes, he wanted to help her. He wanted to touch her cunt. He yearned to immerse himself in the shiny hole. He would like to stick one finger, just one finger up her for a start.

She was sprawled over the chair, taking it easy, like a lazy cat. She was in control of the show. She thought, I am a screen goddess and he is the audience, stuffing his frightened face with popcorn. I am here above you, more powerful than you sat in the front row, like a grubby train-spotting fool. She opened her legs wider still. She shielded nothing from him. There, take a look at that! She was spread legged, spread beaver, all for his delectation. You can look, look as much as you like, but you can't touch. Not yet! She felt hornier by the second. She could see his horn, his peeping arousal, and she wanted

48

them to come, together but separate, at the same time, but far away. She was a gaping hole waiting for him.

But then Jennifer appeared like an unwelcome apparition. She walked over and put her arms round Tom, like a deadly python. She kissed Tom on his head. It was the way you would kiss a small boy. Not the way Sophie would kiss him – if she ever had the chance. Jennifer looked at Sophie with cold pale eyes thick with mascara. There was real animosity in her folded arms and tight lips. And in Tom's version of the game, a Jennifer is worth more than a Sophie; perhaps worth more than two Sophies, or even a line of Sophies.

'Hello,' murmured Sophie.

Jennifer had no need to say anything – her body language was screaming volumes: he's mine!

The Captain crept about the laundry room, among the sacks of clothes. He rifled through the bags, searching for name tags, and then he found hers. He rummaged through the garments, the evening gowns, the lingerie, the tracksuit bottoms, then found what he was looking for: underwear, and not just any underwear, but a blue lacy G-string. The Captain put it to his mouth and inhaled. Deep. Just as he began a tremulous breath out, he heard someone coming in to the room, spoiling his moment. He had to rush away with them in his pocket. He carried nothing else, no keys or small change that would destroy the line of his trousers – but he kept the used panties there. On the way to the restaurant, he passed his inferiors and he thought gleefully about what he had in his pocket. He felt them with his fingers as he talked to people. His fingers rubbed her gusset. And even that gave him a hard-on.

He took his seat at the table, his table, but couldn't concentrate; there were women all around him and he couldn't help thinking, maybe, maybe, they're all soaking wet. As luck would have it, the young girl next to him was the perfect lady. He could see she wouldn't say no – she was that demure, that well brought up. He put his hand to her skirt; he could be well brought up too. She looked him right in the eyes; she knew what he was up to, but she wanted it, she wanted him to fish inside her undies. He crept up her thighs. Oh God, she was wearing those new hold-ups, joy of joys, no gusset to navigate, just silk material and then silkier skin, the space between the legs, a space that must be colonised, that must be captured. He slid to the knickers; shame he couldn't see what colour they were. (Pretend that they are blue, like the ones in my pocket, the ones I rub between my fingers.) He was poking upwards. Ignoring that cloth, proceeding upwards, sending the cloth aside, feeling the profusion of hair, a hairy bush, just what he liked. Tighter than a virgin; maybe, somehow, she still was. You never know.

She felt his finger move up her and knew she should resist, for decency's sake she should resist – she was a newly-wed woman, after all. But she had had a hard day, her husband ignored her; why not have a little fun with the Captain? It felt better than when her husband did it. Her husband was so perfunctory in his actions, so over-confident, without knowing why. Her husband with whom she must fake orgasms or he said there was something wrong with her. She liked this man; he was a Captain, after all, and that made him good. She could dream, couldn't she? He was handsome, and not like a pervert, and not an older man, not a man the same age as her father, but a man who would make her come, and forgive her for coming quickly. Her knuckles turned pink on the fashion handbag. She chewed her beads. She was glad of them – otherwise she knew she would whinny like a horse.

He had his whole hand in her, spectacularly, rubbing her all over, front and middle, front, oh yes, the neglected front. Her knife and fork cluttered down on the plate. The food lay abandoned. No responsibility. The finger worked her awake. No longer sleepwalking, no longer half-dead, but now, a sexual being, a woman with an animal instinct, the instinct to enjoy, to contain him and enjoy him, and to let go. He made her come. He felt her shudder, her judder, just as the dessert trolley surged forward, and the gateaux and the sorbets appeared to be running past them. The waitress squirted cream on his dish.

He wished he could plant a flag there. As soon as the meal was over, he couldn't wait to get back to his quarters, and he actually ran down the corridors, and when some passengers saw him, they got all excited and thought there was a crisis.

Then, when he got back to his cabin, he took out the knickers, her lovely stained knickers, and he tied them around his now aching cock. Mmm. His balls were full and heavy. He had to come soon. He promised himself he would, soon. Oh God, he couldn't wait. He couldn't choose between his bed and his sofa.

He chose a small chair, one he barely fitted in, but he crammed himself in. He squeezed himself in, wishing he could squeeze himself into her. He wished his whole body was the size of the tip of his fingers and he could just live in that warm place, making the woman come and tremble unaware. He took out Sophie's photo. He rubbed his finger – yes, that finger – over the matte surface.

He thought she looked hot; he thought she was the sort of girl who fucked anyone. Who started fucking at fourteen and never stopped. The village slapper, a farm girl, promiscuous because of her proximity to animals; saw the pigs rutting and wanted to squeal the same tune. He thought she was a naughty girl but that he could sleep with her, and he would teach her what an orgasm really was. His thoughts swam between Sophie and the girl at his table – her orgasm, her ecstasy.

The girl at the table and Sophie, four breasts pressing on him, two flaming holes gaping for him. Two women. They became one blurry face, one blurry, grinding, humping body. The knickers were wet on his cock and he had the other woman's smell on his thumbs. He had never felt so wanted in his life. The chair was too tight

51

for his purposes. He lay down and watched himself in the mirror. Oh yes, he had a big cock. Yes, the biggest in the world, yes, the biggest. They all thought so, they all moistened for him, weakened for him. The knickers were wrapped around his cock. They rocked him up and down; they were his bow on the present. He felt fantastic. He tightened the bow, controlling the blood circulation, and his cock looked so red and angry and powerful, he could have anyone. He knew any woman would cream to see that. He pumped up and down his fantastic organ and released the panties just at that moment, so that he could stuff them into his mouth just as he came, the perfect white arch in the air. He fancied it looked like floating doves of peace.

# Chapter Ten

When Mick agreed to take a walk round the top deck with her, Sophie had visions of him teaching her about the stars, reminiscing about being a kid, perhaps talking about a time he realised that there were other worlds, other universes. She pictured him courting her romantically, his dark eyes twinkling with humour. She saw him holding her round the waist, kissing her under a harvest moon. Maybe they would do it on the deck itself. Out in the open, the wind in their hair. But, although she knew she would love every snatched second wriggling under lifeboats, or standing at starboard cadging a surreptitious feel of his dick, sometimes you want a bit of class, a bit of sophistication. Why pitch a tent when you can afford a hotel? Maybe they could do it in the Captain's quarters; Mick was resourceful enough, he could find a way. She imagined pushing the Captain's things on to the floor, his papers, his maps, his pens, all dashed to the ground, and then her and Mick on the desk, fucking forever, fucking like pirates on the high seas. Or perhaps he could come to her room, or she could go to his and sink into his silk sheets, sink into him as though he was quicksand, but she would never need to come up for air.

It had to happen soon; it had to.

But instead, Mick had said, 'Sorry, Sophie, perhaps we should meet in the morning? It's safer that way – you understand.'

Sophie wished Mick wouldn't keep their contact to a minimum. He made her feel like a leper. Of course he was right; if they were seen together, it would be suspicious, but he didn't need to be so fucking aloof with her and yet so friendly with everyone else. The more she saw him out and about with different women, the more she felt the anger tremor inside her, rumbling like a dormant volcano. They were meant to be working together, yet he was flirting and playing, going through the female passengers like a casting director goes through ambitious actresses.

Although it was early, the top deck was awash with bodies anxious to take tans homes. They had 'done' some of the Caribbean islands; they had got their photos taken; now they needed to look brown. Their tans would last three days – the wrinkles would be there for a lifetime, but getting darker skin was as much a holiday requirement as the 'Weather is fantastic' postcards and the T-shirts for the in-laws and the key rings for the kids not yet old enough to have their own keys. A dark figure in purple underpants that failed to conceal anything was reading a mystery story. A woman had her legs open very wide, revealing curls of pubic hair.

Two teenagers strutting along in bikinis yelled out, 'Hi, Mick!'

'Hey!' he yelled promptly, as though returning a tennis serve.

They cooed and giggled at him, like he was some fucking pop star.

'You haven't been wasting your time,' Sophie said bitterly, and then she hated herself. It wasn't her business how he spent his free time. It had nothing to do with her. They were only partners in the old sense of the word. It was just that she hadn't realised how thick and gorgeous his thighs were. They were real bruisers' thighs; he had legs like a boxer's. He saw her looking but tactfully pretended he hadn't noticed.

For his part, he kept forgetting how pretty she was, only to find that each time he saw her again he was forcefully reminded. Then he remembered hearing her on the phone that time, obviously to some lover or other, and he knew that she was playing a game – she was a risk-taker like him.

Sophie pointed out a redhead lying on her side, her hipbones protruding. She was wearing black film-star-style sunglasses and reading a magazine.

'Look at that body,' she said admiringly. (An old trick; Sophie wanted to show that she wasn't jealous of all women per se.) But Mick grimaced recognition – it was the woman from the other night. Sophie noticed his guilty expression.

'You didn't!'

'Well, I don't want to get involved with anyone, so . . .' His voice trailed off uselessly.

'You didn't, Mick, did you?' She tried to make her voice light, as if she didn't care, but it annoyed her. Why did he have to shit on their doorstep?

'I may have,' he said modestly.

A roar came up. A cry, a yell, and then there were the alarm bells and shouting and shuffling. The sounds of doors being opened and slammed shut.

'Dolphin!'

Mick turned to Sophie, the redhead forgotten, his eyes bright with pleasure. Sophie felt the knot in her stomach tighten. The deck was soon swarming with spectators. Even the most committed lie-in-late guests staggered out for the sight. Some of the men were clad just in pyjama bottoms. The women had more carefully covered up, in jogging pants and T-shirts.

The dolphins smiled as they jumped through the spray. They seemed to relish the ship's arrival, to want to play with it. They slipped across the water, showing off. Sophie borrowed some binoculars and leaned against the side to look. But she couldn't concentrate on anything

55

but him. Why did he have to be so gorgeous – and why did he have to be so evasive? She took in the softness of his skin and the way the sun caught his hair, the way his lips jutted out and the soft hollow between mouth and nose. And then she thought about him with her, the redhead over there.

'You had sex with her?' she pursued.

'What do you think?'

'I can't imagine.'

Mick said nothing. He was thinking, you can talk! But he said nothing. She realised he had coloured an uncharacteristic pink.

'She's a lucky woman.'

Before Mick could reply, the ship's photographer approached and trained his lens upon them.

'Photo, together?' he shouted. He worked on commission – and he did well. All the holidaymakers wanted to convince themselves that they were having fun and it was worth all the money.

'No!' Sophie and Mick yelled in horrified unison. The photographer backed off, uneasy and shaken. A few other people turned round to gape.

'All right, no need to shout.'

Mick tried his Neville Chamberlain. 'Sorry, mate, it's just that we look a bit rough this morning.'

'Speak for yourself,' Sophie said fake-merrily. The photographer scratched his stubble and walked away muttering to himself.

'I think,' Mick said, trying uselessly to conceal the excruciating embarrassment he felt, 'I had better go. We don't want anyone else to see us together.'

'No, wait.' Sophie hated sounding desperate, but she was. In front of everyone else, she had to wear this mask of innocence; with him, she could reveal slightly more of herself, even if it wasn't a lot.

'Why are you doing this? Is it just for the money?'

'Sure, why else?'

She said cautiously, 'Maybe you like adventures?'

'I suppose I do.' He grinned at her and then pulled back quickly, telling himself: Do not get involved.

'And you? Why this? Why gambling?'

'What's a nice girl like me doing in a job like this?' She smiled. If she had been given a quid each time she was asked that, she wouldn't need to be doing this at all.

'Exactly.' He really did want to know.

You could say she grew up in casinos. Was weaned on cards and roulette. Her parents were gamblers. They played everything without discrimination, from Spot the Ball to the horses. They dressed up to go out and win money, her mother smelling overly of perfume and her father jiggling his car keys with anticipation. And then, they began to lose. And once the decline began, it never stopped. They lost everything. The fast cars, the house in the country, the flat in the city. After her mother committed suicide – in her note she said she would rather die than be poor – Sophie was sent to live with an aunt who said that her parents had sold their soul to the devil.

I'm never going to gamble, Sophie had sworn to herself with that exquisite certainty of twelve-year-olds. But she was attracted irresistibly to the lifestyle. Her first boyfriend, when she was just sixteen, was a card sharp. He had a tattoo of a joker on his back. She went with him to get it done; he flailed on the couch like a drowning fish, but he was trying to look brave.

He called his car the passion wagon, and when she was ensconced in the passenger seat, he would lean over. The first time he did it, she thought he was going to assist with her seat belt, but he had caught hold of a gadget and had whipped the seats down and clambered over her. He said that was why he bought that car. But the first time they did it, he made her get on top of him. (So even from the first time, she was on top.)

They had sex after he had been gambling, at four in the morning. He said that was the time most people die. She went off him as soon as he declared undying love for her. (They all adored her too quickly. How dull was that? 'There must be a guy with a bigger cock out there,'

57

she and her friends used to say.) But by that time, her passion for the cards had been re-ignited, although she had decided she would work on the other side. She was eighteen when she turned professional; she told them she was twenty-one. By the time they found out, she was the best croupier they had ever seen and they couldn't let her go. The casino was in her blood. The cards were in her veins.

As for the boats, well, that was just a way to see the world (and to find all those guys with the bigger cocks). As for the scam, it had been boiling inside her for years. She had been asked a thousand times if she was interested in making 'a little extra', and each time she turned it down. Petty theft and inconsequential crimes did not appeal; she decided that when she snapped she would go for the jugular. And she did not want to work for anyone else. The Triads, the Yakuza, the Yardies, they all wanted a piece of the action, but she knew that the only way to score, to really make it, was to go freelance. That way, you did it just the one time but you made sure you did it all in one night, with your own team, your own moves. Only that way could you really, really, really rock the boat.

'I never wanted to do anything else,' she said.

'What will you do with the money, Mick?'

'I don't know,' he said, although he did. He knew well. 'How about you?'

Perhaps she would be a female Ronnie Biggs. She would be able to afford a place in the sun – a tropical island maybe, where rich smooth, thunder-thighed men serve sex on the beach and drinks by the pool. Men who managed to wear those tiny trunks without looking stupid – foreign men, *bien sûr*! She would pick one to spend a night here with, one to spend a night there with. Pick them like chocolates from a selection box and throw away the marzipan ones. They would come with oily pecs (or was it biceps – she could never remember the name of muscles, only the feel), pick her up over their buff shoulders and eat her like she was candyfloss. She and Mick would become legends. In five years' – ten years' – time, people would talk about the team that organised the scam on the *Prince Albert* that netted them enough money to retire.

But that wasn't the only reason.

How could she begin to explain about Josh and everything? How could she explain that loving him had burned a hole in her heart and that she would die rather than let him down? No, she wouldn't explain. He didn't want to hear.

'I don't know either.'

Mick felt a horrid unease.

'Thursday night then. Are you sure the inspector isn't going to report us? And what about the cashier?'

'I'll fix it,' she said. 'It's going well.'

'Are you sure?'

'Positive,' she lied. 'Won't I see you before then, just to confirm everything?'

'OK.' He walked off before she could ask when. She wished he would relax a bit. He relaxed with everyone else; why couldn't he charm her a little?

'Enjoy the dolphins?'

The Captain was right behind her. She wondered how long had he been there and whether he had seen her and Mick together. She couldn't think that it mattered. There were so many members of staff, so many passengers, surely the Captain didn't even remember who she was.

'Yes, it's wonderful to see them so up close.'

A spray of water hit his shirt. Why did he have to look so freshly laundered even at this time of day? The peak of the cap was perfectly placed on his head. Some heads do hats well; they have the ears and the foreheads for it. The Captain certainly did. The white of his shirt emphasised the white of his teeth and the whites of his eyes. He had been strolling round the deck, chatting with the passengers, charming the women, and each one that he spoke to wished they had time to moisturise. When he caught her looking at him, the Captain raised his eyes quizzically. He made her uneasy but she couldn't work out why. Perhaps it was his age, or his status, but it was as if he knew a wealth of secrets about her – things that even she didn't know.

'Beautiful creature, Sophie Hemingway.'

He was undressing her with his eyes. Sophie looked up and forced a laugh. So he did know her name. She could smell the danger.

# Chapter Eleven

$S$ ophie disembarked again at the next port. She walked along the pier, on to dusty roads, enjoying the island atmosphere. She had heard that there was a carnival, apparently based on superstition to expel 'foreign devils', but in the twelve years she had been travelling, she had never found it. However, it was market day and the traders were shouting warm hellos. She strolled away from the harbour, pondering at fruit stalls, fresh fish stalls, and stalls of hand-made cotton bags, dolls and wooden instruments. She toyed vaguely with the idea of buying Mick a present – even though she didn't know what he liked and knew that he would resent any further obligation to her.

The road was never ending and was leading further and further into the countryside. The trees thickened and grew darker. Just when she thought she had come to an end, there were more stalls, more people to bargain with. The heat seemed to pervade every part of her and she grew heavier with it. Her throat was drier than sandpaper and her head was buzzing. The task of selecting a gift for Mick began to agitate her. It became his fault she was spending her day off looking for something to appease him – it was his fault she felt lousy, unwanted, defeated even.

As she walked wearily through, the local people began offering her a sparkling green drink. They had jugs of it and were pouring it into cups like eggcups. Sophie would have preferred water but they seemed intent on getting her to drink, so she accepted a cupful of the strange emerald substance. She might as well. She was so hot – any oasis in a desert. The sun was blasting down and the air was moist and soon she had no idea what to buy, nor any inclination to shop any more. The drink tasted stronger than mint, but maybe it was from the same family, and it burned the back of her throat, not immediately, but about three seconds after swallowing.

'More, more,' her benefactor said, gesturing. He wouldn't keep still but was jiggling from one bare foot to another, as though dancing on a live train line. She tried to give him some money but he wouldn't accept it.

'More, more,' he insisted, and she found herself giggling. Wasn't this meant to be the other way round?

And then she found herself in the middle of a fiesta. There were people all around her, dancing, gyrating. And the women, the women were wearing tiny hot pants and halter-tops, shaking their bodies, their shoulders, their muscular thighs. There were carriages too and some were three men high, decorated with peacock feathers, a thousand eyes, all colours of the rainbow. Sophie watched them and felt an unfamiliar excitement grow inside her. This was a barrage of flesh, passion and thrills. Different colours, textures and shapes flashed before her, different sounds echoed and reverberated. Someone held out a bamboo stick and, as they jiggled along, some of the women limboed beneath it. Their dark skin glistened with sweat, their mouths contorted into great big smiles. Their legs, their knees, their thighs came through first, as they arched themselves right back, their necks low. Sophie didn't know how they did it.

At the next stall, she accepted another glass of the green liquor. All thoughts of shopping, of the *Prince Albert*, even of Mick, vanished in a blur of goodwill and happiness.

Sophie began to dance. She had to dance. First her feet were tapping shyly, the way her parents used to on summer holiday discos, and then with more vigour. Soon she was leaping around. Why not? She moved her arms in the air, reaching for the sky now.

There were big, big men around her, clapping, bending and twisting. There was no stopping her now. She felt the burn in her throat and then in the pit of her stomach, and then all over. It was a warm generous spreading. She was whirling, a whirling dervish. Her mouth hung open and her eyes narrowed sensuously. Come on. She was hot, so hot, so when someone offered her more of the lovely green poison, she gulped it down so fast that little trickles escaped either side of her mouth. She wiped it on her wrists and then licked it off. She pulled off her T-shirt – she was wearing a pretty blue bra underneath – and wrapped it round her waist and then, when she saw that she was still overdressed, she peeled off her trousers and stuffed them into her string bag. Her knickers didn't match, somehow she had mislaid her favourite blue ones, but the ones she was wearing were a pretty pink.

The men danced with her, moving over her, their arms around her yet not touching her. And the drums beat faster – they were rising, and raging, and Sophie couldn't control her thighs from twitching and her arse from shaking. And, please somebody, take hold of me, please. She moved and wriggled but the beats were accelerating and she couldn't keep up without laughing. The women around her were thrusting their pelvises out at the men, fast and hard, in and out, working their butts. Hands raised and clapping. There were two guys opposite Sophie, two big guys, and she could see their cocks, hard as anything, long like truncheons and they were waving them at her, but they weren't intimidating or scary, but wonderful, and she wondered what it would be like to shake, shake, shake her arse on top of such a beautiful sight.

She collapsed. It felt like a million small hands were on her. She was held horizontally in the air and she couldn't stop the pleasure that ricocheted through her. She could hear the screaming adulation of the crowd. She could smell the ganja and the sweat of the guys who were carrying her aloft, but even all that was blotted out by the unbearable thirst between her legs. She was jerking and twisting and writhing like a foreign devil. She was shouting, but she didn't know what, and then she was screaming incoherently as a thousand small fingers plucked out her pleasures. And then her thirst was sated.

# Chapter Twelve

*A*fter the day on deck when he and Sophie had met for a second time, Mick went down with cabin fever, and he had it bad. It was like that time after Christmas and before the New Year, an in-between, purgatory time. He had nothing to do but wait. Wait for Thursday night, when he could do the business and then he would be off the ship by Friday.

But he couldn't wait. He felt queasy and he couldn't get rid of the idea that they were heading for disaster. OK, so he had watched the *Poseidon Adventure* one too many times, but still ... Until Friday, he was stuck. He looked blearily out of the ship's portholes and felt trapped by the immensity of the ocean, by the way it seemed to merge into the sky. There was no escape. He should perhaps have disembarked at the last port. There was some crazy carnival on the island, which he had heard turned into something of a fuck fest. But whenever he went to the usual tourist destinations, he always felt like a voyeur. He had seen other passengers take photos of poverty, of funerals, of pain, without a thought that these were real people involved. It offended Mick's sensibilities. At least on the ship the passengers stayed amongst themselves, even if at times it felt like a floating prison. He had to get off at the next port anyway, to meet someone, or, as he put it, he had to see a man about a dog.

He felt like having some uncomplicated fun. He had to keep away from Sophie but that would be difficult. She was everywhere – in the pool when he wanted to swim, in the bar when he wanted to drink. The only way of avoiding her was to hide behind someone else.

The girl in the newsagent's was pretty in that pinky-white way that Mick didn't usually go for. She also had bad pockets of skin, but her features were wide and inviting. And Mick liked an invitation. He was in a melancholy mood. This was no way to live, he told himself. Ducking and diving was dangerous – which he liked – and it was unpredictable – which he also liked – but in its danger and unpredictability it was also somehow dull. It had turned into a routine like everything else. There is nothing exciting about conning the house if you've done it five times before. You might as well be an accountant. He consoled himself that this was the final one. After this, he would be free – as free as a soul like his would allow.

Above the counter a sign read PLEASE ASK FOR ASSISTANCE.

OK, Mick thought mischievously, I will. There was no one else in the shop. The weather was too warm for all but the most avid shoppers. And the girl appeared to be alone. And she looked bored stupid.

'Which magazine would you recommend?'

He laid out a selection of top-shelf magazines and spread them as he would a deck of cards. She stood up uneasily. Anyone else would have been branded a pervert, hounded out of the shop, but Mick had the looks and the easy manner to avoid such a fate.

Which one would turn her on? he wondered. He reckoned he was pretty good at sussing people out from the way they looked: their class, their job, their tastes; what movies they like, what music or what food. But one thing that's hard to guess is their sexuality. Was she a take-it-up-the-arse girl, a blow-job fan, an I-must-have-my-breasts-fondled type or a screamer? You couldn't tell, although in Mick's experience, the more the women tried to appear sexy, the less they actually were, which was why he had his doubts about Sophie.

He could feel the heat as the girl switched her gaze between him, the magazines and back to him again. The tension seemed to radiate from her. On one magazine cover there was a picture of a woman draped over the bonnet of a white sports car. She was wearing thigh-high black leather boots and fishnet stockings. On another, a woman was spread wide, licking a lollipop. Funny, that image never did it for him. Perhaps he had become hardened to it. Ha ha. Yes, he had porn fatigue. The next cover was good though. A woman in a doctor's coat was spanking a woman in a nurse's outfit. This one stuck, clinging to his sexual memory. Mick thought there weren't just two sides of the brain – there was a third side, where the maddest thoughts about sex lived and prospered.

The sales girl was flustered. Mick wondered if she really had been bored stupid, or if she was simply stupid. Finally, she picked out a magazine. On the cover, a woman was cupping her enormous breasts and looking directly ahead. She had lethal-looking nails. Her nipples were half covered, half concealed by a purple negligee. Her legs were twisted beneath her, allowing just a tanta-lising glimpse of white panty.

'Maybe this one?' she said. She said it in a way that made it a question. Her hand was resting on the woman's breast. On purpose? he wondered. She flicked through the pages, idly, but Mick knew that she wanted to examine it further, and probably would, once he left the shop.

It was, Mick conceded, a fair choice.

'Do you fancy going out some time?'

'We're not allowed to sleep with the passengers,' she said coyly. She was still holding on to the magazine.

'Who's asking to sleep with you?' He smiled.

\* \* \*

It was a quiet night at the casino. Many of the passengers were exhausted after their brief spell off the ship and had gone to bed early. Only a few of the more determined gamblers remained.

Tom was unexpectedly put in charge of Sophie's table. The rota was usually fixed but it had changed that night because a couple of croupiers had taken off early to go to the disco, where some over-optimistic manager had organised a talent contest. Sophie hoped it would be a quiet night. She too was exhausted after the twists and turns of the day and she needed as few players around as possible to work on Tom.

When no one approached the table, she started to deal herself a game of patience. She shouldn't have been allowed but Tom didn't have the heart – or the balls – to tell her to stop.

The cards clattered on the table. Even against herself, Sophie found that she was losing, so she decided to cheat. But that didn't improve the situation, so she re-shuffled and dealt again. Once she had the cards out, she proceeded to play – with one hand. She was good at playing with one hand. She moved into phase two of the plan.

She was quiet, too quiet, and Tom's apprehension grew. Since the last time, when she had been so dirty, so thrilling, talking to him like that, flashing at him like that, he had been left wondering what trick she would pull next. What rabbit would she pull out of her hat? She was like a magician – although, on second thoughts, her sex appeal was more that of the saucy assistant. (He would love to see her in stockings, suspenders, top hat and tails.) He had seen her enthral some of the punters with card tricks and he wondered what sleight of hand lay in store for him.

He looked over coyly and then, when he saw what she was up to, his eyes widened. While one hand was turning the cards over on the table with a neat efficiency borne of years of practice, her other hand was circling her breast. She was touching her tits, circling them enticingly and fingering first one and then the other. Her nipples hardened beneath the cloth of her evening dress, but at the same time, she carried on dealing the cards face up. The reds on to the blacks and the blacks on to the reds. She was doing well now.

Tom wanted to touch her breasts; he wanted to so badly that it hurt, but he managed to hold back. Sophie knew that this was the time to press him. He had resisted valiantly, but he would be hers. She had known all along that the scam wasn't going to be plain sailing but if there was anything Sophie loved, it was a challenge.

She took her hand away from her breast and, just as he let out a barely imperceptible sigh of relief, she snaked it up her dress and inside her knickers.

Tom couldn't believe it! She was rubbing herself there. Christ, she really was masturbating. He had never seen a woman play with herself before – not Jennifer, not anyone. This so simple a gift that a woman can give a man had so far eluded him – until now. This was better than the stupid talent contest. The talent in that dress was better than anything they could produce out there.

He saw the material rise and shake, rise and shake. It was beautiful but crazy. How dare she be so audacious? And she was looking at him, licking her lips predatorily, looking at him as though it was him that turned her on, as though it was him that made her so wet that she just had to explore.

And he too couldn't help himself. You wouldn't have been able to either. He slid his hand down his trousers. He didn't look at her; he looked straight ahead, like he wasn't doing anything odd at all. No, really, he always wanked in the middle of the casino.

Sophie noticed the effect she was having and it added to her already considerable pleasure; after all, it's not every day of the week you get to masturbate in a room full of strangers. She slipped her fingers to her panties. Oh, she loved seeing his eyes widen like that and, yes, his pupils were dilated – and hers too. Teasing him, she licked her fingers one by one, before she took them for a walk to the forest between her legs. She wanted him to see everything.

She was biting down on her lips and, was it his imagination, or was she making little noises too? Hot noises, arousal noises, like the women in porn films make. Her hands moved faster and faster. She arched her back. Her legs were open. Wanton. Wanting.

Tom pressed himself with hurried fingers. His cock was huge, pushing at his trousers, aching to be held. She was gagging for it, hungry for him. He had never seen anything like this. No, he had. It reminded him of the red light district on one of the islands. Him and Jennifer parading around hand in hand, pretending to be unshockable, but really they were shaking. When Jennifer looked away, the local women had teased him with their stilettos and long curling tongues. When Jennifer had held back to let someone pass, one of them whispered to him, 'I fuck better than her'. And he couldn't sleep for ages for thinking about their bodies and their wild ways. And he knew he wouldn't know what to do with them – but, no matter, they would know what to do with him.

Tom's erection reached its zenith. Fuck! He couldn't help but work it, bringing his hand back and forth, back and forth. His wrist was making the oh-so-familiar movements while his eyes were fixed on the unfamiliar sight.

He thought about the times he spied on his sister's friend when they had sleepovers at their house. The girls used to dance around the room in their bras and knickers, singing into hairbrushes. They dipped and turned and, at the same time, they were screaming with laughter. There was this dance they did back then that involved shaking their shoulders vigorously forward and back. Their perky breasts jiggled out of their trainer bras. New, just-grown breasts, just discovered; perhaps they knew that he was watching, perhaps they knew . . .

He saw the shape, the fucking horny outline of her fingers under the dress. The dress billowed out where she was at the controls. She was frenzied now, pleased with herself, reliving the carnival, the strange island men, reliving every erotic moment she ever had; thinking of Tom in front of her with his hand down his pants, thinking of Mick sucking at her pussy, thinking of every man she ever knew taking her, turning her over, screwing her, fucking her. It had nothing to do with love; it was all about pure physical sensations – keep the cunt happy and the rest will surely follow. Look after the pussy and the cocks will take care of themselves.

And someone was walking over, a customer, a player, but she wasn't stopping now. Her fingers were fighting, batting, wet and soaking, stroking.

What a sight, thought Tom, and he could barely believe his eyes. They say it makes you blind, but who cares? Give it to me, baby.

The player arrived, holding out a crisp fifty-dollar bill. Sophie casually straightened her dress and took the money. She started to deal the cards, one for him, one for the house. He wanted to make money fast but he was a poor player. He had the bottle but he didn't have the know-how. He wouldn't stick at seventeen but took another card. Bust. The house won.

Was it only Tom who realised why her fingers were so shiny?

# Chapter Thirteen

Sophie was also working on Moira – or perhaps, you might say, Moira was working on Sophie. Although Moira had originally dissed Sophie's idea, Sophie hadn't offended her. On the contrary, Moira often liked to chat with Sophie, her eyes wandering curiously over her face, as though trying to read something.

It was Moira's idea to have one of their chats in the jacuzzi. Sophie was happy to comply because everyone knew that the risk of damage to the skin from sunbeds was considerable.

Sophie also had nice memories of hot tubs. Once, Matthew, a gay friend of hers, had asked her to be his 'beard'. He had wanted a 'girlfriend' to take to a family wedding – to make sure no one guessed that he was having an affair with a step-uncle. Later that night, the step-uncle had driven them back to his place. He was rich, a producer or something, and they had sat outside in the open-air jacuzzi. The night air had felt velvety on her shoulders. Sophie had watched the two men kissing. It had turned her on. It was so, so macho, their jaws working at each other and their hard chests pressed against each other like it was a war. So different from the way a man kisses a woman. The step-uncle had got her friend against the side of the jacuzzi. His hands were all over him.

Matthew's erection was magnificent. Then the step-uncle had bent down and blown him off. His expertise was incredible. She had watched Matthew, unable to contain his mounting pleasure, whine and roar. The big man's hands had cupped the balls and held the bottom of the shaft, but he only used his tongue, seeking out that sensitive vein at the back of Matthew's innocent cock. Then Matthew had been turned round and the step-uncle had fiddled with his buttocks and then entered him from behind. Sophie had wanted to cover her ears from the sound of Matthew's extraordinary groans. He was a lost boy. Then, when he was satisfied, the step-uncle had started on Sophie. He had squeezed her against the side and laughed into her bosom.

Matthew never spoke to her again.

The two girls lay side by side companionably as the water gurgled and splashed around them. Sometimes their thighs banged together, but Sophie shifted herself away. She could see Moira's buoyant breasts bobbing around her. She tried to imagine what Mick or Tom would feel if they saw them, all giggling, with their arses turned red by the heat. Perhaps there was a keyhole and they could see in. What would they think? She liked the idea of them pressing themselves against the glass just to have a look at the two girls in the hot tub. How lovely it would be to have men stare. She felt the spray rush up between her legs, so warm and soothing. She closed her eyes and held on to the rail. It felt good.

Moira was wriggling in the water like an eel. It looked to Sophie as if she had positioned herself over the hot stream. The water must have been flowing into her, massaging her there. Moira kept smiling, bobbing around insouciantly. Underwater, her skin turned white, whiter than ice cream.

'I had a croupier friend once. She looked a bit like you actually.'

'Oh yes?'

'The funny thing was, she was a virgin.'

'Why was that funny?'

'Well, she was a croupier – and you would think that she had more experience, wouldn't you?'

Sophie supposed so.

'Anyway, we were doing a cruise off California when she met this guy, and I don't know whether to tell you this or not . . .'

Sophie shrugged. She rose out of the water and then repositioned herself back down. Moira was certainly hogging the hot stream bit.

'Well, she was determined that he wouldn't find out that she was a cherry, so she asked me to teach her about sex. Can you believe that she had never even masturbated before?'

No, Sophie couldn't believe it. Moira continued.

'I showed her how she might touch herself. I got my powder compact and persuaded her to look at herself. I pointed out the parts that he might like to reach. I showed her what might feel nice. She began to stroke herself gently, her eyes wide. She said that she never really got wet before. Isn't that incredible in this day and age?'

'Yes,' Sophie responded uneasily. Well, it was incredible – in any day and age.

'She was kneeling against the wall, showing me her wet slit. And she didn't know what was happening. Her hands were shaking hard with vibrating power, and then her whole body was trembling, and her hands were working like the clappers, and then she was squealing as she came. She said to me, "Moira, sex is wonderful," and I said, "Honey, that wasn't sex, that was masturbation."'

Moira laughed heartily at her recollection, so Sophie chuckled too.

'So I said to her, "You know what happens in sex is that he puts his penis inside you?" "I know that," she said patiently, as if I were the idiot, "but how?" Wasn't she the funniest thing?'

Sophie agreed that she really was.

'God, she was so wooden. Well, she said, "Moira, please show me what it will feel like." I told her not to be so stupid, but she was really desperate, really crazy, so I said I would do my best. I got out my vibrator, told her to pretend that it was his cock, and I got her to lie down with her legs splayed. I would have liked to have gagged her but figured she should learn to walk before she ran. I made her open herself to me and then, when I got a good measure of how hot and wet she was, I started with the thing. She was pulling me on to her and I fell. She was clutching me, digging her nails into my back, clawing at me, pulling me into her, even though it was not me that was going into her but the vibrator. I tried to pull back, to catch my breath, but she was insatiable, rocking like a drug fiend, slamming her pelvis back and forth like there was no tomorrow and then she came, her legs twitching around my back. And, thankfully, I was released just before suffocation. Isn't that mad?'

'That's very interesting,' Sophie said pleasantly. She wondered if she should eliminate Moira from the game plan. The woman seemed to have no interest in talking shop – all she wanted to chat about was her strange affairs. If there had been more time, Sophie would have been tempted to tackle another cashier. As it was, she was stuck with this oddball.

'Is that all? Interesting?'

'How do you mean?'

'Nothing. I'll tell you the rest another time maybe . . .'

Moira's toes were tickling hers. There were risks involved with jacuzzis too (although these weren't necessarily health risks). Moira turned the water up, so that it came out really fast. She lay back over the spray, and Sophie could have sworn that she lowered her bikini bottoms.

The Captain followed Sophie around like a star-struck adolescent. He watched her promenade on the deck, he watched her eat in the staff canteen and he watched her deal in the casino. He made excuses to himself, such as I have to go to the casino tonight to see how things are going, or I have to check that the staff food is adequate, but the truth was, he had to see her. She is day to my night, he told himself. For the first time in his life, he found himself writing poetry; she is the captain of my heart, she is the ocean and I am the ship. His pen flew across the page as he gained inspiration. Without her, I am . . . I am . . . but a fish without water.

He remembered every word she had said to him, clinging to them as though they were the speeches of a prophet. She had said, 'The *Prince Albert* has a good reputation.' Perhaps she was referring to him. And that same afternoon, that precious afternoon when he had been so close to her, she had said something else very encouraging: 'I prefer working the floor.' Did she mean she liked fucking on the floor – hard and fast on the ground, so that his knees would graze over? And then, just the other day, she had said, 'Yes, it's wonderful to see them so up close,' and he wondered if that was a code for something. Maybe, cryptically, she was referring to him – maybe she had meant to say, 'It's wonderful to see you so up close.' Or, 'I would like to see your cock up close.' Maybe that's what it was.

He wanted her so much. Just the thought of her nearly had him exploding in his jockeys. He remembered that once, a woman had told him the most attractive quality in a lover was that he was 'ardent'. He had misheard. 'Hardent?' he had repeated, thinking it was a new word for a stiff cock. 'Enthusiasm,' she had explained, 'you know, when a man is really up for it.' Well, Sophie, look at me, I'm eager. I'm an eager beaver – honey, I'm eager for your beaver.

It was unusual for him to leave the ship and he had to concoct a sequence of lies to cover his tracks. He told them he had business – well, he did. Sexual business. You can only wank over someone's knickers for so long – sooner or later you want to move up – or in. Knicker-sniffing is, in its own sweet way, a gateway drug. He knew there was plenty of choice of women on the islands. The trade was so much more open than back in Britain.

He first saw a prostitute when he was fifteen. He sat in the small hallway of a terraced house in Catford with his hands clasped around his jelly knees to stop them from shaking. From the rooms upstairs came a cacophony of moans and wails that sounded to him like the cry of lost dogs desperate to get home. The red cloth lampshade shook above him and the shelves of books rattled. The whole house seemed to be trembling. For the young men, the anticipation was exquisite. In fact, it was all too much for him; he shot his load right there on the wooden waiting room chair. It was so unexpected, so unrequited, yet he couldn't help it. He couldn't hold back. Not with the sounds of the women panting, their begging for more.

The next night, the same thing almost happened. He covered his ears and stared at the rising between his legs. 'Stay down, stay down,' he mumbled, as though ordering an errant puppy.

Finally, 'Suzie will see you now.' At the time, Suzie Wong was all the rage and he was expecting an Asian girl. Instead, a little Mexican greeted him. Since then he had harboured a great affection for South American lay-dees.

And here he was, indulging that affection.

This woman was Brazilian. She was wearing a pink shift dress that barely covered her petite protruding boobies. She made no attempt to hide them – and her ease with her nudity somehow irritated him at the same time as it appealed to him. She didn't care who saw her curves – she was a dirty girl. She was the kind of girl who would let anyone play with her like she was a toy. She was wearing slippers with a pink ball of fluff attached to the front. That ball of fluff drove him wild. Drove him insane, even more than her cries for him to do it to her.

'Wow, what is it?' she said, gazing at his equipment.

'That, my sweet, is all for you.'

He realised that, although young, she was well versed. She probably said the same things to him as she had said to the other sailors. All that stuff about him being a big boy, the biggest boy, well, it was rubbish really, but the fluff on her slippers sold it to him.

The challenge was to make her really feel it, to feel that even if he wasn't a paying customer then she would still fuck him. And her challenge was to make him forget that he had paid through the nose – or through the cock – for this dubious pleasure.

She got on her hands and knees and he raised the dress from the back. He launched. As he did so, a thousand memories whirred in his brain, in his prick: I name this ship the *Prince Albert*, cracking the champagne bottle against the side. He was inside her. He loved it this way; it was so feral, so real.

As he drove harder and harder up her, the girl squeezed him. She had the most powerful muscles he had ever had the fortune to discover. She could have made mince meat in there.

'I want to make mister feel good,' she had murmured, her head pressed on the floor.

'Oh hey, I feel good, I feel damn fucking good!'

The Captain couldn't hold back from shouting, 'Your snatch is so tight.'

'I try very hard,' she said, and she clenched his prick so hard, he thought he might die.

'Screw me,' he'd demanded, and she grew red, even her shoulders turned a shade darker, as she went pump, pump, pump against his cock. She was squeezing him as if he were a tube of paste.

'Ride up and down my hot rod,' he commanded, and she did, vigorously squirming.

He snaked his long tongue into her ear and made her shiver with pleasure. He manhandled her, twisting her from side to side. She was gloriously compliant. Her tits dangled low and pretty.

He loved to stand, while they, the women, were bent over. It was like riding a horse, him erect in the saddle,

and like a horse, sometimes, they were out of control –
you couldn't hold them back, but had to ride, ride, ride
with them.

'Queen me,' he said. 'Cover me from head to toe with
your warm sticky slit. Be my eiderdown, be my quilt. I
want to wrap myself in you.'

The girl rocked up and down at him, pulling herself
on and off with an incredible dexterity and tightening
her little hole each time. Her arse was smiling at him.
Her breasts hung in front of him deliciously. He could
take it no more – the pressure on his cock was tremendous. He crushed himself into her, oblivious to her cries.
The whole world was wiped out, reduced to one swooping motion between the Brazilian girl's silk thighs.

'Oh, Sophie,' he wept as he exploded. 'You are my
everything!'

The staff of the *Prince Albert* got in deep trouble if they
missed a boat. They had to hitch a lift on another vessel
and then a panel of staff would judge their excuses – but
when the Captain was three hours late because he had
been fondling the budding breasts of the island's budding service industry, there was nothing anyone could
do. He was the boss – it's the boss's prerogative. The
boat was held up in harbour for three hours. The guests
were fit to riot.

The Captain promised he would make it up to them
all. Mostly, though, he resolved to find Sophie and get
her to admit that she was in love with him, once and for
all.

# Chapter Fourteen

$S$he saw him in the Sunset Bar. Destiny was propelling them together. Fate was playing tricks on them. Her hopeless attraction only increased each time she saw him.

'Hey, Mick!'

Mick looked round cautiously. She thought it was a little over the top, all this cloak-and-dagger stuff, but then he grinned his fantastic grin at her and she would have forgiven him anything.

'Hello, beautiful,' he said.

But he was with someone, the girl from the duty-free shop. They were standing intimately, yes, like they had slept together. You can always tell. It was the confidence, the assured way they handled each other. He disentangled himself from the girl's arms, whispered something and then slapped her dismissively on the bottom. The girl left demurely, without so much as a squeak.

'And I thought you weren't getting involved with anyone . . .' Sophie said.

'She's just a friend.'

'Looked like it,' she said sarcastically. 'There are rules about passengers fraternising with staff, didn't you know?'

'I'll be off then,' he said huffily.

'No.' She pawed at his sleeve. 'Please stay awhile. Let's talk.'

She convinced him by ordering a bottle of rum. He got them a table and insisted that she took the fancy armchair while he took the uncomfortable footstool against the wall. He is a gentleman, she thought.

She had decided to get him drunk. She wanted to see the side of him kept hidden in the day. When people drink a lot, the great closet doors of the mind open far wider than when sober; the skeletons all tumble out. The drunk become themselves – only more so. She wondered how Mick would be. She didn't have him down as an aggressive drinker – she knew enough of that kind, the kind of men whose brains disappear into their fists. Nor was he the kind who got jarringly horny, men who let their cocks make all their decisions for them. No, drunk, Mick would probably get cooler and cooler, until he froze over. Sophie was just a silly drunk. The daft side that she managed to subdue when sober triumphed given the right amount of whiskeys, wines and beers. But Mick didn't seem to mind. Innuendoes and double entendres bubbled forth between them. They were flirting, yes; it wouldn't be long now . . .

While Sophie was making jokes about the passengers, she was imagining him inside her. As he fiddled with the ashtray, she dreamed his fingers were on her. She wondered what his face looked like when he came. Everything seemed to acquire a glorious air of obscenity. In every helpless sentence, minding-their-own-business words, such as 'jug' or 'steam room', were imbued with the stain of soft porn.

And Sophie was working on him, tempting him.

'Why don't you take a risk now and then, have a little gamble?' she encouraged, making big eyes at him.

He stood up and held out his hand, all gallant. 'OK, let's go take a risk.'

'This wasn't exactly what I had in mind,' said Sophie after Mick had led her to the main hall. It had been transformed into a bingo emporium for the evening and was teeming with grey-haired gamblers with biros hanging round their necks.

'Have a little gamble, you said.' He played the innocent. 'I thought this is what you wanted.'

Sophie couldn't work it out. Either he really was dumb or he was pretending to be. Neither made sense.

'How many can you do at once?' he asked as he was handing over money for their cards.

'Lots,' she said with bravado. What the hell was he talking about?

He got her six sheets of paper, filled with squares of numbers.

'I'll stick to one,' he said.

'A one-girl guy?' she flirted. She may have lost the battle, but not the war.

'A one-paper guy,' he corrected. She realised when they had sat down that he would only have to look at one sheet at a time, whereas she had shot herself in the foot and would have to attempt the maximum, which would give her very little chance to concentrate on him.

They were on plastic chairs and it was uncomfortable, and not at all romantic. Sophie didn't exactly need flowers or chocolates to feel sexy, but the caller's cheesy jokes and the smell of fried onions really didn't do the trick. Mick looked quite at home, however, as he hovered, pen in hand, over his sheet. The compère announced the prizes and then the game began, while Sophie was still twittering. Mick asked her to be quiet or they wouldn't be able to keep up.

'Two fat ladies, eighty-eight.'

'More than two, I reckon,' Mick murmured, looking at some of the passengers as they squelched over the side of their chairs.

Sophie uncomfortably shifted from one buttock to another. Did Mick have a thing against hefty people? Was that what it was all about?

'Forty-four, knock on the door.'

'Twenty-one, my age.' Ha ha.

For want of anything better to do, Sophie scribbled

through the numbers. She wasn't doing too badly after all – 46, she needed 46. The caller shouted out 89, 45, oh so close, 15 and then 46!

'I've got it, I mean "line!"' yelped Sophie.

'They've already got a line,' hissed Mick urgently. 'Now we are looking for a full house.'

The other passengers were all tutting her. Mick laughed and laughed.

'Have you never played bingo before?'

'Not for years.' She used to say that watching paint dry (if it were a sweet magnolia or African violet) would be more interesting than this. But if he liked it then she would bloody well make the effort.

'N-n-nineteen,' bellowed the caller, followed by, 'Legs eleven!' He looked at Sophie and added, 'To the lady over there with the nice legs.'

A few people turned round.

'He said I had nice legs,' gushed Sophie.

'Well, you have,' Mick said, and Sophie forgot to mark down the next numbers. Mick took her finger and led it to the paper. She felt the electricity of his touch – it felt like her hair was standing on end. She was finding it hard to concentrate. Mick seemed to fill the space so well; he blotted all other life forms out of the picture.

'You missed a number,' he murmured.

'Did I?' Sophie responded, fruitlessly surveying her paper. 'I think I'll sit out this round.'

'Sixteen, sweet sixteen, and never been kissed.'

Sophie and Mick smiled at each other.

'Twenty-four, knock on the door.'

'He said that for forty-four,' Mick whispered into her ear, and his breath seemed to connect straight to that place between her legs. All show at playing bingo had been abandoned now. While the others scribbled and squinted over their papers, counting how many numbers needed to be filled, Sophie leaned back on the plastic seating, feeling almost breathless. Could she, dared she, open her thighs a little wider, just to show that he was invited in? It had worked with Tom; why wouldn't it work with him?

'Sixty-nine,' yelled the caller. 'My favourite!' The hall erupted into giggles.

But Mick looked at her sheet, refusing to meet her eye. The moment had been lost.

'Mick,' said Sophie urgently, 'I'm not sure I can do this.'

He laughed evasively. 'Look, you didn't mark that number off either.'

By midnight, Sophie had fallen in love with him.

Mick looked shocked when he realised the time. They had spent a whole three hours together – he should go, now. He gathered his jacket, his wallet, his travel pills and his cigarettes and started towards the door.

Sophie held back.

'I think you dropped something,' she murmured. She pressed her room key into his hand, leaving a little indentation on his palm. His arse looked perfect in jeans, not too generous, not too mean, and she was wondering what the stubble he had acquired in the few hours since she had last seen him would feel like against her face and elsewhere. And she thought, this is a cruise, after all. What are you supposed to do on a cruise ship, if not cruise?

Mick knew better than to say 'no.' His hands were warm.

'Thank you,' he said uncertainly.

'Tonight?'

'Yes?'

'I want . . . I want to see you.'

'Yes?'

That would be as much as she could get out of him. As Sophie turned to leave, the ship lurched sideways and Sophie slipped, just slightly, but she grabbed hold of him to stop her falling. Mick yanked her up. She raised his fingers and caught one easily between her lips. Heard him sigh, knew that she had affected him. Knew that the rocking movement of the boat, combined with the touch of her, were enough. He would be as aroused as she was. She gently nibbled the finger in her mouth, wrapped her tongue around it. Pretend it was his cock. He would know what she was thinking. It always works. Sucking fingers, not quite a blow job, more of a blow hobby; a promise of good things coming to those who wait.

'I'll see you,' he said.

'Yes, later,' she said. 'I can't wait.'

She was hammering the point home now, she knew, but . . .


She showered quickly, not allowing herself the time to luxuriate in the hot spray. Later, they would; later, they could. She searched her drawers for razors; trimmed her bush into a heart shape. When she was growing up there was a neighbour who trimmed his hedges into the shapes of animals – a parade of camels and donkeys and so on. One Christmas he had even carved reindeers and a sleigh out of the hedges in the back garden. His son was very handsome and Sophie used to think that she and her friends might offer their bushes up to him to practise on. She used to imagine sneaking over the hedge and into his bedroom, where she would lie prone and in a state of immense anticipation before the work would begin. Unable to contain himself he would eventually fling his scissors aside and tell her that he loved her. As Sophie shaved herself, she smiled at these sweet teenage reminiscences. She splashed on some body lotion; she made sure she smelled nice and that her skin was as smooth as possible.

As for clothes, she deliberated at her underwear drawers. She could put on so many different identities, so many different themes. She tried on a black cotton bra that set off her milky skin just so, but decided it was too simple. There are times when a girl might as well try hard – and this was one of those times. She chose a red lacy set. She looked dramatic, experienced – like a woman who knew what she wanted. At last, she was going to have him. She was almost trembling with anticipation. The base of the knicker was damp after a few seconds.

She looked in the mirror. It wasn't enough. Why not go the whole hog? A suspender belt, perhaps? She pulled on red fishnet stockings. Do men like fishnets because women look caught?

She clicked on the suspenders and admired herself in the mirror.

There is a strange tension when the body knows it is about to be fucked, like the calm before the storm. She wanted to touch herself, but she held off. The anticipation is the pleasure, she told herself, but she knew that, in this case, the doing would be the even greater pleasure.

She liked the idea of them out in the corridor, her palms flat against the wall, the attack on her skirt and then her panties ripped down as he came at her from behind. No, how about them in the casino perhaps, under the table, his cock in her mouth, her cunt in his face. Now, there was an idea. She could sixty-nine for hours, holding off the orgasm for as long as possible and then, when the pleasure reached its umpteenth peak, she would demand change, a quick shift of gear, and then his cock covered with her saliva could be swiftly inserted into her wet pussy. He would stay fully dressed, yes, in an evening suit, as he stuck his tongue on her clit; he would make sweet clamorous noises as he burrowed at her. He would demand that she spread her legs wider and wider, and she would pull his cock into her mouth, clenching his buttocks to her, driving him in and out. She waited and she waited. She pretended she wasn't waiting but she was, of course, she was.

How should she greet him? Would he want a drink first or should they go straight to it, straight at it, doggy style on the glass table? She would love that. She would love it if he caught her by the flanks and pumped himself inside her, without so much as a by your leave. She wouldn't mind if he pressed her nose against the surface and yanked her hair. She wouldn't mind if he bit her neck, leaving cool blue love tattoos. She wouldn't mind anything – as long as he wanted her.

When he didn't come, she had to make do with another friend – a bottle of whiskey. The Bastard. How dare he make her feel like this? He was deliberately making her feel bad. Just like trumps.

Sophie remembered how Mick's mouth felt on her skin. Hard and wet, powerful. He wanted her as much as she wanted him, she was sure of it. But the scam was what they were here for.

Getting laid had to be second to that. But it came a very close second.

She had to think of the money. The scam *über alles*. At least that was still going ahead.

Mick's stomach was churning. It was desperate. He was desperate. Sophie was driving him mad. It was as though he recognised her – but that was impossible because they had never met before. She was familiar to him, not in a dull way, but in a way that made him feel incredibly relaxed. Now that he knew her, everything had fallen into place. He liked the way she walked, her buoyant bottom twitching along the corridor, the way her small hand felt in his. That night in the bar, when he had seen his dolly-bird in the clinging minidress and Sophie side by side, he had known that there was no comparison. His feelings for Sophie were off the scale. OK, so her humour was slightly hit and miss, but she was so hot. Sophie Hemingway made Marilyn Monroe look like a convent girl, made Angelica Huston look gutless. But it wasn't just the curve of her buttocks, or even the brightness of her smile that made him feel lost; it was her aura. He wanted to be surrounded, to cave in to that. But he couldn't.

He wanted to run away. But that was what had got him here. And you can't run away from yourself.

She had asked him what he was going to do with the money. How could he tell her? She would laugh at him; everyone laughed at him. And who was this Josh who was masterminding the whole thing? Was she some angel to his Charlie or something even more sinister? Either way, it looked like the money was going to end up in someone else's hands – that's even if they got that far.

He looked forward to disembarking at the next port. After all, everyone needs a Plan B – especially if Plan A relied on a woman like Sophie.

His cock hardened in his hands. He wondered what he should think about. He rotated his fantasies because he didn't want to be unfair to any of the main stars. He didn't want to show favouritism by featuring some more than others. Recently, he had been completely biased. Once again, he put Sophie on top, him as the filling in the middle, and Jennifer underneath. (Sorry, Tom.) Of course, the girls went wild for him. They arched their backs and their eyes were glazed. They shouted his name and pulled at his skin. They were wet, wet and slippery, and they were both out of control. He saw Sophie's face, her eyes closed, gasping for air, like a fish out of water. Mick, please, Mick. He accelerated his hand. He felt his cock shudder, and then the salty come spat forward between his fingers like a victory parade.

was masterminding the whole thing? Was she some angel to the Chorus or something; a religious student? Either way, Tom liked her. At that moment, he saw the ocean. He felt himself to have a greater clarity too.

# Chapter Fifteen

$S$ophie dragged herself through the sit-ups, the arm-bends, the leg-bends, the whatever-you-call-them-bends and then sat looking out the gym portholes as the ocean knocked against the side of the ship. She had the mother of all hangovers, and working out was not a cure that she would recommend to anyone. However, the sky was a perfect blue. And the view was so much clearer than in the city. Come to think of it, everything seemed to have a greater clarity in post-alcoholic enlightenment.

Her life, her past, even her future. Her world stretched ahead of her, full of possibilities, an open sea. Amazing how being on the sea for this long affected your psyche. Living on water gave you weightlessness. There were so many lessons to be learned from this time spent on the ocean. She realised the futility of fighting against the current and the importance of swimming with it. Tom was the weakest link – but he would be persuaded. She could persuade him. And Moira too; bizarre Moira, with the even more bizarre friends, would tumble. And all she had to do was to stop thinking about Mick in that way and accept that he wasn't *the* one – he was just *a* one.

She used to fantasise about having sex with men in gyms. It was all that huffing and puffing and all that panting that set her off. The way the men's muscles strained and their veins bulged. It was the effort involved that excited her, the sheer exertion of a kind that is usually confined to the bedroom that was the turn on.

Her quarry arrived promptly, as she knew he would. Tom was fastidious not only about his body, but about time as well. Sophie hoped no other member of staff was going to turn up. Rule 25 said that if there were more than three staff members in the gym at any one time then one of them had to leave. If Sophie had been a religious kind of girl, she would have prayed that they wouldn't be interrupted before the deed was done.

She parked herself on the mat next to Tom, where he was doing an extensive series of stretches that formed part of his warm-up. Unusually for a man, Tom's warm-ups were extremely long-winded in comparison with his actual workout. But he had a strict routine of running, the stationary bike, sit-ups, free-weights and bench presses. He was a little concerned that his top half did not match his more buff bottom half, and he was now training hard on his arms to redress the imbalance. Jennifer had indicated that the triangular look was not an option.

'Hi,' he said meekly.

Ahead of them, three big guys attempting to lift a heavy set of weights were grunting and snorting like boars after truffles.

Sophie could also be timely. She threw off her T-shirt, revealing a black-fringed sports bra, which displayed her tits like ripe buns. Tom wished that he could dive in there, plunge into that so-beautiful line of cleavage and put some white icing on top. He packed the thoughts away. Think of Jenny-Wenny, think of Jenny-Fur. But he could smell Sophie's perspiration and see the dark circles under her arms. It was lovely.

Then she pulled her knicker strap high and pushed her shorts lower, so that he could glimpse the tantalising bit of string.

'You're wearing a G-string,' he said, but then, embar-

90

rassed, he chewed his nails. He wanted to pull out his tongue and give it to the cat. (Or the pussy.)

'Yes,' she said, looking down and giggling.

'It's black,' he said.

'It certainly is.'

They stared at each other. And then they both said at the same time, 'I like black. Do you like black?' And then they both laughed.

'Black's my favourite colour,' Tom finished. 'For underwear I mean.'

'What kind of underwear do you like best?'

Oh, these questions! He had been waiting to talk about these things all his life, and now he had the chance. His cock was stirring with pleasure.

'I like sporty, stretchy stuff. Lycra. With G-strings, I like to tug them really tight, so they ride up the arse, rubbing all over.'

'Hmm, sports bras are good but, sometimes, I like to wear really delicate, lacy stuff, you know, where the nipple is almost pushing through the gaps in the material. And I like it when it's kind of tight and restricting.'

Oh God, it was wonderful to listen to her. He wanted his Jenny-Wenny to talk to him like this. He wanted Jenny to say those words, but instead he had got someone else. Which was more overwhelming, the desire for the adventure itself or the desire for the person? Tom was struggling.

'I like to pull the bra down, so, as you –' Tom gulped; should he say 'you' or 'she'? '– are still wearing them underneath your titties, your nipples are totally exposed.'

'Oh yes. I love the way that looks with my tits sticking out over the top of the bra. It looks so dirty somehow. Old-fashioned even.'

'I like fucking with underwear still on, just pulled to the side, just ripped away to let me at your body with my mouth or my cock.'

'What about basques, do you like them?'

'You mean those things with the strings?'

'Yes, all laced up, old-fashioned style.'

'Yeah, that would be fantastic, if your tits poked out on top. Yeah, like a French maid?'

'Exactly. You get that great curve, where the waist goes in and then out for the tits. And I like stockings and suspenders too. I feel fantastic when I wear them. Just really hot. I can't get enough of them.'

'Oh, shit,' he said gruffly, 'so do I. I love the way the upper thigh looks, the bare bit, the open fleshy plane, before the action starts again.'

'I love wearing them. I might put them on tonight, just walk round my room a bit, look in the mirror, you know.'

Tom paused thoughtfully. 'But I also like little skirts and . . . and tight blouses.'

'Oh yes, that's horny too, like a little uniform? The look cries out for someone to put you over their knee and give you a good spanking.'

'I like those loose kind of knickers . . .'

'French knickers?'

'Yeah, they are kind of baggy and they seem to just invite someone to sneak up a finger . . .'

'To explore the honey pot. I know exactly what you mean. White satin ones, with a white teddy top, that's good.'

'What's a teddy top?'

'The loose ones, like a vest, that just glide over the breasts, just glide over like a tongue.'

'This is getting a bit –' said Tom, suddenly self-aware. What was he doing?

'Close to the knuckle?' suggested Sophie.

The words echoed around Tom's head. Close to the knuckle, honey; take it further . . .

'I suppose I'm a breast man actually,' he added self-consciously.

'What do you think of mine?'

Perhaps 'How often do you think of them?' would have been a better question – at least Tom would have had a ready answer: every day, and every minute of every day. They say men think of sex about every five minutes. What they don't say is that they think of tits every two. The swell of them, the way they seemed to be looking at him, saying to him, yes, feel me, squeeze me. The temptation of them was too much to resist.

'They're lovely.'

'Would you like to touch them?'

'What, here?'

'No one's looking,' she encouraged. They weren't. The big chaps were far too interested in their own reflection to pay any mind to the inert couple in the corner.

He reached out his hand and he was a small boy once again, invited to play doctors and nurses with the neighbourhood girls. Show me yours and I'll show you mine. He reached out unsteadily. Her fingers met his and guided them to her breasts. She was warm, and then he could feel that hard, protruding nipple. For one weird moment he thought of his favourite sweets, Liquorice Allsorts. She was so moist and lovely, wet cotton wool, but not soggy, just moist.

'How does it feel?'

'Fantastic!'

'Really?'

'Yes!'

He had turned monosyllabic. Unable to think straight, talk straight. He didn't even dare do what he wanted to do, which was to clasp that titty really tight. He didn't want her to change his mind.

He leaned tentatively towards her. He had followed his cues admirably. He kissed her. At first it was a shock, a strange tongue in his mouth, but then he couldn't get enough of it. He was searching her mouth with his tongue, struggling against her but with her. Hard, passionate kisses, the kisses of people who fancy each other but don't know each other, and don't really want to. He was kissing her so forcefully that he was biting her, and she had to come up for air. He loved it.

'Do you like it?' he asked. He had to know. He had to hear her say it. Otherwise, what was the point?

'Oh God, yes,' she said between breaths, 'oh yes.'

And then the spell was broken.

'I'm sorry, I can't,' he said.

Sophie wanted to scream, 'Yes, you can. Yes, you fucking can.' But instead she said carefully, 'OK, whatever you want.'

'I'm sorry.'

She wiped her lips and stared up at him doe-eyed. She couldn't leave it at that.

'My nipples are rock hard.'

He gave a groan and then whipped her into his arms again. His tongue was trailing a sweet trail inside her mouth. And then from somewhere came a super amount of willpower rising like Godzilla. Tom pulled back, and this time she knew that she had lost him for that night, if not for always.

Tom couldn't face going back to the cabin. The room he shared with Jennifer had never felt so small. He thought he would die of claustrophobia or of longing. He walked around the deck, watching the honeymoon couples saunter hand in hand. How uncomplicated they appeared, how lucky they were. He wished, no, he yearned to feel simple, undiluted love again.

When he eventually returned, Jenny was lounging on the bed.

'Tom, honey, Jenny-Wenny can't sleep. Could baby-wayby make me feel better?'

Tom was glad to alleviate his emotional discontent with a practical solution. He hugged her, the gratitude flooding through him. Out in the world he was surrounded by danger, predatory sharks; here in his cabin, with her, he was safe. He dutifully massaged her back. She had a magnificent back; Jennifer had a magnificent everything. He explored the slopes, the curves, the sharp bits and the smooth bits, as he wandered down into the small of her back and beyond. And he tried not to think of Sophie.

'Do you like it?' he asked. 'Is this OK?'

'Mmm,' she said vaguely.

'Do you like my fingers on your skin?'

'Uh huh.'

(Jennifer wished he wouldn't talk so much sometimes. He hardly ever chatted; he hated gossip, which was why it was a mystery that he suddenly discovered his voice when he was under the covers.)

Tom continued the long deep strokes. Every muscle was worked, every limb tendered. He liked to think he knew what he was doing.

'Does it feel good, Jen?' he urged.

'Uh huh,' she murmured. Why wouldn't he just get on with it?

'Do you like me touching you, honey?' he asked. He would try just one last time to get her to say it aloud.

'Yes,' she answered awkwardly.

He knew she wasn't really interested. He wondered what things Sophie would say if he massaged her back. She would probably holler. She would probably flail and drown in his hands, telling him what to do, ordering him around. He stopped quickly, withdrawing from his thoughts. He added more lotion to his palms. He shouldn't have been thinking like that ... It was just, well, Sophie smelled of sex, and Jennifer smelled of some artificial substance that came in small glass pyramids or crystal bottles and cost her week's wages.

He was hard. He stroked the crack of her arse with his cock and she groaned. He couldn't tell if that was a not-again groan or a do-it-some-more groan, so he waited and then did it again. This time there was no response.

'Jenny?'

She was asleep. Conked out like a car that wouldn't start on a winter morning. Tom surveyed her sleeping body. His mates had given Jennifer the accolade 'sex on legs', and that had made him happy, although he sometimes thought: if only you knew. She did look sexy, there was no denying that. And it was him she wanted to marry, no one else.

He could do what he liked with her, surely he could, couldn't he? There was nothing in the rules to say that he couldn't. If she said no, he wouldn't – but if she said nothing, that was more ambiguous – it was left to him to decide. She looked beautiful; her fine profile, her snub nose pressed on the pillow. He picked her hair up, exposing the white nape of her neck. He brushed it with his lips.

'Jenny?'

Yes, she was fast asleep. He wondered why we say fast asleep, when her sleep was so slow, so sensual, her breathing deep and unhurried. He angled himself over her. He wanted to squeeze that arse, squeeze it till the juice ran down her legs, but he couldn't wake her up.

He knew she wouldn't like what he was going to do next. But she wouldn't know. He angled himself over her, one hand on the small of her back, among the delicious golden hairs. Look at that arse! He almost said it aloud. For fuck's sake, look at that smooth, shiny arse. He had one hand on his ever-ripening cock; the other was holding him up, press-up style on the mattress. He pumped his dick up and down. He imagined he was going to come inside her, thinking how tight it was, and narrow. And he is big, so big. He was coming. He squealed with excitement, and managed to suffocate his come inside a tissue.

Jennifer let out a little snore.

# Chapter Sixteen

*S*ophie put on the goggles and closed her eyes. The exact same moment that the sunbed clicked on, she thought she heard something. But no, there was nothing. She waited an obligatory five minutes and then, when her thighs were sweating and her buttocks were hot against the surface, she tentatively moved her hands down.

'Sophie Hemingway!'

Moira was peering over at her. Moira took the second bed and said she was glad to see her. She wondered if Sophie wanted to come dancing with her.

'I used to be a dancer,' Moira said. 'I used to work on a big showboat in New Orleans. Didn't you know? Then I damaged my ankle – so now I'm stuck at the casino.'

'Don't you like being a cashier?'

'The money is not very good . . .'

Sophie bit her lip. Was this a good time to ask if she would join in the scam? She looked at Moira's dreamy face highlighted in the orange light and decided not.

'But then I meet the most interesting people and have plenty of hot experiences. Croupiers are an entertaining bunch.'

'What happened to the girl that looked like me?'

'Where was I? Oh yes, I was telling her that she had

97

learned about masturbation and, well, what can we call it? Mutual masturbation; now she had to learn what to do when there are two people involved. I said, "You have to do something for your guy too." Although, Sophie, don't you think, he probably wouldn't complain if his girlfriend orgasmed with such velocity every time he touched her? Who could fail to be flattered? If not flattened.'

Sophie laughed appreciatively.

'I said, "I want you to give me pleasure now." To tell the truth, I'd had no qualms left at all. They had all packed their bags and flown away. She had gone for it and, now, so should I. "But you are a woman," she said dumbly. "Same difference," I said. "What you have to do is read my signs – see how I enjoy some things and not others. To help you, I am going to wear a blindfold. And this means you can do with me what you like." "Shall I use the dildo?" "Not straight away," I suggested. God, she was dumb. She loosely bound my wrists. I tried to sound encouraging but, really, I was not particularly optimistic. I didn't think she was going to get the hang of this. She might thrash around and come with a bang, but if all she was going to do was lie back and think of England then . . . "Where shall I start?" she asked. "There are no rules," I told her. "It's not like doh, ray, me."'

Sophie grinned. Moira was evidently relishing the storytelling. She swung around animatedly on the sunbed.

'She came to my breasts; she licked around them; she rooted for my nipple and sucked tight. I began to relax. OK, maybe it was beginner's luck, or maybe she was a vacuum cleaner in a past life, but she was soon doing a very good job. I could feel bolts of pleasure extend all over my body. I was feeling good. Horny even. I opened my legs, hoping that she would take the hint. She didn't at first. I let her go on for a few minutes and then, when I was afraid that the pain would outweigh the pleasure, I said, "Don't forget there are many parts of the anatomy that like to be touched." "Oh yes," she said, "I was enjoying it so much, watching and feeling your nipple harden in my mouth . . ." Actually, Sophie, she did look awfully like you.

'"You might want to touch me, you know, where I touched you," I said. "OK," she said amicably. She trailed her fingers over me, very delicately. It was lovely feeling fingers fluttering on my thighs, and then she reached upwards to my exposed bush. "Shall I touch you here?" she asked. "Why not?" I said. I suppose I had resigned myself to the fact that I was going to have to talk her through the whole thing. She stole inside my pussy and I told her how I liked it. I have to say she was a quicker learner than most of the men – and most men have been doing it for years – she had only started that day. And she responded with a fluency that was most unlike the beginner she was. I couldn't stop arching my back towards her stroke and I was begging her to keep going now. Just a little further, just a little more. She rubbed me fine.'

'So what happened then?' asked Sophie, because she felt it was expected of her.

'"I'm almost there," I said . . . and then she stopped. "Moira," she murmured, and I thought, Oh, God, what is she going to request now? Couldn't she just obey orders for a change! "I have a strange urge," she said. "What is it?" I asked wearily. I was almost getting off on her fingers; did she have to spoil everything? "I want to lick you all over." "If you like," I said nonchalantly, "whatever you like."'

'So did she?' asked Sophie. Not because she felt it was expected of her, but because she wanted to know.

'Oh yes. It was a good experience. You should try it, Sophie. I think you would be a good lesbian.'

'Why do you say that?' Sophie said coolly. She didn't know whether to be annoyed or flattered. A good lesbian? She didn't think so!

'I just reckon that you would, don't you?'

'Not really.'

'You have to be a risk-taker, that's all. Just dare to challenge. Aren't you that kind of woman?'

99

Sophie looked away. She remembered the afternoon in the jacuzzi and the way Moira had moved her body. And the story she had told her. If you listened closely, you might have heard the penny drop.

Tom found the letter in his locker. He knew he shouldn't open it. Shouldn't, shouldn't, mustn't. It would only give him the raging horn. He dangled the note over the waste bin. He knew it was from Sophie, and he didn't dare open that box of tricks. He had a horrid sinking feeling but, at the same time, he felt as though he had been pushed up to the surface.

He remembered a story his English teacher had once told him. His English teacher wore tight black skirts that creased and stretched ever so slightly over a tiny bump of tummy. The skirts had a slit up the back and she wore black stockings, although they were probably tights, he never did get a glimpse above the knee, but they were superb anyway. They were (what are they called with those big holes as large as a little finger?) gorgeous. He remembered that she had a slight West Country accent and that the way she said her R's kept him spellbound. He never told the other boys, they would have laughed, for she was at least, well, fairly middle-aged, but they probably felt the same. She was passionate about the Greeks, and she would get seriously excited about Beowulf.

He would volunteer to go to the stockroom with her, not because he seriously thought anything might happen, but because he could watch her as she bent over, getting those towers of books, ordering him around, advising him what to read or not. 'Tom, this is grrreat. Tom, can you carrry this for me?' He held the books to conceal his teenage erections. And he pretended he was more interested than he was. But when she told him that story, that story about the sailors, he was interested; it had captured something in him then. For the first time, he understood, saw the purpose in what the writer was trying to say, and for the first (and last) time in his reading career, he thought, I am not alone.

He read how the ship approached the infamous area with gathering trepidation. He read how the captain ordered each man to be lashed against the masts, how the captain himself had tied them, moving rapidly from one man to the next, as the water moved them relentlessly to certain seduction. Finally the captain tied himself up as they approached the danger zone. And then the sirens began to sing. And wail, soothe and plead, and each man heard something different, but each man heard temptation. And one man's torment was so great that he freed himself to dive into the sea and then to drown.

When the teacher read it, Tom's hard-on was so big, he thought the desk would rise up, and in the sirens he saw all women, and in the captain he saw himself. Would he ever be strong enough to resist? No, he had the willpower of a gnu. He would have been the idiot who worked himself free and drowned in the process.

He parted the envelope softly, as though it were part of her body. He thought about her licking the edges, her pink tongue peeping from between the ruby lips. That idea alone made him horny – the letter even more so . . .

*I want you. I want your tongue running over my face, creeping into my mouth. My tongue and your tongue entwined, mirroring what your cock will do. Mouths mirroring the fucking, yours on mine, mine on yours, inseparable, wet, inescapable fucking passion. I want you to ram your cock at me, down my throat, in my cunt, up my arse. I want you to eat me out.*

Tom gulped. He was in big trouble. To get his mind off it, to get his mind off *her*, he retreated to his cabin and did hard and fast sit-ups. Feet locked under the bed, his stomach muscles were trembling. His fists were clenched like oranges. After two hundred, he went and threw up over the ship's railings.

When he told Jennifer that he had been sick, she asked him if it was something he had eaten.

The following day, on the way to Sophie's cabin, Tom saw a horrible thing. A bird flew into the window. Dashed, it became a tangle of feathers and blood. Poor little bird. Tom almost turned around. But he didn't. He hammered on Sophie's door. He had tried to resist. Fuck, he had tried. He didn't want to be there. He knew it was a fucking bad idea; he knew it in his head, his gut, his very soul, but his balls ached and his cock was shouting at him, 'Why not? You deserve it! She wants you, you great big tight-arsed prick-fucker!'

Jennifer was at work. Jennifer, sweet Jennifer, who just wasn't hot enough. God knows he had tried to heat her up, but there was nothing there. He was a Boy Scout all over again, fruitlessly rubbing bits of wood together and expecting them to spark. But it just didn't happen. He whispered stuff in her ear and she said it tickled; he tickled her and she complained that it scratched.

And then he thought of Sophie. He thought of her arse as she stretched out over the green baize. Fuckable Sophie. And the rude words she said. Jennifer would say that she was crude. Jennifer didn't say things like 'I want you to fuck me.' She said, 'Shall we go to bed now?' with her head cocked to one side like a puppy.

He couldn't get Sophie's legs out of his mind. Forget haunted houses, a pair of gorgeous thighs was spooking him. That's where he wanted to stick his head. And Jennifer was stingy with the oral. Stingy, no, she was properly Scrooge-like in her attention to his genitalia. Jennifer didn't see the point, now that they were engaged. God knows what she would do (or wouldn't do) when they were married.

Sophie wanted him to fuck her! That was what she said! Jesus H Christ! And if that wasn't the final straw that broke the camel's back then the fact that Jennifer had refused to kiss him on the lips that morning, because he had sneaked in an early cigarette, was.

'Who is it?'

'It's Tom. Can I come in?'

Sophie jubilantly opened her cabin door. Victory! Tom looked more dishevelled than she had ever seen him. He was leaning against the doorframe as though without it he would bellyflop to the floor. Again she could feel the rock of the floor beneath her feet, that sensuous sway of the lovers making out. Perhaps he could feel it too.

Now he was inside the room, he felt more petrified than ever. Sophie smelled of sex, of between the legs, of that peculiar white stuff. He remembered the first time he ever sniffed it. A babysitter used to come to their house to look after him. She used to send him to bed early and then raid their fridge, put the TV on loud and go through his parents' book collection. One time, though, she had shooed him to bed extra early. He could feel her anxiety, feel that she wanted him out the way, which only made him all the more reluctant to go. He remembered the doorbell ringing and, an hour later, he went sleepily downstairs to get a drink. It used to annoy her when he did that, but he did it nevertheless. That time, though, she didn't spring up to tell him off; instead, he saw her there. Now, he wasn't sure if he remembered correctly, but he thinks she was sitting on top of a man. Both of them were naked.

He had seen all of her naked body: the slant of her back; the broad sweep of her hips; her shoulders; and she was making a noise like she was hurt, and she was moving around on top of him like she wanted to get off but then decided to sit down again, and she did that several times, getting faster and faster. And then she had wiped herself and thrown the tissue carelessly in the bin. The condom wrapper was wet and there were tissues over the floor from where she had wiped herself. The sight didn't stay with him, but the smell did.

Sophie locked the door once Tom had crossed the threshold, and the click was deafening. He was standing really close to her. Sophie stepped back. He smelled gorgeous; he looked even better in casual clothes than in his tuxedo. No, that wasn't possible. He looked equally stunning.

'What is it?' Now she could afford to be cool.

'Your letter,' he mumbled.

'Did you like it?' She was still not looking at him.

'I . . . enjoyed it very much.'

'I didn't know if you would be offended.'

'I wasn't offended; I was flattered.'

'It's quite difficult to do . . . you know, to be honest.'

'I appreciate it.'

His knuckles were white with tension.

'What about Jennifer?' she asked. The deception of Jennifer was fundamental to the success of the plan – only if she had some power over Tom, only then, would he agree to the scam.

'She won't find out,' he said, but it was more of a question than a promise.

'What if she did?' Sophie pushed. She had to know how important it was to him, how far he would go to protect her.

'She won't,' he said.

Sophie was satisfied. The business could commence.

'You should undress.'

He didn't know it would be like this. He stared at her nervously.

'Take off your top,' she said.

He unbuttoned his shirt. A scientific experiment once showed that a man's pupils dilate most at the sight of a woman in a bikini. The same experiment suggested that a woman's eyes dilate most at the sight of a baby. Wrong. They did not test a woman's eyes when she sees a handsome, well-built man undo his white shirt. Sophie's pupils expanded as Tom stripped off. All this was for her benefit, at her command. He had black hair in a T-shape over that well-shaped chest, and his arms were huge, twice the size of hers. There was a thick line of black hair leading down to his white pants.

'And your trousers.'

He pulled down his cords.

'And . . .' She raised one eyebrow at his pants. 'You might as well get rid of those – you won't be needing them.'

He wanted her to do it to him, to be the responsible one. Please, miss, it wasn't my fault. He stood awkwardly in front of her, naked. Wasn't she going to do anything? His cock was at the undecided stage, whether to go up or whether to go down. Up. It was going up.

He held his breath. Perhaps she was laughing at him. He felt like a fool. Finally, after he thought it was all a terrible mistake, she sank to her knees in front of it. His voice was throaty.

'What are you going to do?'

'I'm going to suck you.'

'How?'

'I want to suck you, I want to . . .'

She leaned forwards and, very gently with her magic tongue, she licked the vein that ran on the underside. She licked right up to the point where it fattened out, right up to the glorious poking head. She had to lick it, had to tongue the shaft of him, put her hands on his balls, tickle the veins, take it all in her mouth, so that there was nowhere to go but inwards and upwards.

'Hello, sailor,' she murmured. 'Hello, seaman.'

'Tell me what you're feeling,' he requested, and he put his hand on her hair, not tight enough to make her annoyed, but just firm enough to make her feel appreciated.

She was feeling wet. And hot. And single-minded. She was going to straddle his thick shaft and paddle all the way to the Orinoco. So what if this was business? Who was to say that you couldn't enjoy your job? She nibbled the trunk then gazed up at him.

'I feel horny.'

'You look horny. You look fucking incredible.'

She worked the nob in and out of her mouth. He groaned. She wasn't laughing at him. They were laughing together. She started unbuttoning her own clothes, all the while not letting up the fantastic caressing of his prick. She hitched up her skirt without any time wasting, no procrastination, for there had been too much foreplay and no real action already. She wasn't that big on warm-ups.

She held him firm at the base, worked him up and down, and kept the head wet with her tongue. He stood out at 90 degrees from his body, which meant (Sophie did a quick calculation borne of years of practice) that the best position – that is the position most likely to do it for her – would be her on top.

He tried to help pull her clothes off but gave up. He couldn't do anything but enjoy the way she took care of him.

'Oh God, oh God.'

She had everything off. Everything but those skinny knickers and a tight vest.

'Oh God, let's fuck, quick, do it, now,' he burst.

She held him down by the right shoulder and, with her free hand, she started pulling off her camisole. She released herself from her top, so that he could watch the fall of her breasts. Watch, but do not touch. Not yet. She kept her knickers on but tugged them apart, so that he could see the thin landing strip of her pubic hair. And then she pushed him on her dressing table stool and climbed aboard. As she felt his hot cock burrow into her, she couldn't contain a gasp. He was busily contorting his features, trying not to come too soon. She rotated over him, grinding into him. She felt her tits, because they were her own, and because she knew from his eyes that the sight of her was tremendous, and she let one hand touch his lips, and he licked her finger as though she were a princess and he a mere servant boy and that was all she would deign to give him.

She had him over the table. And then when she was atop him, on top of the world, she asked him to pass her a cigarette. It was not because she liked them, nor because she wanted to share what was his, but because she wanted to show him that she was the boss. And then, buckling and straddling over him, she fucked him, she fucked him the way the ocean fucks the ocean bed, and he pulled at her flanks, and then they came tumbling together with a roar like clouds clashing together.

He grew addicted, poor Tom. After that first time, he fled back to his cabin. But the damage was done. You know when you are younger and you think sex is just about putting it in, shaking it about and you turn around? Well, that was the night when he realised what all the fuss was about. He begged Sophie to come to his cabin when Jennifer was at work in the beauty salon, eloquently dishing out hairdos and advice.

She was wearing an all-in-one with short sleeves. Her breasts pressed against the string, like satsumas in a sack, and you could see her bush through the material. He adored it. He turned real passionate, uncontrollable. He pushed the straps off her shoulders and poured himself over her.

Sophie lay beneath him, her knees pulled up so they nearly jabbed out her own eyes. What a display! What a pussy! He never knew 'missionary' could feel this good.

'Oh, you're so tight.' Her snatch consumed him.

'More, more.' Her tongue was all over him. 'Don't stop!' She was a cannibal.

'Louder,' he begged. He liked his efforts to be appreciated, not just physically, but verbally too.

So she screamed for more. And soon, she wasn't pretending, she was really screaming. And at the last minute, as she started to jiggle frantically and to rip him closer to her, he rose like a sceptre and slammed himself inside her writhing fruit. The sex was incredible, but the look in his eyes grew darker and darker, the hope grew dimmer.

He gnawed her to the bone. They fucked until they were raw. They didn't bother pretending they had anything else in common. They liked fucking. Each other. That was it.

Next, she got on top of him but facing away. He

watched her back and arse. She watched the blank wall, and dreamed that she was screwing someone else. He put his fingers round to her clit as she thumped up and down, and she leaned forwards, her head close to his ankles to make sure the cock went as deep as it could, as hard as it would. And he lifted her up and down, and up and down, and she felt like a rocket about to take off. She put her hand between her legs, past his hand, down to hang on to his balls, and he gasped with the additional unexpected pleasures. And she massaged him there as he cried that she mustn't stop. She felt his hard cock surge up her. And her pleasure escalated to an incredible pitch, an obscene level, and she charged against him, with him, under him, over him and around him.

And then, after they had tossed and turned on his and Jennifer's pristine sheets, he told her to leave.

'I can't believe what we just did,' he said, and he sank his face in the pillow as he had done between her legs. He was ashamed of himself, for being with her. He was turning into his father, he said.

'What would Jenny do if she found out?'

'She won't find out,' he said. He hated it when other people called her Jenny – that was his name for her, not the world's.

'What if someone told her?'

'She wouldn't believe them,' he said, and he was convinced of it. He and Jennifer simply weren't the sort to have affairs.

She wouldn't believe it, huh? thought Sophie. She hadn't counted on that.

# Chapter Seventeen

*T*hat night, the casino was swinging. The tables were packed with both players and spectators and, as more and more people arrived, and more and more money exchanged hands, the excitement mounted. Someone was going to get rich tonight. Sophie loved working when it was like this. It was like watching a show, but participating at the same time. The staff couldn't empty the ashtrays quick enough and the room was foggy with the blur of smoke. One man was winning on the roulette. He wanted to gamble on, to double his money, but his wife didn't. She threatened to walk out. She told him to stop. She told him verbally and then with her expression, which bled disapproval. He called her bluff, not even looking behind him to acknowledge her. She stayed. He put $10,000 on red. Two to one. A 50 per cent chance of winning. He lost. The woman didn't even look furious any more. She just picked up her bag and left.

Moira was working, counting out the winnings with little enthusiasm. When she saw Sophie, she blew her a big fat kiss. Sophie grimaced. Moira was so unpredictable. She didn't know what the girl would do next. Mick came in. This time, he was with a dark girl. He tried to avoid Sophie; they hadn't seen each other since that night in the bar – the night he blew her out – but the girl he was with dragged him over to Sophie's table.

'Let's play here,' she requested. Her thick eyelashes wouldn't stop fluttering over her pink complacent face and Sophie hated her.

'I don't like roulette,' he said and tried to move her along but she refused.

'I want to play here,' she insisted, hands on hips. Sophie could imagine her stamping her feet like a toddler if her wishes weren't fulfilled. And she was insensitive too. Somehow, she didn't even sense the tension between Mick and Sophie, which, as the minutes ticked by, thickened even further. As the girl placed her bets (in typical beginner's fashion) she was giggling so hard that her whole body was shaking. Sophie spun the wheel, wishing she would spin the girl's head off, and was glad to see that she didn't win. Sophie was aware, so aware of Mick across from her. They both reached for the chips at the same time and Sophie had watched spellbound as Mick's beautiful dark fingers had accidentally closed over hers and then pulled themselves free.

'I'm hungry,' whined the girl.

'Have a sandwich,' Mick advised.

'I need some hot meat inside me,' she said and then smiled salaciously.

Sophie groaned inwardly but Mick led the girl away. He put his arm round her casually and he left without looking back, but, somehow, Sophie had known that he wanted to.

Sophie was transferred over to the blackjack table. She noticed that one of the players was trying to count cards, so that he could anticipate what cards would be put down next. If he was successful, Sophie would have to report him, but he wasn't. Even though he was moving his lips with the effort, and his eyes were glazed with concentration, he kept betting at the wrong time and losing against the house. It requires more ingenuity than that to win, Sophie thought, although she couldn't help sympathising.

During her break, she decided to follow Mick. She knew where he would be.

Mick was an iceman, frosty to the core, but she understood the way his mind worked. He did like her, she was sure of it. The other girls meant nothing to him. As for his behaviour, she couldn't put her finger on it (but she suspected he *wanted* her to).

He was on the deck near where they had met – near 'their place'. How dare he take someone else there? He and the girl were joined together, connected at the pelvis. Her arms were outstretched like a scarecrow, but she wasn't frightening anyone off. On the contrary, she was attracting more attention than she deserved.

Mick had shoved the girl's sweater over her head. He had pulled the cups of her bra down and he had pushed his face into her breasts. He had pushed them together and buried his nose really deep in there like he was sniffing her, and he rubbed her nipples with his big swollen thumbs.

And Sophie said, 'Hello, Mick,' but he ignored her, or maybe he didn't hear. And all she could think was that she wanted him to stop it, stop that, and then maybe, maybe, maybe it will be OK. After all, there were many people around, and what could he do, how far could he go?

But the girl was wearing a miniskirt and, before long, he was pushing that up too. Sophie watched the hem journey northwards. She could see the girl's rounded thighs and then her white cotton panties. He didn't dally; within seconds he had pulled her knickers down, and then he knelt down reverentially before her. At first, it seemed to Sophie that he didn't do anything. He just squatted, facing her pussy, and then, with both hands, he touched her with tender fingers, as though he were modelling clay. The girl sighed and purred, running fervent fingers through his golden hair. And then he parted her lips and licked her down there.

Sophie shivered. Mick kept going on about not getting

involved – but they were involved, whether he liked it or not.

The Captain prowled around the ship in his secret heels. That is, he liked to think he prowled; in fact, his legs were so muscular that he waddled. He knew people looked at him, and he liked to cause a stir. His cap covered a distinguished drizzle of grey hair. It was difficult to guess his age. People also found him difficult to place. After so many years spent at sea, his English was un-accented, his experiences too diverse. The medals and the tightness of the shirt, which might have appeared comical in others, seemed appropriate on him. The Captain's shirt was always impeccably white, although when he sweated, and even the Captain sweated, you could see through to his tan skin. The guests parted as he walked through the corridors, and who could blame him for thinking it was a bit like when the Red Sea parted for Moses?

'He's so handsome!'

'Now, that's what I call a captain.'

If his guests had known what he was thinking as he joined them for their evening meal, they would probably have been less adoring. He sat the attractive women near him, and their unattractive husbands further away. He talked politics and history while making league tables of whom he guessed was fucking the most. He liked the swell at the front of his trousers. Don't think he didn't know that the trousers were just a little too tight over the crotch; not so snug as to be called indecent, but certainly snug enough to get him noticed. A swell like his certainly separated the men from the boys.

Everyone knew that the *Prince Albert* was a fantasy fulfiller. The Captain decided it was high time he fulfilled a few of his. Watching Sophie move, in that silky skirt that skimmed her thighs and a vest top that cut a little into her arms, the Captain had been more than impressed. She was so curvaceous that she was almost chubby, and the Captain disagreed vehemently with

112

chubbiness, but somehow she seemed very appealing. He could lose his finger in that sweet bouncy flesh. A plump arse was an arse that you would never want to leave. He thought about what he would like to do with her.

He had the last croupier, too, only she had left. Only once, but oh yes, he had her. When he had found out about her crime of passion with a passenger, he had called her into his office, reprimanded her until tears had formed in her eyes. But she wouldn't release them, stroppy mare. Not until later, after his dressing down (yes, another dressing down!) and she begged him for punishment. The Captain still reminisced about her wet pussy, the white moons of those buttocks as he held her down over his knees. She meowed like a cat, and when he made her get down to suck him, she groaned and rolled on her back, as though she were waiting to be tickled.

The Captain's purple monster, the vein in his forehead, began to beat its familiar tune.

# *Chapter Eighteen*

*S*ophie hadn't anticipated that, for much of the time, being involved in criminal activities simply meant that she had to keep people sweet. She had to ensure everyone was happy enough not to bother with her – that was 80 per cent of her task. She had to make it up to the staff. There was the photographer, the pit bosses, the managers, the rota organisers. She needed to be kept informed about spies, so she needed tip-offs. It seemed a constant round of being nice to people – definitely not what she had envisaged. And the staff were such a frisky lot. Really. Because the rules governing relations with passengers were so strict, the staff looked to themselves for entertainment and they had grown rather good at it.

The night after she saw Mick with that girl, Sophie organised a gambling den in her cabin. There were six of them to begin with: a steward, a purser, Stephanie – a musician – and two other girls, Teresa and Jo. They were all very drunk. They started playing Newmarket. And the loser, the one who didn't get anything in that round, had to remove an item of clothing. Sophie started out well. She kept on most of her clothes, except for her slingbacks. Then she went on a losing streak. She noticed the purser was watching her the whole time.

Then, Stephanie and the steward said they had had

enough. Stephanie was as pissed as a newt. They went to the sofa and said they were going to watch TV, but when Sophie looked round they weren't watching anything; they were getting frisky. It was acknowledged that they had been dating for the last two months, but still . . . he had his hand down her top. Sophie knew they were turned on by the fact that they were there; she could see the purser was getting even more aroused.

The other girl, Teresa, took off her shirt and her bra, so she was wearing just a skirt. She fell asleep and the other woman, Jo, left. Sophie and the purser continued playing. She could feel competitiveness building inside her, but it made her lose concentration. She lost the next round.

'Take off your bra,' the purser said.

'I won't.'

'You have to. It's the rules.'

Sophie refused and continued hugging herself, but he climbed behind her and started fiddling with her bra hooks. She said she would take off her necklace instead, but he said she had broken the time qualification. So she let him take off her bra. She dealt the next round, and he just stared at her breasts like he had never seen any before.

'Jesus! You've got fantastic tits.'

Stephanie and the steward were still at it. His hand was down her knickers, massaging that hot place between her legs. Sophie could see the soft burr of her fuzz and the way his fingers worked at her hole. She was cooing. She didn't realise they were there; she didn't even know where she was. Teresa slumped on to the floor next to her. She had the whitest legs Sophie had ever seen.

The purser was still staring at Sophie's tits and was now licking his lips. Although his shirt hung down over his pants, she could see he was erect. They started to play. If Sophie lost, she would have to take off her knickers.

Stephanie started groaning louder and louder, and she was flinging herself back against the sofa. She was coming right there and then, in front of them. The purser's eyes, however, were fixed on Sophie.

'Come on, baby, lay your cards.'

'Two of hearts.'

'Show me what you've got.'

Sophie won. Instead of taking off his shirt, as he should have done, the purser came over to her again. The sleeping Teresa sighed and sank even lower. Stephanie was wanking the steward. His huge heavy cock looked like a fat sausage. When the purser put his tongue in her mouth, Sophie wasn't surprised. She had been holding off because she knew the sooner they started, the sooner it would end. And if they managed to hold back just a few minutes more then the pleasures would be all the more sweeter. He wasn't one for holding back though. His hands went direct to her breasts. Then he pulled Sophie up on to the sofa next to Stephanie and the steward.

'All right, mate?' asked the busy steward. His organ was blazing purple. Stephanie gurgled a half hello.

The purser pulled down Sophie's knickers and slotted his fingers up her slit. She let out an anguished cry. He was too quick – she thought she was going to be dry but, no, she was already wet, already welcoming, telling him she wanted him. The purser kneeled at the foot of her and then climbed into her.

Next to her, the steward had crawled on to his prey and was now humping her madly.

'This is good, isn't it?'

'We must do this more often,' the purser replied. He slipped his cock up Sophie's pussy and obliterated the rest of the world, the rest of the party; even the rest of her body bowed to the magnificent power of the cunt. She started fucking him, pushing on and off him. He loved that.

'Easy, tiger,' he said when his cock nearly slid out. She was so wet, like someone had greased her up. He humped and pumped her, and Sophie knew she could have been anyone, any willing girl, yet the thought only excited her more and more, for it was true that she felt about him the same way; he was only a bit of meat, only a cock, a phallus. The steward did the same to Stephanie. They were a team, the dream team, and she could barely stand to watch the delicious sight of those two male buttocks pressing up and down in time.

There was a knock on the door. The purser said 'Oh shit', but he didn't let up screwing, not for a second. She clasped her legs around his neck and fastened on to him.

'Oh yes,' she wailed, and the steward looked up in surprise. He sped up too, pumping into Stephanie as though he were half mad.

'Oh yes, more, more.' And she knew that the steward wanted to fuck her too. The steward wanted a woman as horny as her, and he knew that the purser was a lucky, lucky bastard.

'Fuck me.' And just as she was coming down the home straight, the steward leaned into Sophie and landed his hand on her pubic hair. Moving his finger down, even as the purser rammed her, he found where the skin parts and the cleft begins and, even though he should have been fucking Stephanie, he was fingering Sophie, toying with her clit as if it were some sacred jewel. The little man in the boat started to rock like crazy.

Sophie tightened up and down the purser's rock-hard meat. 'Yes, yes,' she howled at them, and Stephanie's eyes half opened in wonderment, and she felt a crazy abandonment.

The following morning was weird. Sophie struggled to the canteen for the rescue of breakfast, as did Jo, the girl who had left.

'What happened last night?' Jo asked as they healed themselves with black coffee.

'What do you mean?'

'You didn't leave that room all night.'

'Oh, we were all so drunk, we just fell asleep.'

'I'll ask Stephanie,' she said mock-threateningly.

'Honestly, we all fell asleep. When I woke up, the others had gone.'

The purser perched himself next to Sophie in the canteen. He whispered that her pussy had been really tight.

'It's my pelvic floor exercises,' she snarled. He seemed to think that with their fucking they had somehow bonded, made a commitment or something. Nothing could have been further from the truth.

'What are *they*?' he asked, thrilled. He pictured her clenching, warming up for him. Other women had fannies like wizards' sleeves – but her? She was as tight as a guinea pig's arse – and no, since you ask, he didn't know from practical experience, but he could guess.

'They're especially good for women after having . . .' she trailed off. She mustn't give away anything about herself.

He asked, 'Do you feel like I took advantage of you?'

'That you took advantage of *me*?' she echoed. It was funny, because she was the one with the ulterior motives.

He said he wanted to pinch her breasts, to see if what happened last night was true, or just a beautiful dream. She said that it was a dream.

He said that his balls were aching and he was going to explode if he didn't come soon. She said, 'Explode away. What do I care?'

He said that he had a hard-on like he never had before, at the thought of topless card-dealing. She said, 'And . . .?'

He said he wanted to make her come. He wanted to live inside her pussy and never come out again. She said sorry, she was involved with someone else.

He said he would kill himself. She said, 'Whatever.'

He said if it were a passenger, she would get in big trouble. She told him to fuck off.

He said, 'It is, isn't it? Is it that guy who comes into the casino? That blond guy with the black eyes?' She told him to fuck off, again. (Was it that obvious?)

# Chapter Nineteen

*T*hat blond guy with the black eyes was in the sauna with that girl, that ditsy shop assistant. She was wearing a purple polka-dot bikini, which accentuated the magnificent slope of her bosom. Between her breasts, the hollow looked moist and succulent. When Sophie arrived, Mick pulled back rapidly but she could see his hand had been on the girl's thighs. Sophie averted her eyes; she couldn't turn back, not without looking foolish, and so she climbed up to a wooden bench. She could feel the heat cover her like a blanket, and when by accident her leg touched the hot surface and not her towel, she had to suppress a scream.

They stopped talking, abruptly silenced like a TV turned off. The sudden quiet was as oppressive as the temperature was stifling. The girl raised her shoulders stiffly, an animal scenting a predator.

'I'm sorry,' Sophie said archly, 'but this is a public sauna.' The instant she said it, she regretted it. She sounded petty and the words ran around her head, poking fun at her. She attempted to look self-righteous – which was difficult when she was wiping away the sweat from her forehead with the back of her hand.

At least she was blocking further action. One of them would have to leave, but it wouldn't be her. The girl looked set to explode. She looked sorrowfully at Mick and announced that she was going. He said he would see her outside. She slammed the wooden door behind her, leaving Sophie and Mick alone in the cabin. The room was little larger than a cupboard. Sophie relaxed; it was a small victory.

She thought of the time she played sardines at a friend's birthday party. Her teeth had chattered with excitement at the prospect. She got stuck in the cupboard with three boys and she didn't know whose hand belonged to whom. One hand pinched her bottom and another hand came round to the front of her trousers and rubbed her there. There were two more, or perhaps three, hands on her breasts. It was terrible when the girl whose birthday it was discovered them and the game was stopped in favour of sleeping lions.

Trickles of water ran down Mick's neck. It would have been so easy, so easy to lean forward and lick them off. She wanted to taste the juice of his skin. She thought about Scandinavian porn films – big Swedish men with whiskers like walruses; big Swedish women with flapping breasts – but the couple she knew who tried to do it in a sauna got dehydrated and couldn't get up for a week. Maybe Mick would ask her to go somewhere with him. The jacuzzi would be nice.

'Are you following me?' he accused her.

'No,' she said. 'I didn't know you would be here. How would I know?' So he was going to be like this again. Wouldn't he ever let his guard down?

'Look, we really mustn't be seen together.'

'I know that.' Who was going to see them in there?

'Why don't you leave then?'

'I will.'

But he hesitated. Her towel was unravelling and unwinding like a snake shedding its skin. Could he see? Her body was wet and soft. Could he see?

Yes, he could. He rubbed his eyes and stood up wearily. She couldn't help feeling he was putting on a grand act.

'Well, this is too hot for me.'

She didn't know what he meant. Did he mean her or the room? Time to find out.

'You're just doing this to make me want you more,' she ventured. She noticed how the skin on the back of his neck was paler, from where his hair had been cut recently. Saw the contours of his chest and the pale-pink nipples. And she noticed the creases in his fingers and the cuts in his knuckles. Her towel slipped down, revealing one, then both breasts. Her pair of aces. Love me, please. The sweat ran in rivulets down her bosom.

'Doing what?'

'Playing hard to get.'

'I'm not. Don't be ridiculous.'

'That's what it looks like from here.'

'I don't want a relationship, not with you, not with anyone.'

'You're lying.'

He closed his eyes. Blocking her out. It enraged her more.

'Did you sleep with her too?'

He looked angry.

'That's not your business. Look, I'm just in this for the money, no more, no less.'

'I understand that,' she said sullenly.

'What is it that you want, then?'

Sophie explained. When she had finished, he looked at her, and it seemed his face was one big mosaic of incredulity.

'Take photos of you shagging Tom? I don't think so!'

She dressed it up simply. To get Tom to join them, she had to force his hand. Threatening him with the photo evidence was the only way she could do that. OK, so it was blackmail – but it was only blackmail out of necessity. Of course there was a second reason. Of course there was. Perhaps the sight of her with another man would galvanise Mick into action. The green-eyed monster would take up residency and propel him to act. Although probably Mick didn't know what it was to feel jealous –

the only way to make a cold reptile like him feel such an emotion would be to say that she had a million dollars in the bank.

'Well, you've no interest in me, right?' she persisted.

He had a real ugly scowl. 'I don't see how it will work.'

'Of course it will. How can he resist doing it? He's crazy about Jenny – he's petrified she will find out. After this, he'll be putty in my hands.' And so, hopefully, will you, she thought.

'You're sure this is the only way?'

'Positive.'

He looked uneasily at her. Last night, when she had refused to open her cabin door (he was sure she was in there), he had sworn to himself that he would give up on her. Cheat and go.

'You're the boss.'

'Yes, I am, so . . .'

'OK. Have you got a camera?'

# Chapter Twenty

*H*e read the letter over and over again until he had memorised every word. This time, Sophie had gone into even more glorious detail.

*I will rub my tits in your face, climb over you and massage you with oils, and you will gaze up at me in awe. And then I want you to rub your dick between my breasts, tit-fuck me until I cry out and you squirt creamy love-juice all over my face.*

Just one more time, and then he would stop, he told himself. One more time and it would be over and he would be free. OK, so this time the action was premeditated – *very* pre-meditated – rather than spontaneous. The second time (he discounted the session in his cabin) always is. The first time can be an accident, a glorious triumphant accident, but an accident nonetheless. But the second time? There is no such easy excuse. It would take a more powerful man than him to resist. And Tom wasn't powerful by any stretch of the imagination.

Sophie lay on the bed. She was wearing a sailor's dress, like a Japanese schoolgirl's summer uniform, and even back then, sixteen years ago, it had been far too small for her, but she hadn't bothered to get a bigger one because she was leaving school so soon. It was really tight and a little uncomfortable around her breasts. They had grown so big in the fifth form and they used to burst at the buttons all day long.

Tom undid his jacket, pulled his T-shirt over his head and then pulled down his trousers. He was wearing grey cotton underpants and he looked at her cautiously, as though expecting her to laugh, before he lowered them. Just around his cock, his underpants had already turned a darker shade from his pre-come. She could see that he was nervous – his cheeks were flushed and he was biting his lips furiously.

'What if Jennifer finds out?' he kept saying. 'What if, what if?'

Nonetheless, he still came over and started touching her thighs. She was still wearing her socks and he didn't take them off. He couldn't believe how sexy she was. Jennifer wouldn't have done this. Jennifer would say, 'A school uniform? Tom, that's disgusting.' Perhaps that's why it was so wonderful with Sophie. She was disgusting.

He kissed her lips, her cheeks, her chin, and he bit her neck. He was all stirred up, in a hurry. He loved the outfit; it surpassed all his dreams. She looked like her whole purpose in life was to screw him well. She rearranged him. She seemed intent on getting him in all angles, in all ways. Who was he to turn her down? Never had he been with someone so vociferous, so hungry for him. She squirmed against his leg, straddling his thigh and rubbing against him. She was everywhere, giving him everything to play and be played with. Her neck was at his mouth, demanding attention, her breasts in his face, requiring his admiration. When he touched her knee, she sighed as though he had fondled her buttocks, and when he actually kneaded those buttocks, which she was grinding round and round, she groaned as though he were rubbing her clit. So, when he actually got there, his fingers on that little button, that little island of fun, she was ready to explode. She came, and then she was pressing, rabid, desperate for more. He could barely stand the pleasure.

'Show me how you like it,' he said. She scraped her cheek against his chin and felt that stubble, that maleness, and from then on she was lost. She wrapped herself around him; she wanted him inside her, inside her a million times, a million men. She told him to just pull her knickers aside as she wanted to keep them on. He stroked her there – over the material and then above – and she grew wetter. He stole inside her beaver, her wickedly tight little snatch, and he watched her expression. Then she grabbed his fingers possessively and made him do what she wanted because she couldn't mess around with all the coyness. Straight to the point, only there were many points.

'You're soaking!' he said triumphantly.

Not because of you, she thought. 'Go further, go higher, go deeper.' It sounded like a political campaign.

'You're so fucking wet.'

Could Mick hear what he was saying? How good she was?

'Like this, like this. Oh yes, that's the place, that's the spot.'

'You horny girl. I just can't resist you, I can't.'

'I know you can't. You want it just as much as I do. '

'You bitch, you sexy fucking bitch. I can't stop thinking about you.'

'Yes, Tom, do it to me, keep going, just like that.'

'You naughty girl,' he whispered. 'I had to see your underwear, to make you cream in your knickers.'

Tom was nuzzling her shirt, snaking his long tongue in and around her ear. It wasn't just her cunt that was drenched, her whole face was. And it was lovely. She let Tom ravish her, delighting in her own moans. Tom didn't even have to touch her to make her howl with pleasure – but he did touch her, and that made it even better.

And Mick was watching. 'Look at us!' she wanted to

shout. She presented her slimy slit, waiting for a filling. Can you smell me? Can you smell the cream of a hot woman's sex?

Tom swirled his thumbs on her arse cheeks and then pulled them apart, opening her wide, and she loved the fact that Mick was watching. She showed him her pleasure, multiplied five hundred times. She imagined him gripping the camera with all his might, gripping it, frightened to move.

'Do it to me,' she urged, and she knew that Mick wouldn't be sure whom she meant – him or Tom.

Tom was licking her cunt. He said he loved her.

'What?' she murmured. 'I can't hear you.'

She wanted him to shout it out, to let Mick know what she was like. Don't you wish you could taste me too?

Tom snuffled into her, raising her buttocks and squeezing her tight.

Look at me, see how horny I am, see the redness of me, the wetness, the hunger.

He clambered on top of her, desperate.

'Yes, I want you. And you want me.'

'I want you to fuck me.'

'I have to fuck you, I must. I'll die if we don't fuck soon.'

She had become mad, become so horny that she didn't know what she was doing, only that she had to drive down, down, down on his cock. She didn't know where she was. She forgot the camera; she forgot the reason she was doing it. She even forgot the money. All that existed was swallowed in this great time bomb between her legs, the great waiting, the knowledge of the imminent explosion. She worked against him, and he pulled against her, and sometimes they slipped into a rhythm and sometimes they slipped out of rhythm, but none of that mattered, as she came, came, came, laughing at her own hunger.

Only as the ecstasy subsided, leaving her hole gaping wide, did she remember that he was watching. And so she and Tom started again. And this time, as he humped her like a madman – oblivious that his work was being recorded – she clung to him with her legs wrapped round his back, like a koala, and she was clamouring for more. She dug her index finger into Tom's tight little arsehole. Tom jabbered and twitched, unwilling at first, and then so willing, so grateful that he was almost dribbling over her. And then he was off, like a firecracker, ramming and pouring into her.

'You hot cunt – you love it.'

And she shouted back, slapping him with her free hand, giddy up, while the index finger excavated him thoroughly, pressing on that spot. And she thought, this is for you, Mick. It's not just me who gets fucked. And then they were coming together, howling, the two of them for the one of him.

'Can we do it again?' Tom asked hoarsely.

'What?'

'Your fingers – up there . . .' He lay looking at the ceiling. Even after all that – especially after all that – he was too embarrassed to look her in the face.

'I can do better than that,' she said, grinning. (Just you wait, Mick, you are not going to believe this.)

Sophie and Moira danced separately, and then they danced together. At some moments, Moira was so close to Sophie that she thought she could feel her friend's eyelashes brush against her cheek. It was smoochy. But at other times, Moira moved apart from her, quickly too, swivelling up and down, around and around like a spinning top. Then Moira made a song request. 'You'll love this,' she yelled to Sophie and, 'This one reminds me of my old friend. You know, the girl I was telling you about.'

Sophie realised Moira was more fun than she had originally thought, and she was certainly a great dancer. They worked well together – and that boded well for the future. When they played 'I Will Survive', Moira whooped and danced behind Sophie, her arms in the air. 'This is for you,' she said. Moira pretended to feel

Sophie's body and Sophie couldn't stop laughing. A crowd formed around them and clapped along. Sophie started to lose herself in the music, thumping out the bass line. Technically, Moira was the better mover, but Sophie gave her a run for the money and she was confident that she was attracting attention too. She might not have been a disco diva but her breasts bounced at just the right level, just the right amount, and she had this move, this hip-swinging move that made everyone who saw her think of fucking. OK, so the passengers were horny – but coop anyone up for 24–7 in a cage, even a five-star cage, and this is what happens. Forget dirty dancing, this was filthy.

Sophie got tired more quickly. She needed a drink. Moira followed her.

'You are a great dancer, you know,' Sophie said, smiling.

'Thanks.'

Moira didn't look as flattered as Sophie had expected.

'I haven't had a good dance for ages,' Sophie admitted.

Moira grinned. 'I didn't think so,' she said cryptically.

'Where did you learn to dance like that?'

Moira sat down at the bar, her chin in her hands. She snapped an order to the barman as he wiped the glasses clean, and then she started talking in her quiet compelling tones.

'I trained at ballet school. Actually, Sophie, I must tell you all about it. You will love this. We were a class of about sixteen students; all of us wanted to be professional and the standard was very high. You can imagine how competitive it was. Well, one day my teacher asked me to stay behind. She had some special exercises she wanted to show me, something to do with my posture. Firstly, I had to lean against the barre and do the moves for her, just as I had learned. There was nothing strange about that – or so I thought.'

Sophie had been about to suggest that they return to the dance floor but she soon realised that Moira was not in the mood to go anywhere. She clearly wanted to get this story off her chest.

'She told me to watch the mirror. When I saw my reflection, I held up my neck as high as I could, stretched my back and I tried really hard. I wanted to please her, we all did. We all wanted to perform well for her – I suppose that's what made her such a good teacher. She often used to tap our legs with a stick, but this time, she hovered around me. She told me to continue my exercises and said that she was going to watch how my calves and my shins worked. She squatted next to me. I was nervous about kicking her, naturally, but she told me to relax. Then she raised my leg over her shoulder so that it was stretched quite high. "Good girl," she said. It was only then I realised that something was different. I had heard some of the older girls talk about "auditioning for *Swan Lake*" or something, which was highly secret, and I wondered if that wasn't what we were doing. Maybe this was my big chance.

'She got on the floor beneath me. It seemed to me a terribly awkward thing, but there she was gazing skyward, like engineers working on a bridge, and then she was leaning towards me, pulling at my knickers. Before I knew what to think, she had slipped in a finger, and then she was licking and poking, hot jiggery pokery inside my knickers. I stood frozen in position. I didn't know what to do but mostly I was wondering how this would make my posture better.'

Sophie eyed the barman nervously but he gave no sign that he was listening. She returned to her drink. She was thinking, Moira is absolutely mad.

'When she emerged, her face was all shiny. She asked me if I was OK. "I am checking to see that you have the ability to be a ballerina. Do you really want to dance?" she asked me. I nodded again. "Well," she said, "you have to learn endurance, to learn about each part of your body, and to concentrate only on that small part, and to hold that small part forever." She dropped down on her knees and again was lost between my legs. She licked and nuzzled me. I told myself to concentrate but her hair distracted me. She had tied it up in a bun and it was merrily bobbing around my thighs like a leftover dough-nut. I gripped the barre tightly. My face was red and my eyes were sparkling like illuminations. Then I felt her hands move more determinedly. She let her fingers dance on my front opening, as though she was looking for something. And then my clit was rubbed and nuzzled, warmed and stimulated in her endlessly working lips. The mouth kept suction on me, pulling and pulsating at my clit. I felt raw. Juice was pouring out of me, on to her, my dance teacher's face, and yet she seemed to like it.

'She was making all these murmuring noises of approval, and when for one moment she detached herself from me, she commanded, "Keep thinking of that place," and so I did. I thought of what she was doing there, doing to me with her tongue, her mouth and her fingers, and I thought of that small part of me that had never felt bigger, and then my body was shuddering, juddering, like a car grinding to a halt, and I felt this peace all over.'

The barman dropped a glass and it smashed into tiny pieces on the floor. He bent down scarlet-faced. Moira raised her eyes heavenward but otherwise ignored him.

'The teacher said, "I'm just going to wash my face. I'll bring back a towel." I just stood there, gazing at my reflection. I felt like a puppet, like someone else was controlling my arms and legs. The piano player found me. He played piano twice a week for us. Apparently he too had been a dancer once, but he had destroyed the muscles in his legs through overstraining. My hands were locked round the barre and my knuckles were white. He detached my fingers and carried me over to his piano. First he nuzzled at my legs. I was still in shock, I suppose, and I was already filled with cream because of her, and the smell of my excitement was quite over-whelming. My knickers, of course, were over by the barre, but I was still wearing my beautiful pink dancing shoes. I loved the way the ribbons did up around my legs. He nibbled and guzzled and fingered my slit and then he ate me, over the top, properly, his face got really stuck in. The teacher returned and stood next to us approvingly. "Think of that place," she instructed. "Think of your posture, your balance, and that place." His face was larger than hers, and his moustache was bushy, and I could feel the individual hairs spike, yet caress, my crack. My legs were wrapped around his head, my toes dangling on to the keys. He was sitting proud in the seat and I writhed around him until I was twitching with pleasure and gushing liquid sex. It was a very comfortable position – I recommend it.'

'I'll remember that,' Sophie muttered. She felt very uneasy. A cocktail of jealousy, excitement and fear was cascading through her. The barman was busying himself at the till but it was obvious that he was working as quietly as possible so that he could listen to what Moira was saying. She could hear Moira swallowing. It sounded very loud – but very private.

And then Moira cupped her face and kissed her full on the lips. Her hands came round aggressively and Sophie had no option but to let herself be kissed. It didn't feel bad, it didn't feel bad at all, and Sophie closed her eyes to enjoy it more. Moira moved her hand from her cheek and put it to the front of Sophie's T-shirt. Sophie held her breath, ready to endure. And then Moira turned her head away, ordering a G and T from the speechless and increasingly red-faced barman. When Moira looked back, her eyes were narrow.

'You'll have to be more persuasive than that, Sophie Hemingway.'

'What?'

'I know what you are up to,' Moira added, smirking.

'What do you mean?'

'You know full well what I mean. It's no coincidence that you have been snuggling up to me. Are you still doing it?'

'Doing what?'

'The cheating, the stealing, the scam, whatever you want to call it.'

Sophie wished Moira would lower her voice. The barman was still within earshot. She whispered, 'Yes, more than ever.'

'Look, I don't want to know who is involved but I assume everything is sorted. You have a player, an inspector and now all you need is little old me,' bleated Moira.

'Ssshhh. Everything is being sorted,' Sophie corrected quietly. 'Sorted' was too strong a word at this very precarious stage but if she could convince Moira that the other pieces were in place then it was a necessity. 'And yes, I do still need you.'

'Well, what's in it for me?'

'Money.'

'Money?'

'Yeah, lots. A four-way cut.'

'Sophie, you may be very beautiful, but you can be stupid.'

'What do you mean?'

'I'm not interested in money. You must have realised that by now.'

'Well, if you're not interested in the money then there is no point continuing.'

Moira paused for effect. 'I'm not entirely averse to helping you.'

'I don't get what you mean.'

'I mean I will help you . . . because I like you.'

Sophie trembled. Moira had laid her cards on the table, and now it was up to her to play.

# Chapter Twenty-One

'*D* oesn't look good, does it, Tom?'
It did look good. It looked fucking amazing. The pictures Mick had taken showed everything, every little bit of them, in all their screwing glory. There was a whole film – 36 exposures – and, as Sophie pored over them, the memories came flooding back, and she couldn't help feeling excited. So excited that she might as well have been there doing it again.

It wasn't the first time she had let someone take photos of her having sex. In fact, she had gone better than that. She once went out with a ship's photographer who had videoed all their couplings, and then they watched them on playback whenever they went to bed. She loved being fucked while watching herself being fucked on the screen. She loved to watch herself over his shoulders, her lips contorted with pleasure.

In the end, they had argued. He wanted to have sex without the videos and, to tell the truth, it didn't cut the mustard without that little extra.

'I'll show all my mates,' he had threatened her, which showed how little he knew about her.

'Go on then,' she had taunted. 'I would bloody love them to see it.'

Mick had said nothing when he handed them over. No, he had said, 'Here they are.' That was all.

She had picked just four photos. Four would be enough to do the trick with Tom.

'I have something to show you, Tom. Something very interesting,' she had said.

And he had decided what he would do with her the next time she tried it on. He had resolved to be very clear, very strong about it.

'I'm sorry, I'm ... um ... not interested,' he had muttered into his sleeve.

'My cabin, later on,' she had told him.

Number one depicted her sucking him. His face was clearly in view. You couldn't see her face though; all you could see was her hair in pigtails and blue velvet ribbons. He was standing with his hands on her shoulders. She was kneeling and you could see the white soles of her feet, somehow innocent in contrast to the act itself. When she had sucked him he had been close to tears: 'Don't stop, don't even think about stopping,' he had insisted as she worked his boner in and out.

In number two, she was straddling him. Again you couldn't see her properly. Tom was lying down, his eyes firmly closed, his mouth open and ecstatic; a black hole of pleasure, clear to behold. Just after that, she had gripped his nipples tight, too tight, and he had writhed in pain. Even from the picture, the one-dimensional picture, you could feel the heat.

Number three showed him entering her from behind, doggy style. All her body was exposed, but again, her face was obscured. The upturned heart of her bottom was the main focus of the shot. This captured the moment he had told her to screw him hard, harder. She remembered how his voice had caught with the agony of asking her. Seconds later he had bitten her neck – she still had the love stain. Seconds later, too, she was out of control – she had forgot the camera, had forgot why she was doing this and had given herself up to him, begging him to masturbate her to a grand finale. He had grown confident, cocky, making her say what she wanted him to do, making her shout.

Number four was the most incriminating of them all. It showed her entering him with the dildo. It was exotic, erotic, absurd. He was bent over on all fours like a beast, and she stood behind him like a man. The dildo was half-inserted, half-exposed to the air. He had been reluctant at first, at least he put on a show of reluctance, but after she had convinced him with kisses and licks, he had allowed her to bend him over. She had opened him wide and entered him. She could barely contain her glee. This was how he deserved it. In the picture, even more than the view of the invasion of his buttocks and the stiffness of his swollen cock, it was Tom's face that held you. That expression of extreme mix of horror and ecstasy – the anticipation and the satisfaction all at once. And her, all you could see of her were her legs, her torso clad in that weenie sailor dress and her prying hands.

From this angle, she looked like a small girl.

No, it didn't look good for him.

'It's about money, isn't it?' he sighed. And for a moment she felt sorry for him.

'I'm afraid it is.'

'Did you hate doing it with me?'

'Tom, I loved it,' she said sincerely.

It was funny. Here she was blackmailing him, and yet all he was worried about was that he had been used. 'If you want,' she added, 'we can do it again.'

'I don't know,' he said. And she didn't know if he meant he didn't know what was happening, or he wasn't sure about her suggestion.

'I mean, we can keep it separate from the other. No cameras, no threats, just good old-fashioned fucking.'

Tom felt his resolve soften and his prick harden.

'I can't help feeling used,' he sighed.

'Surely it's better that someone wants to use you than that no one wants to use you at all?' Sophie suggested kindly.

'If I don't do what you want, you'll really show Jenny the pictures?'

'Got it in one.'

'And you still think we can have sex?'

'Uh huh.'

'I . . . I feel really bad about this.'

She slid her hand along his shaft.

'I know it's hard.'

He nodded apologetically, looking down at his pants.

'I mean it's difficult, but, Tom, you have needs.' (Needs! Listen to her!) Sophie enfolded him in her benevolent arms. Christ, this was better than she had hoped. He had agreed to the scam *and* he was still up for shagging her. Excellent. And why not? Mick was screwing around like there was no tomorrow.

After the energy and violence of the photo session, this was a less hurried affair. Tom murmured contentment and covered her with grateful touches.

'You're wonderful,' he whispered. 'You're incredible.' Who could fail to be flattered?

She seemed to have earned his respect. She told him to get down, get it out. She bullied him, and he received each command with joy. When she touched him, he responded rapturously.

Who gave a fuck about love? Who gave a fuck about Mick? It was best to keep them all in separate boxes – friends, fucks and nobodies. OK, when the fucking harvestings were slim, the friends and the fucks crossed over, but there was never any of that sentimentality, that stupidity that came along with love.

Tom ran his fingers up her thighs, and his tongue was hanging out like a slobbering dog.

'Oh, Sophie,' he purred ecstatically. 'This is madness.'

'You,' she said, 'are a very dirty boy, and I am going to have to show you just how dirty you are.'

'Please,' he muttered.

She smacked him and coaxed him into her.

'You think you can get away with anything, but you

need a girl like me. Now put your fingers here. That's right.'

'I do,' he whimpered, his hands right up her. She touched that place between his balls and his anus – that secret, hidden place.

'Sophie, you're the best. I'll do anything you say. Just don't let Jenny find out.' She twisted into position, raised her ankles around him.

'I won't. If you don't.' His cock screamed up her cunt.

'Don't tell Jenny,' he murmured, telling himself it would be the last time he would mention her, but as he felt her clench around him, he could barely control himself.

'Don't tell her, but it feels so good.' He had lost all control, all sense of honour. Everything had ceased to exist but Sophie and her hot slit. Fuck, how did she manage to do this to him? Could Sophie be blamed for feeling a little triumphant?

After they had sex, he looked at the pictures again, and his cock stiffened. Hard-on revisited.

'I don't know what to say,' he said.

'Don't say anything,' she suggested.

'Who took them?'

'No one important,' she said, and it near killed her to say it.

'They won't tell Jenny, will they?' he insisted.

'Come here,' she said. She bit his lower lip when he kissed her, and he trembled.

This time, he took an interest in her arse. He turned her over and kissed and licked her there. It was very earthy, very sexual and very, very effective. His fingers probed her; he certainly wasn't afraid to get his hands dirty. His tongue was cold up her hole. She knew, just knew, that he wanted her to do it to him. Tit-for-tat sex.

'Now you,' she said, and she produced a dildo, only this was bigger than the last one. He was thrilled. And if he protested a little, she knew that it was half-hearted. He wanted to be blackmailed, oh yes, oh yes, oh yes he did. His eyes said it all.

137

When he left her room that night, he was heavy with satisfaction and too tired to walk straight. And he knew that he was in big shit now that he had agreed to her demands, but he couldn't see a way out.

Sophie and Moira met in the canteen. It was the first time they had been together since the night in the disco and Sophie was uncharacteristically nervous.

It was hard serving the food with one hand, and Moira kept trying to assist by loading up Sophie's plate with things that she wasn't sure that she wanted. Sophie tackled the salads and cold meats. She was aware, so aware of Moira helping herself to the buffet next to her. One time, they both reached for the salad dressing spoon at the same time. Moira retracted quickly.

Over lunch, Moira gave no hint that she was lusting after Sophie. Instead, she munched blithely on her food and even went back for seconds. Sophie watched her retreating figure admiringly. She decided she wouldn't say anything if Moira didn't.

'You're very quiet,' Moira commented, smirking.

'I'm tired,' lied Sophie.

Moira asked Sophie if she would come with her to the sunbed rooms, but she didn't seem particularly upset when Sophie refused. They poured the waste from their trays into the bins. Moira scraped her plate clean and it made a high-pitched squeaking noise that made them both laugh. It's amazing what you need to break the ice, Sophie thought. She decided to go forth. Faint heart never won fair lady and all that.

'Have you always been a lesbian, Moira?' she asked boldly. Sophie remembered a girl running around at school yelling 'I'm a lesbian,' when she meant to say 'I'm a Libra.'

'I was bi-'

Sophie thought she was going to say 'I was by the door' or something but she didn't.

'-sexual. Do you have a problem with that?'

'Goodness, no,' said Sophie. 'Some of my best friends

138

are gay.' Disaster! she thought later, when she relived the awkward moment in her head. What a dumbarse thing to say!

'So you like both men and women then?'

Sophie thought that was a bit like keeping your options open, like saying you believe in God, Allah, Buddha and the rest of them. Surely it wasn't fair?

'It's not so strange. You like men, don't you? But I bet sometimes you think about women too.'

Sophie burned.

But Moira continued undaunted, 'I used to be bi but, actually, now I think – in fact I'm sure – that I'm gay.'

'Is it –' Sophie swallowed hard and Moira grabbed the tray out of her hands because it looked like Sophie was going to drop it '– because of me?'

'Because of you what?'

'That you are one hundred per cent gay now?'

'You mean, have you converted me?'

'Uh huh.'

'You're crazy.'

Moira's laughter pealed behind her, as Sophie fled. She would have liked to have flung herself over the side of the ship and never be seen again. How could she have been so stupid, so arrogant?

The Captain had been watching them. Or rather, he had been watching Sophie. He loved to see her eat. It was such a rare pleasure to see a woman stuff herself with food. Sophie seemed to go wild with a lust to fill herself up. Watching a woman eat was like seeing a woman masturbate. So few of them seemed to think they deserved it; they seemed to think they weren't good enough.

The best moment was when Sophie was eating a tomato. She picked it up, plump, ripe, red, from the plate and toyed with it. She was deep in conversation, but as she was talking she prodded and pressed the sides. Then she sunk her teeth into the skin, breaking the firm surface. He saw the mush in her mouth. The juice slipped out of the side. The Captain's balls tightened at the vision of her. She slid her wrist over the juice. Her mouth was slightly open, the tongue peeping out sensuously, and then she went in for another bite. The pips came tumbling out, and one, oh lucky pip, landed on her breast, just above her nipple.

He would love to see Sophie masturbate and eat at the same time. The two glories at once. Perhaps she would slot strawberries first in the pussy and then in the mouth. Alternating: pussy and mouth, pussy and mouth. Dunked in chocolate, dipped in juice. Have her roll on to it, squelching and screwing whatever she could.

A few minutes later, she was out on the deck on her own. Good, the other girl, that girl with the silly fake tan, had disappeared. There was once a time when the Captain would have fallen for Moira – not any more. He was smitten with Sophie.

He crept up to her, stood alongside her, watching the waves as they smashed against the ship, his ship.

'Oh hello,' she said conversationally. She was shocked that the Captain had came alongside her. She didn't know how to address him. Was she required to say sir?

'I saw you in the canteen,' he said presently.

'Oh.'

The Captain seemed to expect her to say something else. 'Did you enjoy your lunch?' she asked.

He was so busy imagining eating out her pussy that he nearly did not reply. Eat in or takeaway? He was wondering. Takeaway, he would say, and then you can have some more in the morning, reheated. Plus you can relax more at home.

'I did not,' he added proudly. 'I don't have time.'

'Don't have time to eat?' she echoed. She wondered why someone who didn't have time for lunch was dilly-dallying out here, in the sunshine, talking to her.

The Captain went back to his quarters, refreshed by their meeting, and more earnest about her than ever before. In his exultant state, he dashed off some poems.

You give me the appetite for love, I will fit you like a glove.

You are the windmill to my wind, Flask to my hot water. No, he scribbled, my container.

Sophie. He had to have her soon. He had to fuck the hell out of her, make her eyeballs roll and her arms wave with frenzy. He wrapped a tourniquet around his cock and tightened and tightened it until his eyes began to water.

# Chapter Twenty-Two

*T*hey hadn't arranged to meet but she knew he would be there, cutting through the water, charging up and down the lanes. He was overtaking the slow swimmers and making everyone wish that they exercised that little more often and ate that little less at the grand buffets.

She had walked the length of the pool slowly, careful not to slip on the tiled surface. She was trying to spot him, trying to give him a chance to see her. But the only people who looked up were a plump matron in a flowery swimming cap and an old man in high shorts who was as wizened as a raisin. Mick didn't see her. He avoided seeing her with such skill that she could only think that he was ignoring her.

She left her towel on a sunlounger and walked over to the steps of the pool. Dipping first one toe, then a foot, she lowered herself in. Shit, the water was cold.

Finally, she was underwater. She kept her eyes closed down there. When she came up again she was shivering and panting. She swam to the deep end, where she trod water and waited. Mick hauled himself up and executed a perfect arch. He swam heavy strokes up to the shallow end and grabbed hold of the side. The bastard. Was he trying to prove something by ignoring her?

He was playing hard to get, and it was working.

'Hey!' she called.

He looked genuinely surprised to see her. Good actor, she thought.

'Hey, you,' he responded.

'Can we talk here?' she said with a healthy scoop of sarcasm, but he ignored that too, or maybe he didn't get it.

'Sure.'

'Tom has agreed to everything.'

'And Moira?'

'I'm working on it.'

'What does that mean?'

'I'll fix it,' she boasted. 'I always do.'

'Don't get me involved this time,' he warned.

'Don't tell me you didn't enjoy it!'

He didn't reply.

'You did, didn't you?'

For once, he didn't move away. He merely looked at her, steadily holding her gaze.

'You loved taking the photos, didn't you?' she repeated. 'I bet you loved looking down the viewfinder, zooming in and out on us. Did you think I looked hot with my legs open wide?'

'You looked all right,' he said weakly.

'Did you think I looked good with him inside me, pumping up and down? You loved watching me fucking him. It turned you on.'

He wanted to tell her, yes, he had been excited. Yes, he went back to his cabin where he masturbated like a madman and yelped out rude words as though he had Tourette's syndrome or something. He had hibernated the whole day. He couldn't face anyone. He kept going over and over the way she looked doing Tom, and the rapture on her face. It was too much. If she was trying to make him jealous then it had worked. Of course it had frigging worked. Did she think he was made of stone?

She swam through the tunnel of his legs. He felt the water draw back. Slipstream. He held his breath, as though it was him who was submerged. She emerged

143

from behind him. He turned around to look. She came up like some gleaming, radiant mermaid, water glistening crystal on her eyelashes. Eyes closed in private ecstasy, as if she were in bed. As if she were in bed with him. He moved towards her, caught her lip with his teeth.

The surface of the lip tasted of salt, chlorine, other chemicals. Only when he drove deeper could he sense the taste of her. He was bruising her lips with his. Firm bites, not hard enough to draw blood, but hard enough to be felt. Hard enough so that she knew, she really knew, that she had been kissed.

'What are you doing to me?' he whispered.

Their bodies moved together in the water. She felt like she was dissolving into him. His fingers were making circles on her kneecap. Then he whispered into her ear, and his breath seemed to connect straight to that place between her legs. All show at reluctance was abandoned now. She was breathless.

'Not here,' she said. Her voice was strangled.

'Yes, here,' he said, like there was nowhere else to go.

Could she, dare she, open her thighs a little wider just to show that he was invited in? His hand was on the top of her thigh and she could only watch in happy terror. He plucked down her bikini bottoms and secured himself a place against her pubic hair.

'I've been dreaming of this forever. Oh yes.'

She kept saying his name in her head, over and over again.

'When I was fucking Tom I thought about you.'

'I know you did.'

'I was so wet then . . .'

'I know.'

'. . . because I knew you were watching me.'

'You're even wetter now.'

'Yes, yes I am. I can't believe this – finally, your finger is inside me.'

She admired his coolness. She trusted him. She guided his fingers against her; he didn't need a travelogue but she wanted to get it right.

144

'I've been waiting for this for so long.'

She was struggling against his hand, squirming against his nail. She wasn't going to come like this. She wanted the real thing. Real fucking, real lovemaking, and wasn't she entitled to it? The body may be comprised mostly of water but there, in the pool, she felt like she was made of fire. She was fumbling for him, but whenever she came too close, he took her hand. At one point, he held her arm around her back like a judo hold. But still he wouldn't let up playing with her, rubbing her, taking her.

'Let's concentrate on you.'

'No, I –'

'Yes, you, honey. I want to make you come.'

As she tried to interrupt again, he kissed her silent. 'You're going to come.'

No, she wasn't going to come, not here, not now. She was beating his back, beating him to push harder inside her. And then she turned to scratching him, ripping the skin of his back up and down. 'I'm not coming. I'm not, I'm not,' she sighed. But it was too late. She gave up to a clamouring, frightening orgasm.

After that, when she was all soft and cuddly, she wanted to tell him the real reason she was there. But she didn't.

'Thank you.' She kicked her legs gleefully in the water.

'My pleasure.'

'Did I scratch you?'

'It's all right.' He smiled. 'Wild cat!'

She rubbed against him. Oh yes, yes please. Call me a wild cat again.

'It's your turn, let me touch you.'

She didn't care that there were still swimmers swooping up and down the lanes. Let them enjoy the view. Her fingers were running determinedly to his swimming trunks. Catching the side, swooping them lower, lower.

'Stop, stop!' His fingers gripped her, firm compared to the fluidity of the pool.

'Why not?' she giggled. He was a player, a risk-taker; she knew that.

'I would rather we were just friends.'

Just good friends? It was pathetic!

'You're joking.' She peered at his face. No, he wasn't joking. This time there was no humour in his expression.

'No, I'm not joking. I hope you don't mind.'

'Of course I don't mind. Why should I?'

What did he mean, he would rather they were friends? Did he find her unattractive or something?

'I'm going back to my room,' he said.

But it wasn't fair. She wanted him inside her. How could he deny her now? Why shouldn't his cock go where his fingers had been?

'Please, let me come too.'

'You already did!' At last, he broke into a grin.

'What about tomorrow?'

Once you cross the border from shame to begging shamelessly, there's no going back.

'Tomorrow is another day,' he said, winking enigmatically.

And then, in that moment, as she was frozen, waiting for more, he disappeared, powering down to the deep end and then hauling himself out. His legs looked long and gangly on the little ladder. Little drops of water like tears flew from his shoulders.

Yet, she couldn't resist. She shouted out.

'I don't give second chances!' The swimmers all looked at her. They even stopped their ploughing through the water, just so that they could stand gawking at her, looking at a scandal in the making.

'Really, I thought this was my third, or was it my fourth?' He was mocking her.

'It's your last chance. I don't need this,' Sophie stormed back at him. Let them stare – idiots.

'Fine!'

'Fine!'

Only when he was safe, on the tiled surface, shaking the water out of his hair, did he dare look back at her.

# Chapter Twenty-Three

Moira stood outside the entrance of the Anchor Bar with her head held high and her chest pushed out, looking down her nose at all the passengers. Sophie admired that – Moira was only a cashier but she acted as though she owned the ship. She was a woman after her own heart. And what excellent posture!

Sophie had weighed up Moira's offer. The cashier was prepared to help; that was clear. But the question of payment had not been fully resolved. It seemed that Moira wanted to be paid off in kind. How difficult could it be? Sophie wondered. It would mean just letting her do stuff to her and, after the shenanigans, or the non-shenanigans, with Mick, it was nice that she was actually wanted. And, after all, Moira hadn't been hit with the ugly stick. If Sophie weighed everything up, even if she had to endure that, it would be worth it. And it was entirely plausible that Moira didn't want to be touched, that she would just be happy to do a bit of touching.

It took Sophie back to a time when she and her best friend from school had decided to try out some experiments. They were great scientists. They were forever mixing things. She had inserted things up her. They had both pretended to be very methodical about it, very sensible. At least Sophie was pretending to be sensible.

In her mind she was going wild and her heart was thumping in a way it never did when they used Bunsen burners in chemistry. They had pulled down their knickers, and she had seen the other girl's red-blonde bush, like an embroidered flower. They had opened their legs and worked toothbrushes, hairbrushes, everything and anything long and rectangular inside themselves. The girl had said, 'Have you ever tried with your fingers?' and Sophie had said no, truthfully, she never had, and then the girl had said that she would if Sophie did. And Sophie had come with her eyes closed. Afterwards, she couldn't stop thinking about it, although they never discussed it again.

'Do you want to go to your room then?' Sophie asked after they had done the hellos and the air kissing.

'Oh my!' smirked Moira. 'Do you have to be so clinical? Can't we have a nice time together?' She looked at her watch. 'Let's go and see a film. The night is young.'

'And so are we.'

This time Moira laughed aloud.

'Do you know what's on tonight?' asked Sophie.

'A documentary about wildlife.'

'Oh Christ, do you still want to go?'

'Hmmm, well – I've always been drawn to the wild side of things.'

The hall was already in blackness. Sophie had night blindness but Moira held her hand and guided her confidently to a seat. Sophie was surprised when she let go of her hand once they had sat down. She could hear the sweet sigh of her breathing and felt the hairs on her arm prickle when Moira leaned across to check if she was OK.

The film started tamely enough with the eating habits of beetles. Sophie closed her eyes. She had been working hard and it was pleasant to drift away to the soothing tone of the narrator. When she came round, she was leaning on Moira's shoulder and Moira had slipped a protective arm round her.

On screen, some hippos humped each other from

behind. The male thrust but the female held her own as he moved in and out. And they let out this fierce guttural cry. Moira moved her face towards her and smiled.

'Falling asleep?'

'Mmm,' Sophie murmured. In the darkness of the theatre, Moira's teeth shone very white. Sophie could hear her breathe and see the rise and fall of her chest. Then, in a swift unexpected movement, Moira grabbed Sophie's wrist and put her hand into her lap. It felt warm and damp there, the material so flimsy. Sophie had a revelation: Moira wasn't wearing knickers. Moira was using the same tricks that Sophie had used on Tom. Only it wasn't going to work on Sophie. She didn't even know what to do with her fingers in her lap. She just left them there, disabled, leaning. She didn't know whether she should tuck her fingers between the gap, as though perhaps she was making a bed, or if it was just by chance that Moira had placed her hand there, on that secret spot, and that she should move it away. She did neither. She just let her hand lie soft and pliant.

Sophie remembered the first time she touched a boy there. It was at home in front of after-school TV. Their legs were tucked under the table, their fingers darting about like little fishes. She took hold of his cock and worked her wrists up and down. It was bulbous and purple and she was astonished at the angle with which it reared its head. She moved her fingers up and down until he grabbed them, made them work much faster and then warm milky come spat out from its top, like a snake's tongue. They would do it in front of *Blue Peter* and *Grange Hill*, but if he paid too much attention to the TV, she would sulk.

On the screen, a tiger prowled through a forest. Its stripy marmalade face was stern and predatory. Moira, however, wasn't paying much attention to it.

'Instinct, eh, it's a very powerful thing.' Moira's mouth was so close to Sophie's that she almost understood the words by feeling the shapes they made on her lips. She squeezed agreement into Moira's thigh. But still Moira gave no clues about what to do next, so eventually she withdrew her hand and put it in her own lap.

'So free of inhibition, aren't they?'

'They are,' agreed Sophie. She didn't know what to say. She was unsure how to behave. So often had she been the one to press her case eagerly, to do the seducing. It was weird to be the seducee. It was as though she had given over her map and compass to Moira and was totally dependent on her to get home.

'It's a shame we're not more like animals,' Moira said, giving Sophie a meaningful stare.

These were uncharted waters and Sophie felt excited, but it was not a particularly sexual excitement. The thought of Moira creeping into her knickers was strange. But then she could let her do that. Let her defile her. (No, what was the term? Deflower her?) If that was what she wanted to do. It wouldn't be bad, certainly not. In fact, she probably would get off on it. It was only if Moira wanted her to reciprocate that problems might arise. But she was surely worldly enough to understand that Sophie didn't swing that way.

'I'm going back to my room now,' Moira said. She was very matter-of-fact.

'Do you want me to . . . come with you?' Sophie asked.

'I don't think so, do you?'

'What about the deal?'

'Oh yes, the deal.' Moira spoke confidently. 'That's all you care about, isn't it? Well, maybe you need a little time . . .'

'No, honestly, tonight is fine. I can . . . whatever you want.'

'Thank you, Sophie.' Moira was laughing at her. 'Actually, I don't want.'

Sophie was so surprised that she couldn't find the words to say goodbye, so she stood there gulping like a goldfish (but with a considerably longer memory). And in her shock, as Moira cannily predicted, she conceived the first real trickle of interest.

150

# Chapter Twenty-Four

Mick disembarked at the next island and, when he returned, he was in a much better mood. In all the years he had been drifting, wandering from one scheme to another, from one woman to another, he had learned one lesson – always cover your back. In more fanciful moments he liked to think he was a reincarnation of a Samurai: aloof, honourable and brave. Perhaps this was why he always took the seat against the wall in a restaurant or bar, for fear of a knife in the back, and he never relied on one source – be it for information, affection or money.

Angie Weatherby, née Graham, was a newly married, newly disappointed 34-year-old blonde receptionist from Atlanta. She had left her husband after four hours of marriage, after finding out how he spent his stag night between the legs of a stripper on the stage in front of all his friends. She had come alone on this cruise. And she set her sights on Mick. Mick knew he was being followed. He knew he was being watched as he executed his ship-famous dives. He felt Angie's eyes on him as he soaked himself down in the public shower. He didn't know what she saw: the arse to die for, or the back that was broad at the top then narrowed magnificently like the Panama

Canal to a trim, slim waist; but he knew she saw something that caught her. She watched him drying off, lolling around like a puppy in the sun, all the while trying to get him to look at her.

Finally he did. He didn't know where to take her. He was fed up with doing it out on deck, but he didn't like going to their rooms because they never would release him; and he wasn't going to allow anyone to stay in his. But he did want to feel her body. She had a great figure, a lovely hourglass shape, like a number 8 – or at least number 0 with a belt on. He liked the traffic-stopping way her bosom thrust out. All tits are equal but some are more equal than others. And these were pretty damn more equal.

He found out where the emergency key to the Captain's office was. He let them in; everything was hunky-dory. He took in the Captain's lavish surroundings: the high back armchair, the laptop on the ornate heavy leather desk, and he laid her on the bearskin rug in front of the fire. Angie squirmed with pleasure. She wished her groom could have seen her then, with some stranger's finger up her pussy. He gave her a good seeing to. Her tits were a little less than had promised – damn those up-lift bras and their false promises – but still ... Enjoy, enjoy, he told her and so she did.

He took the whip off the wall and lashed her peachy buttocks until they were an acre of red stripes, and then he kissed and nuzzled her there, all on the Captain's sacred floor. And when she asked him, with tear-stained grateful cheeks, why he didn't actually fuck her, he said that she was too vulnerable, too raw for that. When she was ready, she would know; until then, she wasn't to feel under any pressure.

Sophie wasn't the first to witness the honeymooners in action. And she certainly wasn't the last. When the Captain went on his daily tour, he found that, once again, the door to 'that room' was ajar. Inside, a woman was sitting at her dressing table, applying lotions to her skin.

Her hair was wet and she was wearing a silk dressing gown. When she saw the Captain reflected in the mirror in front of her, she did not start but merely continued circling the lotion into her face with her thumbs. The Captain stayed quietly where he was.

'Why, hello,' she drawled. She had a husky, too-many-cigarettes voice, and massive cahooneys. 'I seem to have collected myself an audience again.'

The Captain set his cap straight.

'Just checking everything is OK, ma'am.'

'Won't you come in, Captain? It is your ship, after all.'

He pushed open the door so hard that he almost fell in, which wasn't how he intended to make his grand entrance, but it was better than nothing.

'You've caught me in the middle of my ... my ablutions. Isn't that what you military types say?'

The Captain laughed enigmatically.

'We military types would say that I've caught you in the middle of something very interesting, that's what.'

'Well, Captain, do you like what you see?'

She swivelled round and her robe opened. He could see up her legs, into the heart of darkness. She continued creaming the lotion into her face. It was white and greasy – her skin looked very soft, very pliant.

'How would you like to come a little closer for a bird's-eye view?' she added.

'Strictly speaking, a bird's-eye view would be from above.'

'From above, huh? Well, I'm sure something could be arranged.'

He watched her fingers move round and round her cheeks. She wasn't Sophie, but she wasn't bad.

'What is all that stuff?' He gestured towards the creams that even as she talked she was so diligently applying.

'Vitamin E, toner, anti-aging lotions. Do you want to try some?'

The Captain checked his watch – it was nineteen hundred hours; plenty of time – and approached.

She squeezed another tube and the white lotion landed

153

on the end of her finger. He noticed she had fantastically long nails. He liked that. She could do some damage with them. She raised her finger and put a spot of the lotion on the end of his nose. The Captain endured it silently. Then she squeezed the tube again and applied the lotion to his right cheek and then to his left. Very slowly, very gently, she started to rub in the lotion. As she did so, her robe parted wider and her tits were revealed to him in all their glory. She continued to caress his cheeks. His skin dampened. He felt wet, clammy even. It seemed to him that she was echoing other places, other wetnesses.

'Feels good, doesn't it?' she whispered. 'It's all soft and slippery. Rub it in, go on.'

The Captain could wait no more. He grabbed her, visciously, aggressively – he thought, romantically. He took her in his arms and kissed her hard. She pretended to struggle for one second and then relented, falling back into his arms and kissing back with all her might. Their faces squelched together. Her teeth scraped against his and then moved to nibble his lips. He stroked her and sought out the back of her teeth with his tongue. When he pulled away to look at her, she was flushed and moaning her approval. He felt the nails grasp his back determinedly and he almost shouted out in pain. Anti-aging? This would put years on him. He pressed at her with his cock, so she could take a feel of his official member.

'I want you,' he said dramatically.

'You are a fast worker,' she sighed approvingly.

'We military types don't mess around.' He got her hands away from his back – Christ, she was ripping him to shreds – and put them around his cock. Just look what he had got for her! She yelped with pleasure.

'You are enormous,' she exclaimed. 'Is that how you got to be the Captain?'

'This is as big as they come,' he said. He pushed himself closer to her, had to get inside, had to. Who cared that at twenty hundred hours there was a special reception for the salesmen from Texas? Who cared that his face was white with vitamin E lotions? A Captain has a licence to fuck. Her claws were back, scratching lines on his buttocks. He felt her arse too, and it was an arse to die for.

'You, lady, are just the way I like my women.'

She went back to stroke his cock impatiently. He couldn't help worrying that she might dig her nails in there too and cause some real damage.

'Do you want it? Say it then . . .'

'Oh, I do, Captain, I do.'

'Where do you want it?'

'Up me,' she breathed. 'I want it up me.'

But the Captain was disturbed before he could comply with the woman's wishes. His steward appeared, flanked by two police officers. One of them, he couldn't help noticing, was a damn fine filly.

'Captain?' the steward said awkwardly. 'Sorry to bother you when you are so clearly . . . indisposed but they insisted.'

'What is it?' he groaned. If they were anyone else but the police, he might have been driven to murder. The woman backed off and returned to her mirror. She began filing her nails. Her composure was remarkable.

'I hope you don't mind . . . We tried to call but you were . . . occupied. I'm afraid I have some very bad news. It's about a member of your staff . . .'

An announcement went out that all ship and entertainment staff were to convene in the meeting hall at seven o'clock in the morning.

Sophie got up grumpily, her sleep having been disturbed by a nightmare involving Moira, wild animals and working the casino with no clothes on. By the time she arrived, the meeting was already in full swing; the Captain was marching up and down yelling something about 'a disgrace', 'an embarrassment to the *Prince Albert*', and 'disgusting behaviour'. She wondered what on earth had been going on.

155

'Sorry I'm late,' she murmured, as contritely as she could muster.

But he yelled 'Sit down' without even looking up.

She had never seen him so angry. For the first time, she was impressed. Usually the Captain was a constipated control freak. Surprisingly, when he let himself go, he came across as quite attractive.

'I have just found out something dreadful.'

Sophie shivered. Surely they couldn't do her for the scam; for a crime not yet committed? How would anyone know? Could it have been the gossipy barmen, or the over-suspicious purser? None of the team would have spilled the beans, surely? Nerves dashed across her. Perhaps this was what would be talked about in ten years' time – not the gang who conned the casino but the duds who planned to and got caught before they had even done anything. Please, please don't let it be about us. They could be locked up. (Mind you, she wouldn't mind being locked up with Mick; but then there was Josh to think about and all those complications.)

Fuck, she prayed, don't let this be about us.

Then she realised that the fuss couldn't be about the casino because all the staff were gathered there, from the chefs, the musicians and the stewards to the ship's doctors. This surely meant that whatever was going on had to be a ship-wide affair and not just to do with the entertainment staff. Even her purser (if she could call him that) was anxiously whispering. Everyone looked subdued. Actually, Moira was leaning against a pillar at the back of the hall, confidently smoking a cigarette and was the only one who didn't look guilty. She waved at Sophie, who leaned back in her chair. The white rush of panic had been replaced with a casual interest in the proceedings.

'I will let the police explain,' the Captain barked.

A young black policewoman, attempting to hide her prettiness with a stern expression, and an older fat policeman with a moustache stepped forward self-importantly.

'We have reason to believe that someone is trying to

smuggle class A drugs into the United States. This is a federal offence.'

'It's probably more than one person,' the fat cop interrupted, determined to assert his authority.

'Yes,' the woman conceded. 'We know that the person, or persons –' she nodded towards her colleague deferentially '– came aboard after negotiating a deal with an islander. And we are pretty certain that he, or she, is working on this boat.'

'Or "they",' corrected the fat cop pedantically.

Sophie was flooded with relief. Thank God she hadn't done what Simon suggested. If she had been caught with that stash it would have been sayonara for her.

The cops surveyed the room with such suspicious glances that even the most innocent person felt they must have done something wrong.

'The police want to interview you all individually. And if any staff member is involved in this, they will be handed over to their custody without further ado.'

Things began well for Sophie. The pair went through her things chatting brightly as they pulled her clothes from her wardrobe and her suitcases from under her bed. There was nothing incriminating at all, although the fat policeman did look inquisitively at her packs of cards, her backgammon, her dominoes and her chess until she said apologetically, 'I'm a croupier – what can you do?' And he laughed.

The policewoman was harder to charm.

'Where did you disembark?'

Sophie told her. 'And did you associate with any of the locals?' she asked.

'Yes,' admitted Sophie, 'but not closely' (unless you consider burrowing your face in their cock 'close').

'Did you pack these bags yourself?' The policewoman picked disapprovingly at Sophie's suitcase. When she found the dildos, Sophie told herself not to be embarrassed. I'm a sexually active woman, so what? But she couldn't help turning crimson.

'Have you noticed anything suspicious or strange since you have been aboard?'

'In what way strange?' asked Sophie.

The policewoman consulted her notebook and began reciting, 'Anything unusual, out of the ordinary, missing items, noises, anything –'

'Actually,' Sophie interrupted, a little shyly, 'my knickers have gone. I used to have about ten pairs, and now I only have three.'

They wrote it down, but Sophie knew they weren't particularly interested. She couldn't blame them. She wouldn't have been interested either – they had far bigger fish to fry.

They were the height of professionalism. They thanked her for her time and apologised for the inconvenience. Sophie liked them enormously. It was nice to talk to people who were from outside the *Prince Albert*. It was refreshing in a funny kind of way.

They got ready to leave.

'So, what do you think these people planned to do with the drugs once they got to Florida?' Sophie queried, just out of interest.

'How do you know that?'

'What?'

'That the drugs were destined for Florida.'

'I don't know. I'm just guessing.' Fuck, she had put her foot in it. 'That's where it all goes, isn't it?'

They looked at each other and then back at her.

'What do you know?'

'Nothing, honestly!'

'I'm afraid we'll have to search you,' the fat man said. 'Empty your pockets.'

She put her keys, her money and her wallet on the table. Then they indicated that she should stand against the wall with her arms raised. The woman ran her hands up and down her trousers. Up and down her arse.

'I'm afraid I'm going to have to ask you to remove your trousers.'

Sophie did as she was told. She unbuttoned her jeans, lifted her arms in the air and returned to the wall.

'And your top and the bra.'

The woman moved her hands across her breasts, gliding her fingers across her hard little nipples. Sophie shivered. What did the woman hope to find there?

'And your knickers, please.'

Sophie stepped out of her pants and left them on the floor. The fat man snatched them up. Part of the search, it seemed, involved sniffing them.

'Don't you have to wear gloves?'

'Would you rather I did?'

And Sophie had stared hungrily at the woman's fingers and felt a curious swelling between her legs.

'No.'

The woman started looking for the evidence. The fat man held Sophie's arms against the walls – as if she would resist. It felt nice to be so ... so trapped. The woman's fingers slid up her vaginal passage, and then down, up and down. It was a complete invasion, a terrible abuse of authority. It felt terrific. Sophie was wet; she knew the woman's hands would be coated in her cream.

'Is there anything there?' the fat policeman asked.

'Just this.' The woman had accessed Sophie's clit. She was tender to it, circling and massaging the whole area with well-practised fingers. Sophie was holding her breath; she didn't dare let it out. She was full of tension, full of excitement. How dare these two come in here and start demanding this of her? How dare they? And yet, how come this had never happened to her before? This should happen every trip, every week, every day even. She could feel a familiar surge of pleasure, the gradual loss of rationality, and then, just as she was sure she would not be able to contain herself, the woman removed her fingers. She shook them and little droplets of milky liquid flew through the air.

'Have you got anything I can wipe with?' she said to the fat man. With a flourish, he produced a tissue.

'Did you find anything?' At last, Sophie breathed.

'No, I think he'll have to look.'

Sophie almost laughed with joy but she knew better than that. After all, she was a suspect in a major crime. She was a prime suspect; she loved that idea – she was the best suspect of all. The primest, juiciest, sexiest of all the suspects. The man's fingers were much bigger and Sophie held her breath as he clumsily parted her pussy lips and entered her. He pampered her, explored her. Was he a mind reader? He knew what to do. He was wanking her.

'Anything?'

'Nothing.'

He slid out of her. Sophie wanted to tell him to check again. She didn't have to. The policewoman, after extensive examination of her own fingers, which involved putting them in her mouth and sucking them, told her that she was to bend over the table. They would both have to search at the same time. And they were going to check every orifice known (and some not too well known) to man. Sophie bent over shyly.

'Can you touch your toes?' the policewoman asked.

She could.

'Good girl, you're very nimble.'

She grunted her thanks.

'Ready? Here we go.'

The man's hands came at her first, and then the woman's. She was taken care of, stripped down and taken over. Oh, it felt good, so good, so outrageous. He was prying up her arse and she was hollowing out her cunt, friction on the spot, jackpot!

'Oh, God,' she hissed, 'don't stop.'

'Did you say something?'

'Is she telling us where the drugs are?' asked the woman excitedly.

'Mmmeowww, don't, yes, no.'

'What is it, dear?' said the fat man, thrusting deeper and deeper up her hole.

'Don't stop,' she said, and her voice sounded funny.

'If I just rub you here,' he said, and now it was his turn to move his fingers over her clit, 'will you tell us where you hid everything?'

'Please rub me there,' she begged. And he rubbed faster and faster. The policewoman was inside her too, jammed up her arsehole, creeping around, searching for something, and Sophie felt that she had no secrets left; there was nothing about her that they didn't know – but that wasn't a bad thing.

After they left her cabin, Sophie lay down on her bed and wept. She didn't know what she was crying about, but mostly it was relief. She felt better than she had since, since, well, since being in the pool with Mick. Plus, they hadn't found out about the scam. In a roundabout way, things were going pretty well.

# Chapter Twenty-Five

The changing room curtain was so fine that Sophie could see Moira trying on the clothes as though it were a shadow movie. She watched her friend's narrow shoulders wriggle into shirts. She watched the way her body tapered down to the slim waist and then curved out again over the ripe buttock cheeks. She watched her jiggle into a pair of skinny pants.

When Moira emerged from behind the curtains, she commented on how flushed Sophie was.

'Why don't you try on some things too?'

Sophie resisted. Neither of them had enough money to buy anything. The ship's boutiques catered only for the rich clientele and Sophie couldn't bear the ache she got when she fell in love with clothes that she couldn't afford (even though she knew she would be able to afford them soon . . .). But the main reason she didn't want to try on anything was that, unusually for her, she felt self-conscious. Next to the size ten Moira, she felt bumpy and unsavoury.

This time, Moira told Sophie to squeeze in with her. Sophie sat down on the floor of the cubicle and clutched the coat hangers, while Moira tried on a tiny minidress. It was a forlorn little thing on the shelf but when she put it on, it came alive. Moira pranced in front of the long mirror, as though she were mesmerised. Then she lifted the dress up at the back and Sophie couldn't help noticing her little white panties just about to fall off her narrow hips. She bit her lip and agreed, yes, it was the kind of dress you could wear anywhere.

'Go on,' urged Moira. 'It's more fun if we try the clothes on together.'

'OK, how about this?' Sophie succumbed. She grabbed at a vest and went to join her in the little space. There was hardly any room in there but the mirror deluded you into thinking there was.

Moira stood in just her bra and knickers. She kept readjusting the knickers, pulling them this way and that. She wouldn't take her eyes off Sophie. Sophie bit her lip. She didn't really want to take off her top to try the other one on; she felt awkward. She wished there were more shoppers around but they must all have been at lunch. She wondered about the other people who had used this room, today maybe or yesterday. Had anyone fucked up against the looking-glass, hanging on to the hooks for dear life? Had someone pretended to try on outfits but, instead, had they ran their fingers over their hot thighs, dancing down their knickers while their partner waited outside?

Sophie remembered a fantasy that a boyfriend once told her, back in the days when she used to ask them what they wanted and tried to cooperate. These days, she could usually guess. He said he would like to be a security guard. It was an elaborate fantasy and had grown and grown until Sophie thought they had the makings of a short film. He would be, as he put it, caravan trash – trousers high, smoke-stained teeth and fingers – and he would work in a department store, locked in a little room full of cameras.

One day, a beautiful young woman would arrive to try on some clothes of a high-class clothes store. Only she wasn't rich like the other customers, she was just a college student, struggling, but she was beautiful. Near closing time, she would slip an elaborate top over her head. Only, whoops, silly her, she has gained weight from working in a pie shop all summer and, whereas she used to be a skinny eight stone, she is now a meaty twelve stone and has gone up three dress sizes, a fact she had conveniently forgotten. She would get stuck, stuck in this top that would cost all of her college fees and more.

Only the security guard would know anything about it. He would enjoy the pictures of her struggling out of it and then go down to offer his assistance. The top would be over her head, straitjacket to her arms, and revealing all her panties and thighs. 'Can I help you?' he would ask, pleasantly. At first she would be so grateful that he had arrived. Breathless, 'Oh thank you, please get me out of this,' but then she would gradually realise that he had a secret agenda. Rather than releasing her, he would spread her thighs, finger down her panties and help himself to her.

She would be trapped, but ever so obliging. And so careful not to tear the shirt, worth hundreds of pounds, she would do anything he wanted. He could poke, lick and nuzzle while she squirmed with embarrassment and then pleasure. When Sophie had asked why exactly this scenario had so much appeal (back in the days when she tried to analyse everything) he said it was the combination of the clothes, the entrapment, the anonymity and the CCTV camera. Nothing was sexier, he said, than being caught on film.

Sophie wondered if she should try on something that was grossly too small for her, and then Moira would have to liberate her in the same way as her boyfriend had fantasised. Perhaps not. She hoped Moira could read her mind. It would be so much easier that way.

Moira waited and waited. Then she said, 'I had better help you,' and she walked over to her.

Sophie gazed at Moira's slender fingers as they nibbled at her shirt buttons. Moira parted the shirt and it slid to the floor. Sophie was frozen. Instead of handing her the vest, Moira made her turn round. She undid the clasp of

Sophie's bra. The strap pinged and then her breasts were spilling out of the cups. Sophie turned back slowly towards Moira, whose eyes widened at the sight of Sophie's breasts. Then she held out her hands under the curve of her tits. Moira weighed them, as though she were assessing fruit in the greengrocer's.

'They are very big,' she said. Sophie was quivering, but that didn't stop her nipples from hardening up, like water turning to ice. 'Much bigger than mine,' she continued. Her small buds were sticking out, pressing at Sophie.

'I always wanted to have big tits.'

Was this the moment to consolidate the deal? Time was suspended and Sophie felt like an actress who needed direction. She looked from her own breasts to Moira's. The name of this game was pairs – and Sophie never lost. She wanted to push them together, push them at each other. This was the moment. With her eyes firmly shut, Sophie leaned forwards with her lips pouted ready for impact. She felt a twinge of panic when Moira's nipple pressed against hers, and then the fear turned into pleasure. Moira was warm. Her skin was soft and smelled sweet. They would both be wet between the legs, wet and sticky, warm and cuddly. This wasn't going to be so bad. But her lips found no place to land.

'No, I don't think so, not until you are ready.'

'I am,' whined Sophie. 'What do I have to do?'

Moira leaned very close. 'You have to want to.'

'I do!'

'Sophie, you think you can just lie back and think of the money. Well, it's not going to work like that. I'll help you in the scam ... but it doesn't all go your way.'

Sophie blushed. It was true – she had thought she would get away with just being a passive participant – but the more she thought that even that wouldn't happen, the more downcast she felt.

Before Sophie could think of an apt response, Moira had dressed and swept out to the front of the shop.

'It was the perfect fit,' Moira gushed to the woman at

the counter, as Sophie hastily pulled her clothes over her head. 'The colour and the style –' she winked '– were great.' She nodded back to the sales assistant; her lips were flushed, alive. 'She will pay for it.'

Mick was out on the tennis court – with yet another woman. Sophie walked by swiftly, hoping that he hadn't seen her and wishing that she hadn't seen him. It hurt to see Mick with someone else; it was more than a throb of jealousy – it was like being stabbed in the guts. Sophie knew it wasn't the woman's fault – after all, the woman didn't know her, didn't owe her anything, but it was the woman Sophie chose to hate. She watched the woman laughing as she served the ball. They were both fairly useless players – this was obviously more of a date than a contest – and they both spent most of the time retrieving missed balls. Unfortunately, poor play gave the girl plenty of opportunity to flash her wares. Down she went, picking up the balls, her little buttocks facing up to the heavens. And when she wasn't presenting everyone with a view of those slender thighs underneath the tiny tennis skirt, she was marching around, rubbing her arse, as if to say, I bet you would like to do that too.

Mick was laughing. His arms were flailing around as he helplessly tried to return her miss-shots. Sophie wondered what they got up to in bed. The girl probably had lots of stamina – she looked the sort who would grind away for hours upon hours, wearing out her opponents in a war of attrition. She probably liked to fuck in that silly tennis outfit. Well, you would, wouldn't you, if you knew you looked that good? She probably took it up against the net, from behind. It should have been *her* thighs Mick softly parted; it should have been *her* knickers that he slid off – not this silly cow's. Maybe he had sex with her. He wouldn't sleep with her, but he probably slept with ol' Billie Jean over there.

Sophie watched the girl drop her racket and consoled herself that at least she had firmer wrists than her! She wished she had asked Mick to play tennis. Maybe he only liked women who did sports. Maybe he preferred athletic fresh-faced sportswomen to women who spent all night at smoky gaming tables, learning useless card tricks.

She mooched off to the slot machines – that was about as energetic as she was going to get. She pumped money angrily into the slot. Pulled the arm of the machine aggressively and watched mesmerised as the peaches, apples and bananas spun round. Each time, she thought she was going to win. Each time, the machine bleeped out her failure. Maybe she should just give up.

She was down to her last few coins when Mick turned up beside her.

'Enjoy the tennis, Sophie?' he asked softly. She didn't look at him, but she was so glad he was there.

'It wasn't exactly Wimbledon,' she said. Why was she always so rude to him? It was like being seventeen again.

He had been watching her watching him all morning – should I stay or should I go? He knew he shouldn't get involved but that knowledge only increased the feeling that he wanted to rebel, to kick out – and to touch her.

'Is everything all ready for Thursday?'

'More or less,' she said. (Moira-less, yes.)

'I'm looking forward to it.'

'What do you want?' she challenged. She kicked the base of the machine, like that would help. The bastard machine was keeping all her money.

'Did I use up all my chances?' he asked.

Sophie was thrilled but she knew she should wait awhile. Let him sweat, the way he made her.

'Shall we go to my room?' she said after a few minutes had lapsed.

'No, let's stay here,' he said. She didn't know what he meant until he wrapped his arms around her. 'Don't stop playing,' he said.

'Oh, Mick,' she murmured. Oh, God, she felt so horny. And the gentle movement of the ship made it so much worse. All she could think about was having that same movement inside her.

'Let me touch you, babe. I'll make you feel better.'

'How do you know I need to feel better?'

'I can see it in your hands,' he said. She thought later that that was nonsense, but at the time she believed him.

A couple on the next machine looked over at them curiously, but Mick was clever. He was discreet. One hand shot up her T-shirt to press at her pert nipples. The other hand was clambering insistently down her waistband. He whispered into her ear.

'That's all I want. Just to play with your moist pussy. You know you want it.'

She used to have a fantasy about doing it in an auction room. She liked the idea of keeping still, staying calm, while getting shafted from behind. And even though the pleasure would be excruciatingly good, you couldn't even risk a nod, not even a murmur, or you would end up buying a seventeenth-century jug used by Queen Beatrix of Holland, or you might be saddled with a pair of cufflinks. Oh, it was the pressure of keeping still, that exquisite challenge, that did it for her. She would be poked and pressed, hunted and caressed, yet she couldn't show a thing, and the auctioneer would be shouting, 'Do I have any offers? Do I have an advance on eighty, eighty-five? Going, going, gone,' and she would be gone by that point . . . under the hammer.

Mick stood behind her, her tight butt pressed against his crotch. She let her legs fall open carelessly. The couple walked away and a man stood next to them. They had to be careful. Mick gave her some more money to feed the machine. He liked watching her cram the coins into that narrow slot, just like he was cramming his fingers into her slit, waiting for her jackpot.

Sophie felt him fill her up, take her over, and all thoughts of resistance vanished. He was up her. The fruits whizzed round and round, landing and then moving off again. Sophie had given up all cares about the machines and was giving it up to the feeling in her pussy. She had to hold an even keel now, keep control, she told herself, keep a sodding lid on it. But how could she when he was exploring her so well, like he was made to do it, making her so silky, so flowing? It was too much for anyone to ask. She held on to the handle of the machine, let the tension mount, the incredible build-up commence, and he rubbed her to kingdom come as she purred and brayed against him. The shudder of release was so great that, if she had been in an auction room, she would have ended up buying the lot, auctioneer, hammer and all.

The Captain felt his jealousy erupt like a hail of acne. Sophie's face was scarlet. He registered that her face was always a pinker shade of red and it charmed him. Red cheeks, red lips; both top and bottom deck. She was a woman on the edge of a sexual meltdown.

'Sophie,' he said, 'I've been looking for you everywhere. It's time for your review.'

'Now?' she asked incredulously. Every part of her was hot. Every part of her was swollen with desire.

'Yes, now. Come along!' The Captain turned on his heels and snapped down the corridor. Over at the machine where she had been playing, someone had won. A crowd gathered round as the lucky player opened his arms and swallowed up all the money, her money.

Once installed in his study, the Captain flicked an ink pen round and round. Round and round it swirled. In a former life, he fancied he was a hypnotist.

'How are you getting on here on the *Prince Albert*?'

'Fine.' She was swaying. She followed the movement of the Captain's pen on the paper. She tried to apply analysis to the resultant scribbles, but if her memory of graphology served her well then they might be indicating that the Captain was a psychopath.

'The policy on ships is "women first". Do you understand?'

'Yes,' she said faintly. She had no idea what she was talking about. She wondered if seasickness ever took the form of delirium.

If he knew all the plotting she had been doing, not

169

only would she be sent off the *Prince Albert* but also she would probably have to stand trial.

'I have something to discuss with you,' he said abruptly, and his voice was so much lower than before that it almost scraped along the seabed.

'OK,' she whispered.

'There's something I've been wanting to tell you for a while now.'

The idea that he was going to try to have sex with her crossed her mind, like a black cloud on a sunny day. (Or was it like sun breaking through the clouds on a cloudy day?) Sophie felt her mouth go dry. The gold buttons on the Captain's impeccably white shirt glinted and seemed to twirl at her. She wondered if those uniform trousers had a zip or button fly.

'You have passed your trial period with flying colours. Welcome aboard, Sophie.'

She had completely forgotten. When she realised it was just this, she couldn't help cringing. Was she going mad? How could she have thought he would have anything salacious on his mind? This is the Captain of the *Prince Albert* for goodness' sake, not the purser of the *Love Boat*. But then he turned back to her.

'I haven't finished yet.'

Sophie waited. The Captain moved towards her and tilted up her chin.

'Sophie, Sophie, Sophie,' he murmured. Sweet Sophie, with the red lips, the red shiny lips and the swivelling hips. 'I've worked it all out!'

'What?'

'Why you are here, Sophie, I know why you are here.'

Sophie felt her chest constrict. Oh God. Would nothing go right? How had they, no, how had she been so careless? It was as if she had left a trail of clues around the ship. Was she so bad a criminal?

'Look at me.' He said it so tenderly that she would have believed he was a different person. Sophie couldn't bring herself to face him. She hung her head low. How could she have let him find out? The Captain, however, jumped up and whipped the curtains together. The two sides met discordantly. Sophie looked up in amazement.

'I wanted to do that before I kissed you.'

'Before you kissed me?' Sophie echoed.

'How long have you been in love with me?'

'In love?'

'Yes.'

'Ahh.' Sophie had to think quickly. The Captain had grabbed the wrong end of the stick. The very wrong end, and what he had grabbed was ludicrous, it was obscene.

'Tell me when you realised you were in love with me,' he persisted.

'I think it was, um, a few days ago.'

He frowned.

'But that's impossible. It was before you came aboard.'

'Oh yes,' Sophie said quickly. 'It was while I was working on the *Princess Alexandra*. I couldn't stop thinking about you.'

'What did you want me to do to you?'

'Um, everything.'

The Captain leaned forwards. She could smell his aftershave.

'Did you want me to kiss you?'

'Yes,' Sophie said uncertainly. Was that the right answer?

'Did you want me to hold you?'

'I . . . hoped you would, yes.'

'Do you lie in bed thinking of me?' The Captain stared intently. She realised he shaved the bit in between his eyebrows.

'Sometimes, yes.'

'Do you want me to . . . fuck you?'

'I guess so.'

'Then, my darling sweet Sophie, your wish is my command.'

He moved forward and kissed her. She gave up to it. She had no choice. He kissed hard and well, forcefully. He was a man who took care of things. He didn't believe in all that feminist nonsense. In his experience, women want princes not pansies.

She was still aroused. Still wet through. Excitement from one man carries over to the next. She was weak with arousal, willing to submit. She gave up to the lips pressing on hers. They searched out her neck, her ears. Hot whispering there. Disgusting maybe. Arousing, yes, yes. She could feel the strain at his trousers. And with a faint coming back to consciousness, she wanted to touch him.

'I want you to sit on my table on Thursday night.'

'I can't.' She felt horror stricken. Thursday night was *the* night. 'I can't. The Captain shouldn't entertain staff alongside passengers. It's one of the rules.'

'I'm breaking the rules,' he said, looking delighted.

'But not Thursday then. I'm on the late shift; please; sorry.'

'You can work after dinner.'

'What about tonight instead?' she offered desperately.

'No, I can't make it tonight.'

'But you know how strict the casino staff are . . . about their rotas.'

At that, the Captain rose up proud, like a dog on his hind legs, and said, 'Sophie, I am the Captain of the entire ship. Do you think I give a toss about rotas?'

Still, he was impressed with her enthusiasm. Tonight? She was certainly ardent. He walked away euphorically. It had been three whole days since he had had a woman. Women like Sophie don't come along very often.

Sophie left her key for Mick, and a note saying that he was to come. URGENTLY.

# Chapter Twenty-Six

$S$ trange dreams came to Tom; bizarre unwelcome sub-conscious thought explosions that made him shiver for his sanity. He was beginning to fear sleep itself for fear of what it uncovered.

That night, the cards woke up and came to life. They were dancing and taunting and teasing each other. It was a 52-member party, a veritable orgy. The numbers, the mere plebs, paired off and pressed against each other. Sometimes, there was inter-species sex, for example, a seven might go off with an eight, but this was generally frowned upon. There were so many questions raised, questions of consent, of abusing one's authority. Usually, a five would only go with a five, a four would pair off with a four, although the three of spades and the three of clubs were deeply in love, and this put the three of hearts and the three of diamonds in an awkward position because they quite fancied a bit of swinging, but the others wouldn't agree. And the six of clubs refused point-blank to do it with the six of spades. However, it was the higher members of the court that proved more interesting.

The king of spades was in love with the queen of hearts. But she ignored him. He hurled up her dress and burrowed inside, but she despised him for his dark vulgarity. She let the other cards have her, though, sometimes two at a time, even the prince of spades was allowed to dig into her front, and the king of clubs was throbbing behind her. She went for the joker as well. The joker didn't make her laugh, had long since stopped making people laugh, and instead was a rather subdued presence. 'Hide me,' she said, and he wrapped her in his arms, enclosing her in his space. She had her back to him, and he slipped his cock in from behind as she stood there, pressed against him.

Meanwhile, the king of clubs was feeling neglected. Why couldn't he have some action? Why did the hearts hog all the love stuff? It wasn't fair. He had had all the club family, and all the spades, all but the king who, being in love with the queen of hearts, resisted for as long as possible for cardkind. But then he had to have her. She didn't protest, she felt wanted again, but suddenly, just as he was about to come, the ace of spades, the death card, was pushing at him from another angle.

Tom woke up abruptly. He had heard the phrase 'cold sweat' before but never completely understood what it meant until that morning. He lay sleeplessly, waiting for the first glimpses of the sun to ease him to another day, a better day. How was he going to handle this? He kept replaying the dream in his head, until he was sure of what he had seen. That card, he told himself, the ace of spades, wasn't necessarily the death card, but it represented the death, or the end, of something. He decided he would speak to Jennifer. Come clean. That was Jennifer all over really. Come clean – when all he wanted was to come dirty. Jenny would know what to do.

At first the key didn't slide in easily, but he fiddled around a bit and before long he felt the release of tension as the lock unwound. Sophie was sprawled out on her bed, watching cable TV. She was wearing a silk gown with a tasselled belt. He caught a glimpse of thigh between the gaps, the allure of pink skin beneath the velvet. It didn't take long before he realised she was drunk.

'I thought you wanted to talk,' Mick said wearily.

'I do,' she said, the wind taken out of her sails. She did want to talk, but she wanted to talk in his protective arms. Even if he didn't give of himself properly, at least he had given something. If he was going to have sex with everyone, he might just as well have it with her. They weren't just going to be ships that passed in the night. Not if she had anything to do with it. She was rather disturbed by how casually he treated the matter with the Captain.

'It's only dinner – at least he didn't suspect anything between us. That's a relief.'

'But it's Thursday night.' She wanted to impress on him the importance of that. Thursday night! *The* night!

'What's the problem? We can start later – it will only take a little while. '

'I think the Captain is in love with me.'

'You think everyone is in love with you, don't you?' The minute he said it, he wanted to bite off his tongue. It was a nasty thing to say, and it wasn't true. 'Look,' he said more gently, 'you can handle the Captain; just do what you have to do.'

'You want me to sleep with him now?'

'It wasn't my idea that you slept with Tom.'

'But you didn't object, did you?' yelled Sophie. It was the red wine yelling.

'Look, let's not argue; just keep him sweet!'

'I've been keeping the whole bloody ship sweet,' Sophie spluttered.

'Well, that's not my fault, is it?'

'Look, there's another thing I didn't tell you. I've been having some problems with Moira. She ... she's a lesbian.'

'I would have thought you had been there, done that, bought the dungarees.'

Sophie decided to drop the issue and get on to what was really on her mind.

'The other day, in the pool . . .'

'Yes?'

'And at the slot machines . . . you touched me.'

'Uh huh.'

'So, you do find me attractive, don't you?'

Mick looked defeated.

'You do,' she repeated.

'Yes, I do.' He looked like he had admitted selling his grandmother to pay for crack.

'Are you going to stay then?'

'Sophie . . .'

She unwrapped her dressing gown and, leaning against the door, he watched her.

'I'm going to have a shower.'

'And?'

'Would you like to join me?'

Mick didn't move. She knew she had won him over.

'Come on,' she said, and this time she was careful not to plead. Her body could speak for itself.

'Take off your clothes.' He moved towards her nonchalantly. No one told him what to do. And, as it happened, he didn't feel like taking off his clothes. They started kissing. Her heart was thumping. This was it! His tongue was deep in her mouth. She covered him with kisses. She didn't want to let him go.

'Shower?' he said. And she thought, what's wrong with here? But she nodded. She was walking on eggshells, but what a delicious sensation it was. She walked backwards so that she didn't have to separate from him, not for a second. They were kissing and nipping each other. In between the kisses, they smiled into each other's eyes.

In the shower, he turned her so she was facing away from him, and then with one hand he squeezed her arse as though he was pulping a lemon. With the other hand, he sought out her nipples and ran first one and then the other through his fingers. She let out a deep groan. He pressed up against her. It was a shock how well her body fitted into his. She curved inwards where he curved

176

outwards; his body seemed to mould to fit her, like sand rushing in to fill all the crevasses. It almost took his breath away. His trousers grew damp with the water, but still he kept them on.

'Does Tom do this to you?' he asked spitefully. The shower glass steamed up misty white, and inside the temperature was rising. The water pressure was good in these cabins; the spray poured firm on his head.

She could only sigh. His fingers were between her legs and he was up, wasting no time, up her hot pussy. Corkscrewing her in the way only he knew how. He wouldn't forget her tits though. He wouldn't stop pulling and releasing, squeezing tight and soft. His shirt was soaked through. Soaking like she was. She was groaning louder and louder. He turned the water up, but she raised her sighs even louder. The glass was completely fogged.

'Does he?'

'No,' she whispered.

'Louder,' he urged.

'No, he's got no idea what I want.'

'What do you want?'

'This, like this.'

That was what he wanted to hear. His fingers were turning wrinkled by her juices, flicking her clit, holding her down so she couldn't escape the orgasm. He had her against the shower cubicle, but still he wouldn't fuck her. Her hair was slicked back and drenched and little tears of water clung to her cheeks. She came, trembling and jerking under the hot spray, and he thought, I am a master of this.

'Does Tom do this to you?' he repeated. He had to know.

'You should know – you watched us.'

'Does he?'

'No.' She howled again with her pleasure, her head slung back, the water dripping down her face. For a brief moment, he was sure that she was the most beautiful sight in the world, and his fingers were propping her up.

She fell down and he picked her up with his fingers still between her legs. She was wetter than anyone he had ever touched before (but he always thought that).

And still he didn't fuck her.

He licked her. He opened her legs and licked there. He got two pillows: one for her and one for himself and then he turned up the music. He propped her on the sofa and wet her pussy, and he stayed there, drinking in her juices, for hours, waiting until she clenched her fingers around his head, pressed him against her, and pushed up her buttocks to him.

She tumbled on to her bed and he watched her indulgently. Women were always so sweet afterwards, so spaced out.

'Why?'

'Why not?' he said ambiguously.

'Why didn't you make love to me?'

'You know why.'

And he knew, guiltily, that in the midst of his bad behaviour, that almost made him look good.

'When did you first realise that you fancied me?' she asked.

'You were standing on the deck, leaning over the side, holding on to those binoculars when the wind whipped up your skirt. I could see the outline of your tight arse. It was agony seeing you like that. I wanted to touch you so much but I was petrified that I would give the game away.'

He laid her on the bed, parted her lips and put his hands to where she was still soft and tender. He opened her as wide as he could, so her feet poured off the sides of the bed. He wanted to get inside her there, and live there. He wanted to make her happy. He loved hearing her mounting pleasure and the little giggles that she couldn't hold back when he hit the spot. And he ate her all up like before, only this time, like Goldilocks, he fell into an exhausted sleep beside her.

She would enjoy a trouble-free sleep, wake up and remember little about the night before, only that her body felt fantastic. She had been soaked, wrung out, squeezed and all she would want to do would be to lie out to dry. And then, throughout the day, little flashbacks (like acid, only sweeter) would come back to her, and again she would ask herself why.

# Chapter Twenty-Seven

*B*itch, bitch, bitch. She had made him do it. If only he could get the money and run. And keep on running. Or, if only he had met her two months later, after he was fixed, after he was good.

Mick tried to calm down with yoga exercises, but he had to remind himself to breathe. And still he couldn't hide from the simple truth. The problem was desire. He had too much fucking desire. He had tried to put her out of his head, tried to tell himself not to get involved, but while his head agreed with him, his heart was more reluctant.

He sat in the lotus position and concentrated on blocking the world out. He could almost manage the world. It was Sophie who was the problem. He wished he could get off the merry-go-round of the last week, but he needed help to dismount. And he was too proud to ask for help.

He could have fallen in love with Sophie. Only he never wanted to fall in love again. It all ended badly – it all ended with a crucifixion. His. There was so much effort involved in relationships, for such little reward. Better to play around. Better to develop superior means of seduction.

He gave up sex ten years ago. No, rephrase, he gave

up penetrative sex. If anything, his appetite for women since then had doubled. For the first couple of years, he had a permanent hard-on. When he refused it, women pleaded and groaned with him. 'Stick it in, please'; 'Just for a moment'; 'I won't wriggle, I promise'. It was fantastic.

From films and songs he had been led to believe that it was always the man begging for it; it was always the man making promises. So, to find out that it wasn't always that way was a revelation, if not a revolution.

Eventually, women accepted it. And why not? He was good with his hands and he worshipped the breast; round, oval, droopy, pointing up, cross-nippled, teenage, middle-age, all the rage, dry, wet, lactating. He became an expert at oral sex, a master at tongue work. Before long, his reputation was opening legs all over the place, all over his face. The efficacy of the female grapevine never ceased to amaze him, and soon the story spread that he was the best in town. So what if he didn't go all the way? The journey was more than memorable.

One time, two women insisted on sharing him. 'Aren't you going to invite us in, Mick?' But it was they who invited him in. He lapped at their pussies, first one then the other, as they held on to each other, laughing. What he didn't realise was that, although he washed his face, his hair had become warm and sticky with their come, and again what he didn't realise was that it was a scent. In the pub later that evening, three women came on to him and he had the difficult task of deciding who he should like to have next.

There was nothing magical or mysterious about Mick's prowess, whatever his fans thought. Mick's skill lay in the fact that he liked women and wanted them to have a good time. He excelled at being a great consoler. He liked to restore women's confidence with his hot sticky fingers and sweet words. Because he was withholding of his cock, he paid particular attention to other areas; he learned how to spread his fingers, so that he could access all areas. Anal penetration became a speciality – and he was always having an internal wager about this; not on who would or wouldn't let him, because they all did, but how long they would take before they let him. Ten seconds was the fastest. Three weeks was the slowest. —

At about one in the morning, a gentle knocking awoke him; a knocking so gentle that at first he thought it was just the breeze shivering between the cracks, but then he realised that someone was outside.

It was Sophie.

She was wearing a red dressing gown that made her face look pale. Her narrow ankles and bare feet just poked out from beneath the hem. Just the sight of them brought out a weird feeling in him. He had seen many naked women in his time, but none had appeared to him so nude, so delicate or so alluring as her bare feet appeared then. He couldn't help but gaze at the slim toes, with their colourless, even nails, and the swerve of her anklebone.

'I'm sorry,' she whispered. 'Tell me to go if you like but . . . I just want to sleep with you.'

Mick very rarely allowed people to stay. That was his policy. But he wrapped his arms around her and guided her to his bed. She felt soft and comforting. He didn't know how to lie, now that he had a visitor, and he turned away from her to face the wall. She faced the opposite way, but their bottoms touched and he liked that.

'Do you mind if I sleep with the Captain?'

'I trust you,' he said, 'to do what you think is right.'

'I don't mind that you see all those other women,' she said. 'I just don't want you to fall in love with anyone.'

'As if,' he retorted gently. 'I only have eyes for you.'

'It's the rest of you I worry about.'

He didn't think he would fall asleep, but it only seemed like seconds later that it was the next morning – and the room looked different somehow.

# Chapter Twenty-Eight

*T*he ship lurched onwards drunkenly, and the sailing time was brought forward. There was a typhoon warning. The afternoon sessions in the casino and the bingo hall, and the tea dances were all cancelled. The afternoon visit to one of the smaller islands was curtailed.

'Apologies, apologies,' the Captain growled. It was clear he wasn't particularly sorry at all. 'We have to leave, otherwise we'll be stuck here all week.' His tone was such that no one would dare question his decision.

'We can't control nature,' he added, when he saw Sophie. 'We can control lots of things, but Mother Nature is not under our jurisdiction.'

The way he said 'Mother Nature' was simply lecherous. It was as though Mother Nature was reclining on a marble couch eating grapes while the world went to pot. He raised his eyebrows and mouthed the words 'Thursday evening'. She dashed down the corridor away from him – he could have no idea how exposed he made her feel.

On the way to her cabin, Sophie saw the girl who had been playing tennis with Mick; she was sitting on a bench weeping. Sophie walked on by. It gave her a cruel bite of pleasure to see the girl in distress, but then her conscience (or her curiosity) got the better of her. She asked what the matter was.

'Nothing, nothing, nothing,' muttered Angie Weatherby, in a way that suggested there was something.

Sophie got up to go.

'Actually, it's this guy,' she began – and started to cry with more ferocity.

Sophie put her arms around her. If Mick discovered them like this, he would (mistakenly) conclude that Sophie was most magnanimous.

'Ah yes, what's the problem?'

'He's really lovely and we get on really well. We are really close and we do lots of –' the girl smiled up at Sophie '– stuff, but the thing is, he won't sleep with me.'

'A lot of men are like that,' Sophie said vaguely. Her head was spinning. Did the girl mean Mick? 'Do the dirty and then they're out of there. I guess they are afraid of intimacy.'

'No, well, actually, we did sleep together for a couple of hours, but he just won't fuck me.'

'Well, did you try?'

'Yes, I tried.'

Sophie brightened.

'And he still wouldn't?'

'No, he wouldn't.'

'Did you ask why?'

'There must be something wrong with me,' Angie wailed.

He hadn't slept with that woman. And she found Angie's theory about his restraint – something about her being raw and vulnerable – less than convincing. It was all becoming clear: Mick didn't sleep – have sex – with anyone. It wasn't just Sophie whom he played along, it was all the women he saw. The question was, why?

At first, she had thought he didn't want to get involved with her because of the scam. That's what he had said. But that couldn't be the reason he didn't sleep with her. Could he be gay? With some people, when you learn about their homosexuality, it's like the final piece of the

184

jigsaw puzzle has been put in place, but there are others where it just doesn't seem to make sense.

OK, next possibility. Maybe he was a Catholic? A couple of years ago, she had met a man in a pub that didn't believe in sex before marriage. Well, this was like offering a hundred pounds to a gambler – Sophie was hooked on the idea. The touching began in the cab home. 'Everything but,' he murmured. 'We can do everything but.' The taxi driver saw a good amount of that everything. By the end of the evening, they both had won: she had got him to screw her in every orifice except that one. (And her ears, but they don't count, do they?) He didn't screw her there, but he damn near did everywhere else. And he was happy because he still retained his special relationship with the Lord.

Hmm, Mick wasn't a Catholic, though, so that idea also didn't fit. A heroin addict? A friend of hers went out with one – without knowing it – and she said he never came. They did it for hours at a time, bare-backing freely, but he never once shot his load.

No, that didn't work either because Mick wouldn't even let them get that far. In fact, come to think of it, she had never even seen his cock. He was ill? HIV or something? No. That wouldn't account for it. Nothing, nothing seemed to ring true. Except perhaps the one thing she hadn't considered. Maybe he was in love with someone. In which case, she should just try to shove him out of her head and jump into bed with someone else.

Sophie was lying on her bed when Tom knocked on the door. She was going to write a letter to Josh, sweet Josh, but she had decided she wouldn't – not until she had good news. She could never share bad news with anyone, especially not him. It wasn't fair. She would wait until the money was theirs. But it was so weird that, as the day of the scam drew nearer, the money was becoming less and less important, and she had to repeat to herself that that was the reason she was on the *Prince Albert* and not meeting her soulmate. Mick had offered her coffee and helped do up the zip of her dress (even though she could have done it up herself, she had asked him for assistance), but he had been polite. And polite scared her. As for the imminent storm, it had barely made any indentation on her consciousness. Rules four and five concerned lifeboat procedures, and Sophie was fully conversant with them – they were rules she wasn't interested in breaking. Anyway, she had been on the boats long enough to know that the sailors always erred on the side of caution. They would say something was worse than it really was, just to cover their tracks in the unlikely event that it was bad.

She had seen Tom at lunch and he had seemed ordinary, if a little more haggard than usual. But then some staff got cold feet when the weather turned nasty. She had already seen the purser chasing around making much ado about everything. Yet, she wouldn't have thought that Tom was the type to panic. Now, she saw that Jennifer was behind him. And it was Jennifer who spoke first, before Sophie even got a chance to say hello.

'I want to know what happened.'

'About what?' Sophie was caught on the hop.

'Between you and Tom,' Jennifer spat venomously.

'Nothing happened,' assured Sophie. She hoped Tom would corroborate. 'Why do you say that? Is it because of the storm? People often get jittery before a storm but it will be over –'

'I told her,' Tom interrupted lamely.

Boy, did she feel stupid.

Jennifer sat on Sophie's unmade bed. She picked up the book *One Hundred and One Great Card Tricks*, which Sophie had been reading, and then tossed it aside.

'I want in,' she burst.

'In what?'

'The money.'

'I'm sorry, I –'

'I know what it's all about, Sophie, so don't play the innocent, and don't blame it on the weather either,' she added, as she saw Sophie was about to protest and play the paranoia card. 'That's bullshit.'

'All right.' Sophie gave in disarmingly quickly. The money would have to come from her share. Although, God knows, here she was dishing out the supper before it was even cooked!

'OK, that's sorted.'

'No way,' said Jennifer with a heart-stopping finality. Sophie hadn't realised how big she was. Tall and powerful, she took over the room. Tom wriggled like a worm next to her. 'What happened?' Sophie and Tom took the fifth. 'I want to hear it. I won't rest until I do.'

Finally Tom piped up. 'We didn't do anything. I mean, we just did the usual.'

'The usual? I want to know everything.'

'There's nothing to tell.'

'What position did you do it in?'

'The missionary.'

'That's all? Come on, don't give me that.'

'And her on top.'

'And?'

'From behind.'

'Is that it?'

'Anal.'

Jennifer's lips quivered, almost imperceptibly.

'Anal. I see. You fucked her up the arse?'

Not exactly, thought Sophie, I did him with a dildo and he licked me there but he didn't fuck me up the arse. Still, she let it lie.

'And which did you like best?'

Sophie said that she liked it from behind.

Jennifer laughed coolly. 'I bet you do! Tom, which way did you prefer to have her?'

'Um, I liked her on top.'

'No surprises there then. And you like her body, do you, Tom? What bits do you like best?'

'Her tits?' Tom proposed hesitantly.

'And, Sophie, what part of him turns you on the most?'

'I guess his cock. I liked his cock best.'

Jennifer was all folded arms and schoolmarmy tone.

'Christ, you are both so predictable. I want to see what you did together.'

Sophie laughed incredulously.

'If you don't, I'll tell the Captain. It's as simple as that.'

'Look this is –'

'I mean it. I want to see what you did.'

'We just told you.'

'It's not the same. Hearing about it and seeing it in front of you is quite different. You will allow me that.'

Sophie eyed Tom nervously. Could he not do something about her? Tom was shrugging his shoulders rather hopelessly and Sophie felt a rash of contempt for him. Was he a man or a mouse? There was no way Mick or even the Captain would stand for this. At the same time, though, she couldn't help admiring his laidback manner. If he were being tortured, he would be the kind to endure anything.

Jennifer pushed Sophie on the bed. Sophie sprung up, but Jennifer blocked escape. Sophie stayed down, her arms clasped protectively over her breasts. She pulled up her legs foetal style; there was no way she could enjoy this, no way. Tom was gulping furiously. And then he came to her side and put his hand on her waist.

'Sorry,' he murmured, but Jennifer wasn't allowing any sentimentality.

'Get on with it then.'

The bed was rocking like a hammock. Tom wrenched down his trousers and then his pants. His prick was poking out at her. Already, it was long and taut, glistening with love juice. Sophie couldn't believe how turned on he was, under these 'strained' circumstances – but it was nice to see. Sophie relaxed a little; she couldn't help it when she saw a prick that hard.

'Well?' insisted Jennifer. 'I mean it. The Captain will find out about this. And you know what? You could get sent to prison for this.'

Tom's face was close to hers. Sophie kissed him. She might as well. He clumsily slid on top of her. They both went for her knickers at the same time. She let Tom take over, though, and he yanked them down. Then his hand was traversing her pubic hair, going under, going round, going in. Sophie gasped her approval. She brought her knees up and struggled into position. And then she steered him into her. And if she had been surprised at how hard he was then he was even more surprised at how wet she was. She was overflowing with juice. Yes, his cock was covered in welcoming slime. He started working up and down, pressing in and out. Yes, it was a tight fit, yes, it went right in, deep as they come, and then, teasingly, he pulled out again. In and out, in and out. His arse was soon springing up and down and even in the cold light of Jennifer's pale-blue eyes, Sophie couldn't help calling out for more. She was biting her lips, biting her tongue, praying that she wouldn't show the pleasure that stemmed from being bullied. And then they built it up and up, faster, faster, frenzied. It was a straightforward fuck, but it worked. The pressure he applied as he pumped in and out was perfect. Sophie opened her legs as wide as she could and felt the full extent of his throbbing dick. A few more pulses, a few more stabs and then it was over. Shafted.

Tom rolled off her. He wiped his cock dry with his pants. Sophie scissored her legs shut and tried to collect herself. This was just a little embarrassing. It was true what they say about what goes around comes around . . . and what comes around comes again and again.

She stood up and pulled on her knickers. Tom was hastily dressing himself.

'Wait, wait,' Jennifer said crossly. She looked furious, her arms folded across her breasts.

'I'm ashamed – if that's all you can do.'

Tom bit his lip.

'Really, Tom, can't you do any better than that?' Tom wasn't saying anything. 'That was a terrible performance. For someone as . . . as . . . highly sexed as she obviously is, you made a crap job of it. Anyone would think you

189

had never shagged before. Don't tell me, she makes you feel like a virgin again?'

Tom just stood there and took it, not quite on his chin, but on the ear maybe.

'How do you think this reflects on me?'

Sophie and Tom looked uneasily at each other.

'She probably feels sorry for me because I have to sleep with you.'

'Oh no,' Sophie protested, 'I thought he was quite nice.'

'Quite nice?'

'I mean he was wonderful. You must understand, it's difficult to do in front of an audience.' (Especially if that audience is his girlfriend.)

'Rubbish. You feel sorry for me. You think, that poor cow has to go to bed with him every night.'

'No, really,' explained Sophie honestly. 'It hadn't crossed my mind. Besides, what is one man's meat is another man's –'

'Quite. If you don't mind, Sophie, I'm going to teach Tom how to fuck.'

'Don't be ridiculous.' Sophie fumbled for her bra but the damn clasp had been broken. 'How on earth can you teach him that?'

'Oh, you think we are born with it, do you? The ability to make love, you think it's hereditary, do you? Or genetic?'

'I didn't say that,' Sophie argued bravely.

'You think we inherit the skills from our parents?'

'I think . . .' Sophie didn't really know what to think.

'Don't be so stupid – it's learned behaviour. That is, we can all do it naturally, but to be really good at it, you have to be taught.'

'Well . . .'

'And I'm going to teach him. Someone has to.'

'You can do what you like,' said Sophie, pulling on her top. 'Just don't involve me.'

'You forget that I have the power here. I will show him how to make love to a woman.'

'And, you know?' whimpered Tom, at last finding his voice.

'I could make a better job of it than you.'

For the first time, Sophie began to see what Tom saw in Jennifer.

'You think I don't know what you do, wanking behind me, close to my arse, when you think I'm asleep. Well, I'm pretending, you wazzock, only because I can't be bothered to go through the motions. You think you men have to have affairs because your women have gone off sex – well, it's because you are so crap at sex that we stop wanting to do it. Isn't it, Sophie?'

'Well . . .' Sophie had never exactly gone off it, but she could see the girl's point.

'You make me laugh, Tom. Creeping around behind me on the bed, jerking your cock at me as though you are firing a gun. Believe me, it's not a very appetising proposition.'

'I think I'll go,' said Sophie.

'Now, you, get over there, and watch carefully.'

Tom scuttled off to the corner like the class dunce.

'And you . . . you lie down.'

'Hey!' Sophie would try one last time. 'This isn't right; why don't you talk it over? Sometimes a good relationship can –'

'If we wanted counselling, we would ask for it.'

'Oh!'

'I want to show Tom what to do. I could hardly do that at marriage guidance, could I?'

'No.'

'Well then, get down, and why have you put your T-shirt back on?'

There was no answer to that. Sophie submitted once again. She lay on her back on the bed, her eyes flickering everywhere. Jennifer started the proceedings by removing her own sweater. She was wearing a black lacy bra. She was pale skinned, slightly freckled. She pulled at her jeans and wriggled her hips out of them. Her knickers matched the top, only they were transparent, and her pubic hair was pushing against the lace, like mice trapped in a cage.

'Watch me, Tom. This is how to make a woman come.'

'She came before,' pointed out Tom, quite rightly.

'Huh, only because she wanted to. It had nothing to do with you.'

She was right, too. Sophie was ripe for it. Even without Tom pumping away on top of her, she probably could have come. It was horny to be there, to be ordered around by this witch.

Then Jennifer was looming over her, leaning over her, on her. Her hand was surprisingly gentle on her breast.

'OK?' she whispered. Sophie nodded. Jennifer's hand was roaming over her bosom. She had something remarkable about her; it was true. Then suddenly she clasped Sophie's nipple really tight. It was like a thread had been wrapped around it and then tightly pulled, making Sophie cry out in pain. Sophie hated her passionately but then Jennifer ducked down and sucked and it seemed to Sophie like she had never been sucked like that before. It was more suction than suck. Her nipple hardened adoringly. Jennifer sucked and licked with a professional's ease. Sophie's tongue was rolling. Little darts of pleasure were prickling at her. Flurries of excitement ran through her veins. Soon she was writhing on the bed, showing off her contentment. Out of the corner of her eye, she saw Tom had sat up attentively. He was all ears. And eyes. And cock. If he had had paper, he would have been taking notes.

Then Jennifer was dropping down towards Sophie's knickers. She didn't arrive directly but took a circuitous course, over her stomach, down, down, fondling her and opening her wide. But she didn't do anything when Sophie was opened – she just let her be, gaping wide, desperate for something substantial. Sophie would have humped anything. Jennifer put her finger in her mouth. Her cheeks hollowed.

Finally, when Sophie began to think she would end up fucking air, one wet finger was slipped up her pussy.

Sophie tried to avert her eyes from Jennifer's searching glare. Out of the corner of her eye, she saw that Tom was still rock hard. His cock was keenly pointing at them, as if picking them out in an identity parade.

Jennifer now moved swiftly. She pulled Sophie's legs so that they were up pointing to the ceiling and then guzzled at her pussy like a thirsty dog at the water bowl. Oh Jesus, oh fuck. She pulled Sophie's legs so that her knees were pressed against her face, and her pussy was facing upwards. Don't stop. And Jennifer mashed her face in there. And then Jennifer did something that left Sophie speechless – and made sure Tom never thought that his girlfriend was a prude again. She opened Sophie's buttock cheeks and in probed a finger. Don't stop. She was so indelicate, so angry, that it almost hurt. But not quite. Sophie knew she was going to explode – and she didn't want to give Jennifer the satisfaction, but the more she told herself not to, the more the flames of passion inside her were fanned. Fuck, fuck, fuck. Don't stop. As the fingers and the tongue worked in unison, Sophie lost it.

'That's how to fuck a woman, Tom,' Jennifer said defiantly, as Sophie quivered and shook underneath the expert.

Sophie didn't know if it was anger, frustration or what, but Tom was storming over with crashing furious footsteps, and yanking Jennifer's face out from between her thighs. Tom started licking her too. Sophie moaned appreciatively. Why should she care who licked her? She was in a state of shock, but it was a glorious state to be in. To have such things done to her, to be allowed to have her body used in such a magnificent way; it was unbelievable to her. So they both did her together. They opened her legs wide, and sometimes they kissed each other, slathering slobbery French kisses over her juices. The pleasure was mounting inside her, it was incredible, their hands, their tongues, their attention, their competition. They were fighting over her. She was swinging up and down, shoving her pussy up at them, play with me, touch me. She loved the way Jennifer located her clit and nursed there, while Tom went for the deep shots.

Afterwards, Sophie lay prostrate in shock. But they hadn't finished. Jennifer walked over to Tom and pushed him against the wall. He had no escape. Her hands were wrapped around his cock. She looked like she was shaking a bottle of champagne so that she could enjoy the bubbles, and then she was manoeuvring him into place, into her. No foreplay, no preliminaries, nothing. They stood locked together. She rose one leg, then the other, as he held her up by the arse in a remarkable display of athleticism – Tom had clearly grown in confidence in the last five minutes.

Sophie grabbed her clothes and, with difficulty, jammed on her high-heel shoes. She left the two of them wailing and humping frantically like two desperate co-workers at the office Christmas party. Only when she was outside her room did she stop running. She needed to decompress. Fuck, it was like the bends. She needed to get out of there. Her head was full and she needed space to think.

And after all that, she decided, she might as well, she might just as well, contact Moira.

# Chapter Twenty-Nine

*T*hunder is scary when you are on a ship. And the ocean rocked forcefully as though in competition with the weather. The storm clouds were gathering fast. There were rumours of flooding.

The ship staff rushed around, looking uncharacteristically busy. Young sailors trotted up and down the stairs, full of anxiety and excitement. Sophie watched them dreamily. She liked to imagine a whole army of men at the very bottom of the boat, locked up, working furnaces, the sweat pouring off their shoulders in torrents and forming small puddles on the floor. She imagined getting lost and wandering in there by mistake, and they would turn on her. Who are you? What do you want? In their prolonged years of captivity, they would have lost all social skills, and some of them would merely grunt, like latter-day Tarzans. She imagined that, overwhelmed at the vision of her, they might grab her and ravish her. Plunging desperate lips into her neck, fumbling hurried fingers pulling off her clothes and theirs. She would like to lick up their sweat, like a dog. Hard-working men would surely have hard dicks.

Her imagination wasn't simply running away; since the afternoon with Jennifer it had packed its passport and bought a plane ticket to the other side of the world.

* * *

They opened the casino that evening. The managers decided that the best way to approach the oncoming storm was distraction. It was a good idea, for all those who turned out not only had a good time but they also gambled heavily. The table was loaded with chips, as hundred dollar bills were thrust at her from allcomers. There is nothing like the threat of disaster to make people a little more carefree with their money.

Sophie was also distracted from the machinations of the storm; however, her thoughts were not on the cards but on Moira. She kept eyeing the cashier, but Moira was too busy ruffling her hair, reapplying her make-up, to notice.

They closed the casino early because glasses, ashtrays and the lighter members of staff had started sliding. A man with a Hitler moustache didn't want to go back to his cabin and he asked Sophie to accompany him to the bar.

'I'm not allowed out with players,' she said.

He fancied himself a bit of a card.

'C'mon, darling, live a little.'

Sophie judiciously ignored him and made a beeline for the cash desk.

'Moira, come back with me tonight.'

'No!' Moira pouted through the bars.

'Come back to mine,' Sophie whispered.

'I don't think so.'

'I do. I want to consolidate the deal, consummate our relationship.'

'Sophie, I said I would do it anyway,' Moira sighed. 'I don't want to force you into anything.'

'You're not forcing me. I volunteer. I want to. Please.'

Moira looked up at her sceptically.

'Well, this makes a change!' she said.

Sophie continued: 'I don't want to be alone tonight,' she lied. 'This storm stuff has got me really scared.'

Back in Sophie's cabin, Moira stripped down to her tiger-print bikini and then lay back on the bed. She was going to take Sophie at her word – she wanted to see how far Sophie would go. She was tired of leading the brides in their merry dances. Sure, they had just got hitched but some of them were so naïve it was as though they had just been hatched.

Sophie struggled with her bra. Oh God, she was luscious. The pink peaks were in her fingers, in her hands. Her knickers moistened. Moira's breasts were so small, so tender, and so sensitive. Little round balls of pleasure. Moira's head was rocking from side to side. She came alive over Sophie's finger, like a wind-up doll, like she had in the changing room.

'You're not really nervous of the storm, are you?' Moira giggled.

'Not at all.' They smiled knowingly at each other. 'I always sail close to the wind.' Moira's lips were pressing on hers, sliding downwards.

'Really, Sophie,' Moira said, 'you have the most incredible breasts. You should do something with those.'

'What should I do? Hire them out?'

'Let me lick them,' Moira said, and she leaned over and placed a nipple in her mouth. God, she was amazing there, so honest, so true about her arousal. Sophie was squirming, crawling over the quilt to get closer to her because, to tell the truth, her breasts weren't bad either.

She wondered what that idiot in the casino would say if he could see her now. Live a little? She was living a lot, thank you.

Sophie grew bolder and she slipped her hand down Moira's knickers without her asking, finding the place where the flesh parted so beautifully into one opening, one warm sticky opening. That made her shiver, when she rubbed her just lightly up and down, up and down. And she shivered more when, at the same time, she added another finger to her pussy, to pamper the deep hole of her, and then she caressed her buttocks, all at the same time.

'When did you learn all this?' Moira smiled.

'You wouldn't believe it,' Sophie said.

And Moira was doing the same back to her. So they

were both stroking and caressing each other's pussies and it felt lovely, lying with one hand around the woman and one hand in her honey pot. It felt lovely, lovely, lovely, but then Sophie felt really tired all of a sudden. It was almost like sleep paralysis, only she was awake, and she didn't want to move. All she could do was raise her arms over her head.

Moira was climbing on top of her. The plump pink lips were over her, and the dancing hairs were right on top of her and then Moira slid over her face. At first Sophie gagged. Oh God, she didn't want that. She was just building up into a perfectly glorious rhythm when she was suddenly squashed and submitted. Moira's pussy loomed over her, vast and glistening like a spider's web in the morning dew, and then she was raining down on her.

At first, Sophie struggled against her, but there was no escape, really, she was imprisoned by her sex. So she relented. Besides, she was quite curious how it would taste, and what she would do, and all that. Sophie liked the taste, and the way, after just one touch, one stroke with her tongue, Moira was whimpering, wriggling for more. And it was easy to pick up what to do.

And then Moira swivelled round and she was at Sophie's cunt, licking and lapping there. And every lick Moira made felt like an echo of every lick that she made. And it was getting all very wet and very out of control.

Moira was bent over her, and Sophie's tongue was up her hole and her hands were coming round to squeeze her arse, and all Sophie could see was Moira's glorious buttocks as they pressed over her face. Then Moira pulled her over, so that it was Sophie's turn on top – Sophie at the helm. Her cunt was locked over Moira's mouth, or was it Moira's mouth that was secured on Sophie's cunt? Whatever, both were whimpering piteously like small dogs in their simultaneous fondling. Heaven. Moira's tongue was squirming in Sophie's small tight hole and she was doing the same back, and still finding the time to grab and sniff and probe everything else.

Maybe Moira was right all along – Sophie was a good lesbian. She hadn't wanted to be, but she had gone along with it . . . and now . . . she wanted to give her the same pleasure as she was receiving. Giving the other woman pleasure was her pleasure. These were selfless actions for selfish reasons. These were wet, sticky, hot actions. They continued sucking and kissing, kissing and sucking. Sophie was squirming, dying for more. Oh, she couldn't hear what Moira was saying, but it felt incredible. As her fingers pressed up and down her, she thought of Mick. She thought how he would just die to see them like this, two women playing, two women entertaining themselves. She pictured him pressed against the wall, masturbating, wanking at the hot sight of her cunt in another woman's hands. She pictured the pleasure on his beautiful face as he saw how turned on she was. She split herself wide and wider. And then they both seemed to lose contact with the world, and Sophie felt like she was flying, or floating, lost in the storms of her own body.

Afterwards, Sophie knew with a painful certainty that she wasn't going to erase Mick as easily as she had hoped. This was sex-lite – sex for the body conscious. But for the real, full-calorie, gastronomic union, then it had to be him.

'So, you'll do it?' she asked Moira – just for verification.

'I said I would do it anyway. We didn't have to do that, you know.'

'I know. But is that a promise?'

'Yes.'

'How do I know you won't change your mind?'

'I never go back on my word,' Moira said severely. She reapplied her mascara perfectly, without even needing to check the mirror.

The ship rocked beneath them ominously.

The rain thrashed against the library windows. The typhoon was coming. Mick gulped back his fear. He had sent Sophie a note saying that he wanted to meet her. When she arrived, she said, 'You really want to get me between the sheets, don't you?' but he didn't see the funny side.

'I thought here would be the safest place,' he said.

He was no sailor, thought Sophie, looking at the shelves stacked high and ready to topple over. It was quite endearing, really. Poor Mick, his muscles were tight and his eyes red.

He couldn't stand it any more. He was petrified. He had known all along that the ship would come to no good, and now, everyone was running around like blue-arsed flies – none more so than he. He had to tell Sophie how he felt. No more holding back. They might not live to see the evening.

'Look, you may as well know the truth. It's not that I don't like you, it's just that it's impossible, Sophie.'

'Nothing is impossible. Look what we have done. Look what we are doing. We're almost millionaires.'

'I know you don't want to be with me anyway.'

He was so spiky – hedgehog man. How could she get close to him? Only by disarming herself completely. If she rolled over, maybe he would . . .

'Why do you say that?'

'I heard you on the phone to . . . who is it? Joshy?'

It all became very clear. Mick had heard her speak to Josh and jumped to the wrong conclusions. Forget all those stupid speculations about homosexuality and Catholicism. He just thought that she had someone else! But how wrong could he be?

'Josh is my son!' she yelled. 'That's why I need the money. Until I can get the funds, I'm stuck. You think I had someone else?'

She kissed him and, as she drew back from the meeting of their lips, she gave out this deep sigh, and he thought, what passion was it that made her so stirred? It surely could not be him alone. Surely it wasn't personal.

When they kissed, she felt his tongue prickle at her lips, like a small yet gentle thorn, and she let his tongue inside her mouth. As she did so, she felt this great passion in her womb. It was an incredible feeling of openness and need. They kissed more and she couldn't stop, and she clung to him. It was all her; she was the main initiator, the motivator, but she couldn't help herself. It was as if everything was blurry up until then and suddenly she saw the world in clarity, and the revelation was that she had to have him inside her.

The boat rocked and they tumbled against the shelves. She had book dust in her hair. She yelped and clutched him tighter.

'Shh,' he hissed. There was no one else in there, but respecting quiet in a library is ingrained, even more so than in a church. He felt his hunger for her come up like a roar. He hauled her up on to a desk as the chairs around them slid on the wooden floor. He kissed her throat. Ripped open the blouse as she watched him, as though watching a wild animal. She could feel the ship's movements as they cut through the current, as he cut through her tremors. He made her wet. He pressed downwards and her bra was unlocked.

'Oh yes,' she squeaked. She couldn't contain herself.

'Shh,' he murmured, and backed her against the old mahogany bookshelves. Something was snapping. Mick could feel his resolve go 'ping' just as her bra strap gave way. He bent to kiss her breasts and he lifted the nipples up to his mouth, barely aware that her dark eyes were on him, watching him, savouring him. He felt her nipples in his mouth and wanted more. Sophie brought something out in him that the others didn't. The brides, the angry ones, the disappointed ones, they all had something to prove.

Sophie was different. She seemed to be offering not only her body but her complete acceptance too. He reached further and further for her breasts, and as she lay further back on the shelves, a few books cascaded out, plummeting to the floor. As he licked around the fierce red nipple, he caught sight of *Lady Chatterley's Lover* and *How to Make Love to the Same Woman for the Rest of Your Life*. He had to have more. He wanted more than anything to get in there, get in her. Dared he believe that this was his place? That she understood him or that she wanted him for . . . for more than one thing?

'Fuck me,' she murmured. 'Please, fuck me.' She was pulling at his pants, there in the library, with its grandfather clock and collection of old compasses in glass cases. Even if the whole *Prince Albert* went down, it wouldn't be just the band who went on playing but them too, unable to stop themselves.

'I want you,' she said. She had never been like this before. Never so single-minded and determined. It was a revelation, and she was going to bring him down, persuade him, if it was the last thing she did. She pulled him tighter and tighter towards her. Tighter, stuffing him closer to her, as close as two people could go, and yet he kept trying to push back. She threw herself on top of him, and he wriggled out of her grip. Something wasn't right. She plastered his face with hot kisses, trying to snake her tongue through his lips. But he kept his mouth closed. She just yanked her skirt aside. She thought that maybe she went too far then, but she remembered the look in his eyes; this mixture of deep longing and painful self-loathing, the combination of which just drove her on, like a siren. She knew they were going to drown, she knew, yes, that it might all end in tears, it had to, but she knew she couldn't stop. You can't turn back tidal waves.

'Please, Mick, do it to me.'

He liked kissing her. He liked her. Her hair smelled of camomile, but she was all over him now and he couldn't cope. Mick untangled her hands. If this were Cluedo then he would be the victim and she would be Miss Scarlett in the library with a blow job.

'I can't handle this!' he muttered.

Sophie tried again, softer kisses this time. 'I'm sorry, I didn't mean to. I'm just so keen, so . . .' She took a deep breath. 'I'm really into you,' she added awkwardly. Again the ship lurched and they staggered to keep their balance. Mick got up and steadied himself on a chair.

'Let me touch you,' she persisted.

'No!' He flicked her hand away. He was getting angry now.

'I just don't get it.' Sophie spoke quickly and venomously. She felt the dagger of betrayal dig deep. 'If you didn't want me to touch you, why did you make me feel like you did?'

'Look, I can explain.'

Sophie noticed the light swinging first, and then the tables and the shelves were sliding as the shake turned into a full-scale smash. And then the shelves seemed to pour themselves down, and there were books flying, raining down on her head. She couldn't move. She was too overwhelmed. It was Mick who came to his senses the quickest. He yanked himself upright as the collapse continued and he held on to her. The noise was incredible as the ship swayed from one side to the next, a see-saw on the high seas. She was sure they were lost, all was lost. And then she was falling again, and the library was cascading around her.

When Sophie woke up, she was back in her cabin, tucked up in bed. Her clothes were folded on the floor but she was still very properly wearing her T-shirt and underwear. There was a note next to her on the pillow.

*I can do the scam, but nothing else. I'm sorry, but that's how it is. Mick xx*

# Chapter Thirty

*T*here were women who dreamed about the Captain. They dreamed that he paid extra special attention to them and made their sourpuss husbands jealous. Sometimes, they dreamed that he furtively kissed them and sighed hotly into their ears that they deserved more. The more daring ones even dreamed that he showed them how to steer the ship. Their hands would be on the wheel, and he would place his arms around them, moving them starboard.

They sat, eight women round the table, buoyant and giggling. The men too were delighted to be at the Captain's table. They searched out the similarities between them. Such and such university? Yes, a friend went there.

The Captain introduced Sophie as a very important member of staff. She nodded graciously, and wondered how she would get through the evening. This was worse than the storm. He indicated that she should sit to his right. A thin, wan woman sat to his left. Sophie recognised one of the other women at the table as the redhead whom Mick had had. They were served hors d'oeuvres in glass bowls and the Captain kept smiling over at her.

'Miss Hemingway here was quite unfortunate. She was in the library when the storm hit and, of all the rooms aboard, that was the room that sustained the most damage.'

'Oh dear, and did you lose many books?'

The Captain steered conversations with as much aplomb as he steered ships.

'Sophie is not just a pretty face. She does enjoy reading too.'

(If he had known who she was with in the library perhaps he would not have been so generous.)

'I was in the pool when the storm struck,' offered a cross-eyed woman eager to trounce the opposition.

'Sophie likes swimming too, don't you, Sophie?'

Sophie smiled majestically and tackled her melon balls. They slid down a treat.

The Captain was meddling. He spread his fingers over her knees and dug his thumb in, swirling up towards her thighs. Sophie raised her eyes to the rest of the guests, but they were busily exchanging 'Where were you when the storm hit?' stories. (And a remarkable amount of them had been on the toilet.) The Captain was trespassing further. He pushed up her skirt and fondled her thighs. By the time the waitress had served up the roast potatoes the Captain's fingers were on the top of her thighs.

'Would you like some more?'

'No, that's fine thank you,' she sighed, as the waitress offered her huge slabs of succulent-looking roast beef, cooked in its own juices. She couldn't move for fear that he would go on – for fear that he would stop. His fingers felt so good there. And then, it was crazy, it was lunacy, but he was pressing on her panties, stroking the front of her. She felt him paw down the black lace triangle of her knickers. They were bikini briefs, so tiny that her last boyfriend had insisted on calling them knickerettes. Her pubic triangle was exposed to him, and he was taking full advantage of it. Oh God, she tried to think of something else, types of triangles maybe, but she only could get as far as equilaterals and isosceles before she was thinking about him again. Think of Pythagoras, she told herself sharply; think what he would say. He was

205

tickling her skin, the skin there. And then he was going for gold, launching forwards to her cunt.

'Tuck in everybody,' the Captain said. 'You too, Sophie. What's wrong with your food?'

'Nothing.' Sophie tried to eat, but it was increasingly difficult to swallow.

'Miss Hemingway usually has a fantastic appetite,' the Captain announced to the assembled, 'but tonight, she seems a little off-colour.'

'I'm fine,' she corrected. 'I'm just not used to such rich fillings – I mean foods.'

She couldn't see where his left hand was, so she presumed he was using that one to feel his boner. The only way you would know what Sophie was doing, or rather what was being done to her, was the two dots of colour that appeared high on her cheeks.

The waitress reappeared with the silver platters piled high with meat and huge fat jugs of steaming gravy.

'I'll have it all over,' said the Captain, grinning at the guests. 'Pour it all on, that's it. The sauce makes the dish, I say.'

Everyone except Sophie nodded. Sophie grimaced and wriggled over his fingers.

'That's my girl, you look a little more satisfied,' the Captain said. He added to the woman on the other side of him, 'Eat up, you never know when the storm will strike again.'

The woman couldn't stop giggling. Oh, the Captain was a wit!

He leaned towards Sophie, nodding at the good people all around him, and held a serviette over his mouth as he spoke.

'Suck me,' he ordered.

'Now?'

'Now,' he affirmed.

'I can't,' she said meekly.

'Get down,' he said.

'What, here?'

'Where do you think?' he whispered. 'I am the Captain of this ship, now get down and suck me.'

'Excuse me,' she murmured as she slid to the floor, but no one was listening; they were all too busy savouring the moment.

It was dark down there, and the white curtain of the tablecloth and various legs and feet walled her in. The woman to the right had delicate narrow feet, poised. The man to her left had leather shoes, and red socks with an insignia she didn't recognise. Sophie stumbled into the Captain's lap, her hand on his trousers. She unzipped them – it seemed excruciatingly loud – and then dug in. His cock stretched out to meet her, and then she saw it – the piercing, penetrating the urethra and coming up the side. His was a superb cock; if any deserved decoration, his did. It deserved a medal. It was big, yet cute, seriously upright and very shapely. Sophie clasped it between her hands as though she was praying.

Suddenly the most important thing was that she did this, and she did this well.

He was giving a speech. He called for attention with the spoon on the glass, although they were all mesmerised by him anyway. He made jokes about the typhoon, apologised for the bumpy ride (something to tell their grandchildren about), said that marriage was certainly about hell and high water and so on. Sophie concentrated on his thick shaft. She was wet. She stuffed it into her mouth. She felt the veins with her tongue, circling the head and the trunk of his cock. She felt the ring clicking against her teeth and tickling her tongue, taunting her to go on. She drew his dick in and out her mouth, pushed it right up her cheeks and layered him with hot saliva. And she worked him with her hand too, with a hold on his balls. She would explore the creases and folds of his cock until he would spurt into her mouth. She kept telling herself, I will swallow it down like it is nectar. The other hand she gave to herself.

The Captain was thanking everyone for coming. Thank me for coming, she thought, as she licked his crinkly balls. She was working up to it. The cock demanded greater stimulation and she tugged it vigorously. He was telling the guests that he hoped they had a wonderful night. He was so confident, so outrageous. She wanted him to fuck her. He was moving his hand down to trap her head between his thighs. And she knew – she felt the blood racing to the tip, the wetness – he was going to, going to, going to ... She swallowed the spurt of come as it gushed at her like a hissing tap. She gobbled the Captain's spunk down, cleanly, neatly and efficiently.

He snapped his fingers and told the waitress to clear away the plates. Sophie emerged; she hoped she didn't look as horny as she felt. How do women in the movies manage to do this without looking at all dishevelled?

'Found it!' she gasped, her face flushed and her hair askew. In her palm she held a small gold hoop.

The man to her right took the earring out of her hand and dropped it between his legs.

'Oops,' he said, 'silly me. Can you get that?'

# Chapter Thirty-One

$M$ick was glaring at her as she ran through the casino. Jesus, why did everything happen all at once? She was exhausted – not only with the sex, but also with the strain of the secrecy.

'What the hell took you so long?' he mouthed.

She shot him a you-don't-want-to-know look.

The Captain was following just behind her like a small eager puppy. She couldn't shake him off.

Tom was there, overseeing a roulette table at the back of the room, and yes, Moira was in place at the cashier desk. She didn't meet Sophie's eye but busied herself with the till. Her skin was Seville orange, suggesting that she had been on the sunbeds that afternoon. Sophie thought she looked like a tiger behind the bars, ready to spring.

'Ladies and gentlemen,' she murmured, and perhaps her voice was a little higher than normal, 'place your bets please.'

She was shaking, really trembling, like ash on the edge of a cigarette. I'm not going to be able to go through with it, Sophie thought. But she had to now. The worst thing was that she had devoted so much attention to finding the others who would join in that she hadn't thought about the part she was going to have to play.

Meeting Mick's eyes was the only thing that saved her. Could everyone feel the tension in the air? Could everyone sense something was happening, something to change their lives? She could still feel the Captain's spunk in her mouth. That was the only disappointing thing about the experience – the taste of his come. It was a thin, rather mean-flavoured liquid, whereas Tom's had been much thicker. Mick, of course, had never even let her so much within striking distance, which was odd ... but this wasn't the time to worry about such indulgences.

The inspector behind her had cold fish eyes, and he hated Sophie. Sophie waited for Tom to take over. She waited and waited, but Tom didn't emerge from the back of the room, where he had firmly installed himself. He refused to look up. He was trying to bury his head in his hand. Bastard, he was letting her down. Tension hammered on Mick's face. What was wrong with Tom, the idiot? Why wouldn't he stand behind her? There was no way, absolutely no way, that they could risk cheating with this inspector in place.

'I don't feel too good,' she said to her inspector. 'I need to go to the bathroom.'

'Now?' he asked incredulously. 'Look at this place, it's heaving!'

'And I will be too, all over the table if I don't go now. It's my time of the month,' she added, as a decider.

'Go on then,' he said, won over by the mysteries of women's troubles.

She walked right behind Tom and then purposely tripped so that she smacked into his back. Tom turned round but when he saw it was Sophie, he blanched. She thought she had never seen anyone as white as he was then. He looked like he had been dipped in bleach.

'I want a word with you,' she hissed. She was so angry, so tense, that she didn't realise the implications of what she was doing. 'Now. And if you don't come, there will be big trouble.'

She had a great sense of self-importance. Nothing was going to stand in her way any more.

Tom sheepishly followed her into the women's bathroom. Sophie selected a cubicle, grabbed him by the elbow and slammed the door behind them.

'What the hell do you think you are doing?'

'I can't,' he said, looking shamefaced. 'I can't do it.'

Never before had she met someone so lily-livered. After all they had been through! She wanted to shout at him, shake him; instead she had to be cool.

'I don't have to, anyway. Now that Jennifer knows, I've nothing left to lose . . .'

It was true.

'Tom,' Sophie said diplomatically, 'what about Jennifer? Now that she knows, she will be expecting the money; she wants her cut. You can't back out now.'

'No,' he whispered. 'I can't do it.'

'I'm not asking you to actually do anything,' she said. 'Just to not do anything; just don't report what you see. It's as simple as that.'

'I can't.'

'Yes, you can.'

She dropped to her knees. Only she wasn't begging.

'No,' he said, and covered his prick with his hands.

She pulled down the zipper with her teeth, nuzzling at the cotton there. Her hands were rubbing up and down his thighs.

'No,' he breathed, 'don't do this to me.'

'Do what?'

'Don't . . . don't!'

But how could he say 'don't suck me', or 'don't fuck me'? These were alien words, an alien language that he, no man, had ever properly studied. All he could muster was a feeble 'don't' and each time he said it, his tone was subtly lower, as though descending the keys of the piano, and soon the 'don't-don'ts' were replaced by the 'oh yeses', as though he switched to a different chord.

He was still half-hearted, half-mast. Sophie felt a mixture of anger and compassion. But they only had a few minutes. How long before something else went wrong? A new cashier, or perhaps Mick would get tired?

He was in her mouth. He was defeated – he knew when he was eaten.

'I can't do it, though, the scam I mean.'

He was giving her a mouthful, a piece of his meat.

She gulped him down, covering the whole of his cock with her mouth, and then she stopped, letting it withdraw. She put her finger to her lips and sucked. He was watching her. He didn't want to watch but the tide was too strong; he had to just swim along. She pulled her evening dress up around her. The material gathered about her hips, circling her, embracing her. Underneath she was wearing red stockings, suspenders and see-through black panties. He could see her pubic hair bunching underneath. She fingered down her knickers and touched herself.

'Look at me, Tom.'

He was transfixed. He was a sucker for a pretty lady.

'Look how hot I am for you!'

She opened herself out and started rubbing. Mmm, it felt good. Only a few minutes to do it. She liked a rush job. Fast fucking. Fucking for busy people.

'Do I look horny?' Did she? She didn't need to ask. She only had to look at his face to know that she had struck a chord. His eyes were popping out of his head and his tongue was reaching at his teeth and caressing the tops of each one. He was a total pushover when it came to pussy – and he knew it.

She heard someone open the door to the next cubicle. Then came the sound of a toilet seat being raised. In other circumstances, she might have been put off – but these were desperate times. Indeed it was the sexiest of times, and the least sexy of times.

He tried to fuck her against the door. She had one leg on the ground, the other on the toilet seat. Yes, she was pulled open wide, all space ready to be filled. He pushed her against the door and she felt his cock bang against her. She gripped his arse tight, and tried to raise herself so that he could ease himself up her crack. But each time he tried, they smashed against the door, and the noise that made in the silent stately bathroom was tremendous.

'Is there anyone there?' sang out the voice from the adjacent cubicle.

Sophie's face was red; she sank her teeth into Tom's neck. She could feel his heart marching. And his cock was almost inside her, it was slithering along her crack, waiting for lift-off.

'Don't stop,' he whimpered.

'I can't stop.' She was going to add 'even if I wanted to' but the only sound she could make was a hiss like a balloon emptying of air.

The voice came again from next door. 'Are you OK?'

They were going to be discovered, but the prospect of stopping was just too terrible to contemplate. God damn this door. God damn this ship.

Tom slammed down the toilet seat and belatedly attempted to take control.

'Say that you are OK,' he ordered.

'What?'

'Tell her, tell her you're OK.'

Sophie was thrilled that he was ordering her around, telling her what to do. She couldn't resist. No one could resist.

'I'm fine. Excuse me. I'll be out in a moment.'

'OK, dear.'

Tom sat on the wooden seat cover. He pulled her on top of him, her legs out over his thighs. They were face to face. She was straddling him, lowering herself little by little on to the tip of his cock. As she moved, he nipped at her chin, taking little nibbles of her like she was some chocolate fancy. She bit at his neck, salivating over his Adam's apple. For the first time, she realised how phallic the Adam's apple was. And then, she was down, down, impaled on his cock, and he was up her, up her again. And it was tight. Tighter than ever, and she couldn't fuck him without crying out, could she? He was so stiff, so hard, and he was inside her.

'Do me hard, fuck me.'

'More,' she cried, she couldn't think of anything else, only that she didn't want him to stop.

They say that the average man takes less than five minutes to come, and the average woman takes over twenty minutes. (This means the average man could come, go off, read a book, watch the news and then come back to catch the finale.) Sophie was usually a fifteen-minute girl, twelve on a good night – but that night, she was fast on Tom's heels.

'Do it to me, don't stop, fuck me, Jesus, fuck me, baby.'

From then on, it was her job. She held on to the cistern and worked herself up and down. He pulled at her hips. Pulling at her rhythmically, so that when she pressed down, he pushed up, and she was riding, riding him. She could see the pleasure and fear in his eyes. They screwed faster, no time to waste, no room to dally, up and down, up and down, the pleasure swarming around her body.

He had taken his lessons seriously. His finger curved towards her and she knew it was coming, the hook up her arse, massaging her G-spot, touching her there, there.

'More,' she growled. 'Go deeper, harder, please.'

'Your cunt is so creamy.'

'Please push your finger up me more.'

'My finger is up your arse now, it's right up your arse.'

And then he was jerking up her and she was convulsing around him, and sighing fit for a princess, and somehow he had the presence of mind to pull the flush, to block out the noise, only he had to do it three times because her orgasm was so protracted.

'Ready then?' she asked, when the shaking had stopped.

'Yes,' he said, 'I'll do my best.'

He went back to the casino first. She powdered her cheeks and sprayed her wrists with perfume. She wondered if everyone could smell the fucking on her. But she was buoyant, exuberant. No one could stand in her way now. Tom was now at her table. He didn't look up as she approached. She started to deal for blackjack.

There were three players already there by the time Mick joined. The superstitious players didn't like a newcomer, didn't want someone opening a box, disturbing a good run, but when they looked up and saw it was Mick, they nodded at him. He was a real gambler. Not one of your honeymooning grooms trying to show off.

'Are you going to be lucky for me tonight?' Mick said, as had been arranged.

Sophie murmured, 'I'll do my best, sir,' which meant everything was going as planned – full steam ahead. She held her breath and dived into the game.

'Card.'

'Stand.'

It was a stand-off. Now Sophie had to give him the money, even though it was a draw. She passed it over. Not one of the other gamblers noticed. They were busy talking. She even had to remind one of them to play.

'Card?' she insisted, tapping his box, adding, 'Card again?' when she got no reaction.

It was how Sophie liked it best – real players letting her do the dealing, big money play – only that night, she couldn't rest and enjoy, she had to be alert. The team was in place – a slack inspector, a bent cashier and a player for whom she had everything to cheat for. On a night like this, Sophie had to be seen to be better than usual.

'No more bets please.'

She stacked up the chips, split into fives for easy counting, and pushed them across. Mick's winnings were increasing and no one was saying a word. Finally, Sophie tipped herself. This was her present to the other croupiers. The money would be divided at the end of the week, when she was well away, but why not give them a little boost?

This was the culmination of all her work, and it was so easy. She grew bolder and bolder and shoved Mick three or four times the amount they had agreed. And no one spotted a thing.

Then, at the roulette table, she let him put his bets on late, just as the ball nuzzled home. How could he fail to place his bet in the right place when the right place had already been revealed to him?

Sophie was tempted to think it was running like clock-work, but no, it ran smoother even than that. All her organisation had paid off. The faffing around, the weeks of planning had been worth it. Screwing Tom, Moira, Jennifer, various crew members and the Captain had been great – but it was even better than that. It had served a purpose. The money was, literally, rolling in. She and Mick (even if there were no 'she and Mick') were about to become rather better off than they were before embarking on the *Prince Albert*.

After an hour, Tom accompanied Mick over to the cash desk. His lips were set hard – Sophie thought he was overacting – he looked like he was taking a prisoner to the dock. The chips, their money, were piled high – and no one suspected a thing. Moira was much cooler, of course. She handed over the money and then, audacious as ever, winked her approval. Sophie's heart was thumping so loud that she was sure it would give them all away.

All the while, Mick ignored her, until finally, at the door of the room, he nodded at her, and she felt a great relief. I'm losing it, she thought, dismayed. I don't even care about the stupid scam. I would give it all up for one fucking smile from him.

But the chance never came.

It was a waste of time. She had the money but it all seemed banal, all trite and empty. She had come aboard with one mission, and now, now it was falling apart. Fuck the money, fuck it; all she wanted was to fuck him. Sophie felt flat. She thought she would be euphoric. She thought she would be skipping around, going bananas. She should call Josh. Tell him that they were almost home and dry. The piggy bank was full.

One more day, then she and Mick would disembark. It would be over. The fat lady would have sung.

But Mick hadn't even bothered to tell her that all was well. Perhaps he had screwed her over. She was attacked by doubt. All that crap about him not being able to trust

216

her – it was all a cover. Yes, he had screwed her over – and that was why he wouldn't get involved. She was due thousands of dollars but all she could think about was Mick. Gross. She was beginning to feel sick. A wave of dread came over her, like that Sunday evening feeling when you don't want to go to bed because sleep would only hasten the gallop towards Monday.

# Chapter Thirty-Two

*T*he Captain had watched Sophie intently all evening. He stroked his cheek, and his purple vein was flicking in his forehead. There she goes, he thought, that's my girl. Her cheeks were still flushed. Was it from their invigorating love session before? he wondered arrogantly. Was she still burning from the pleasure of his cock? He thought about inviting her up to his quarters. They could listen to some of his CDs. He thought about having her on his bearskin rug. He himself had hunted down the bear in Alaska. Staring down the horny barrel, his fingers alert on the trigger, he had seen the bear almost swoon at the shot then stagger around before going into free fall. He had lugged his trophy back to base victorious. And all evening his crew had clapped him on the shoulders, telling each other how brave and how manly he was.

She would look beautiful spreadeagled on that white fur. Open legs for the *Prince Albert*. Maybe she would let him bury his head in her fanny. Then he had a better idea – he would have her here, over the tabies. A kind of busman's holiday for her, but still . . .

'Sophie, darling.' Sophie spun round. And the Captain knew he had taken her by surprise. She hadn't been expecting to see him! She must have been thrilled that he

218

had deigned to speak to her again – he didn't bother with most.

'I wanted to tell you how much I enjoyed dinner.'

Enjoyed? Was that the word? He was salivating, couldn't wait to repeat the experience. Oh, he had done it before, had seen dozens of women surrender to his hook, but none came like that. It felt like he was dipping his fingers into a hot, wet cauldron. No wonder it was referred to as a velvet glove; tightly, so tightly yet so tenderly, he had felt his fingers clasped.

'Thank you,' she murmured. A strand of hair had fallen over her eyes and he ached to brush it away. 'It was nothing.'

She was frightened. She didn't know why he was here – hadn't she done enough by serving him at the dining table? Perhaps Mick had abandoned her. Perhaps he had jumped ship. This very moment, he was sailing away, with one of his women: Angie Weatherby, the redhead, or the ditsy shop assistant, most probably.

The Captain moved towards her. He couldn't contain himself, and why should he? He was the Captain of the ship, Captain of the entire fucking universe, why shouldn't he do as he pleased? He took her fingers – he wanted to put them in his mouth, but she pulled them away. Ahh, he knew this; she was playing hard to get. Women did that sometimes, he had heard, but they didn't know their own minds.

'I don't want to . . .'

'Yes, you do.'

He pushed her and she lost her grip and fell back against the tables. One hand was fumbling uselessly behind to find her balance; the other was on his chest pushing him away. He was insatiable; he was a madman. But she couldn't stop the excitement from rising; her pussy was throbbing as though demanding attention. Someone wanted her – even if it was the wrong one. Someone needed her.

He opened her legs wide and then went down there, rubbing his face against her panties. Sophie wondered, can he smell Tom? Can he sense Mick? But no, the Captain was far too busy submerging himself in her creaminess. And fuck, why not? Why not? They could both have lost their jobs. Forget oysters, risk-taking is the best aphrodisiac, and she had taken a few that night.

He licked her out. He licked her over the green velour tables. He saw himself in the mirrors, and he saw the ocean blue lapping against the windows. He saw himself and he loved himself, for he was an exhibitionist by nature. She felt his fingers pulling her wide open to allow him greater access.

'You want me, don't you?'

How could she say no to such arrogant charm? She felt him toy with her clit, and she felt his tongue bring its sweet wetness all over her hole. He pulled her legs apart, so she was all cunt in his mouth, and she wished more than anything in the world that Mick could have seen her then. Descending down a sexual chasm. She started to move up and down, and they were like one thing: his face, her pussy, one thing, one thing with a common goal, and soon, in the sweetest way (and well under five minutes too!) she lost control.

And then, as she recovered from the one great orgasm that smashed through her body, he was opening his trousers, reaching inside for his cock. But it was she who pulled his cock out from his pants, pushing his fingers away. She pampered it, but only for a few seconds because she knew they had to be quick, not just because they were in the middle of the casino, not just because the cleaners would be approaching, but because she couldn't wait any longer. He looked even bigger there in the casino than he had under the table. Perhaps it was because of the mirrors, multiplying him, or perhaps it was because of his power. Either way, the cock was pressing at her, tapping at her sex, tapping and then entering, entering and then filling, filling and then servicing. He made strong strokes, powering up her.

Anyone could catch them, and the fact that he was prepared to take that chance doubled the pleasure. It was like asking for another card at fifteen – a fool's way – but oh so compelling. She drew her legs up around him. She wanted Mick to find them. Mick with the no-option cock. Mick the guy with the disappearing trick. The joker in the pack. And what was she? The queen of fucking hearts.

Here was a man who would service her, who wanted to fuck her. They moved together, rocking and fucking, licking and sucking. They were soaking, squeezing hard. He growled into her ear, instructing her when he wanted her to go faster, when he wanted her to slow down, he was going to come; slow down, slow down, to prolong it, to last for ever. Her feet were over his shoulders and he pressed down into her, pressed on to her, all sticky fingers and thumbs, riding her, adrenaline racing, speed mounting, race driving, mad fucking. Yes, yes, yes.

And then they changed over, and she was on top of him, grinding down on him, and his hands were everywhere, seeking out her crack, her crevasse, and his lips were everywhere too.

'You taste like honey,' he whispered. And then, when she wriggled her snatch over his raging cock, he shouted that she was the best, the tightest, the sexiest woman he had ever known.

'Sophie, you spoil me,' he groaned. And in the middle of all that, all that hot, thrusting wetness, she nearly started to laugh, because it was a funny thing to say: 'Mr Ambassador, you spoil me'. Did he mean he was spoiled and not able to have anyone else after this, or that she was some kind of nanny dishing out the sweets?

'Sophie, don't leave me, don't leave me,' he spluttered as he mashed into her, grinding his cock up her cunt.

'I'm going to . . .' she hissed. She moved faster and faster, feeling the moment approach.

'Oh God, I'm going to . . .' She wanted it now, him and her. 'Come on, come on,' she urged. 'It has to be now, now.'

And then he roared, 'I'm taking you with me, come

with me, Sophie,' and he and she smashed forwards into gorgeous oblivion.

When they were done, she brushed herself down. Small bits of fluff from the baize clung to her dress and the Captain said that he would see her tomorrow.

Not if I see you first, she thought.

# Chapter Thirty-Three

'*S*o, it's over.'

'It's over.'

'I thought you had gone.'

At first, Mick hadn't answered the door. Then the knocks grew in volume and in colour until finally, unable to resist, he opened up. Forget the storm, this was the drowning he had feared; this was the sense of dread. It had nothing to do with the boat capsizing; it was all to do with her, and the way he felt about her. He had lost all sense of hope.

He showed her the money, in neat piles in his suitcases.

'Well, it was fun working with you,' she said. It could have been more fun – but you get what you're given.

'One for you, one for me. And one for Moira and Tom.' He looked about him shiftily. 'You did good, Sophie, you really did. I'm sorry I didn't believe in you.'

'It's fine.' She felt shy. She had to take her chances. She caught his hands in hers, looked him in the eyes.

'You know how I feel about you.'

He looked down. 'I think I have guessed by now.'

If at first you don't succeed, get down on your knees and suck.

'Mick, we've done it. Surely we can celebrate . . .'

He still held her back. His face was ashen. He kept

shaking his head from side to side, regretfully. He was caught between the devil and the deep blue sea. If he told her, she would hate him – and if he didn't, she would hate him.

'What? What is it?' Sophie felt afraid.

'I might as well tell you now. I don't fuck.'

Ideas were whirring around in Sophie's imagination. Was he a virgin?

'This sounds ridiculous, I know it sounds ridiculous, but the truth is ... I ... my cock ...'

'What happened?'

Accident with a butcher's cleaver? She had heard of someone who hung his head out of a train window and was decapitated; perhaps he too had hung out his 'head'? Or what about a circumcision gone wrong? That time, in the pool, she hadn't felt a thing. Not even nearly. Was he like one of those Action Man dolls, all smooth down under?

'Christ, I can hardly bring myself to say the words.'

Sophie waited. She felt like she was trembling on a precipice.

'It's not very big.'

'And?'

'In fact, it's very small. I mean seriously.'

'Wh– How? I mean – you've got such big hands.'

'What's that got to do with it?'

'I don't know ... Um, how do you know?'

'I've been told.'

'By who?'

'I was engaged once to a wonderful girl. It's the only time I've ever been in love.' (Not true. He was in love now, and he knew it.)

'And what happened?'

'She laughed at me.'

'What did she say?'

'She said that my cock was medium when it was ... when it was flaccid, but when it was erect, it was tiny. She said she had never seen a cock grow so little. She

224

said that mine was the only one that actually got smaller when it became erect.'

'And you believed her?'

'Well, she had no reason to lie.'

'No reason . . . except to hurt you.'

'No, she wasn't like that, she was nice.'

He had worshipped the ground she walked on. He would have given his life for her. And at one time, she would have done the same for him. If she said his cock was a weener, then his cock *was* a weener.

Sophie was bewildered. She had never expected this; not from Mick.

'I don't care about your prick,' she said, but he continued as though she hadn't spoken.

'I'm using the money for a penis extension in the States. It's not so unusual in America. They are not as hung up about cosmetic surgery as we are,' he said, wishing he could rephrase that. 'I mean, it's no big deal over there.'

'I said, I don't care about your prick, you prick! All I care about is you. Sex isn't important to me.'

He laughed hollowly.

'The best things come in small packages. It's not the size of the ship but the motion in the ocean.'

They were platitudes, the lot of them. He knew it, and she knew it.

'I'll wait for you,' she said. 'It'll be fixed and we'll get together then.'

'Yeah, maybe,' he said unconvincingly. There was no way he wanted to be with anyone who knew. He was cutting ties with his past, reinventing himself as a man with a big nob.

'Do you mind going now? I want to be alone.'

He always felt better after he told someone – a problem shared is a problem halved, but if you halved his little problem, you would be left with virtually nothing.

The Captain wanted to relive the night with Sophie, by himself, before he sought her out to do it again. He told his steward to set up his room. He was not to be disturbed. He was 'doing some very important paperwork'. It wasn't entirely a lie; he would be working with paper – a big box of king-size tissues.

He loosened his trousers and darkened the room. He had his tissue supply next to him and he felt all comfortable and keen. What a nice way to spend your day. And he was getting paid thousands of dollars for this. His fingers trembled on the remote control button. He rewound the tape right to the beginning. He had set up the CCTV camera in the casino a few days earlier.

The casino was one of the Captain's favourite places – he was still a little boy at heart – and James Bond was his hero (Sean Connery's James Bond, naturally). It was the first time he had done it. He knew of other captains who were camera crazy – cameras in the changing rooms, cameras in the saunas, but he had restrained himself. Until Sophie.

He wanted to see her working. Wanted to luxuriate in those perky breasts straining at the material of her dress. To enjoy the rounded tummy, the tightness over the crotch, covering that simply luscious bush. Come to think of it, he thought, as the tape rewound to the beginning, it might be quite something to hide a camera in the ladies' loos. He could watch her tinkle; watch her wipe. He liked to see her unawares. He imagined her, oblivious of his attentions, tugging on the paper, placing it to her underbelly. She would look gorgeous with her pants at her knees. Perhaps she would rush forward for a quick feel, a surreptitious fanny-finger before coming out to wash her hands, put on make-up or whatever women do in those places that takes up to half an hour. Women behave differently when they know that they are being watched, which was why it was big fun to catch them out.

He watched her arms as they spun the wheel; those beautiful arms with that crest of fair down. Flick, the ball spun against the motion of the wheel, bashing against the sides, ready to settle in its little crack. He knew the odds: 35–1 for the one number, 17–1 for the splits. He watched them place bets on the outsides, the black and the reds, the odds and the evens. He enjoyed a mathematical challenge, loved a bit of calculation.

He looked closely at the video. He couldn't believe it. Something strange was going on. Freeze frame, he was watching it again in slow motion. Adding up the numbers in his head. The payouts were all wrong. No, they weren't just wrong, they were out of all proportion. Odds of 35–1, $350, and she had paid back $150,000.

What the fuck was going on?

Fast forward, on to the blackjack. Either she was duff at arithmetic or something else was up. And it was always the same player – the strange loner with the cock-and-bull story about a dead fiancée – and it was always the same inspector – the one with the beautiful girlfriend.

She wasn't going to get away with it.

227

# Chapter Thirty-Four

*I*t was hot and Sophie had thrown off her sheets. Lying on her front, her arms spread wantonly on the pillows, she looked the picture of abandonment. Her mouth was wide open and her cheeks were flushed. She was dreaming of Mick. Mick's fingers were on her breasts. It felt nice, lovely. She felt a tongue twist in her lips. This was a fantastic dream; they didn't come better than this. Sophie let her legs drift apart. Mick was turning into someone else. She was sixteen again, and the guy at school who everyone fancied had chosen her for the night. The finger rubbed her, very gently, much gentler than the guy at school ever did.

Sophie parted her thighs and helped the finger with one of her own, opening herself out. She would never have done that! She was sighing and groaning loudly now. This was a wonderful dream, and it felt so real, it felt as though someone really was tickling her clit, someone really was making her wet there. She smelled fried chicken, so she knew that it was a dream, a lovely dream. Far-fucking-out. Then the boy was turning into someone else. Tom now, Tom and Jennifer, together, taking her over, doing it for her. And the boat was rocking her from side to side, soft as a lullaby, in the cradle she rocked.

Someone knew what they were doing, and they were doing what they knew.

Sophie felt the delicious tension collect through her body, the fantastic coiling before the uncoiling. The dreamy finger worked her cunt and Sophie sleepily quivered into an orgasm. She felt the wetness form a puddle beneath her and moved away from it, into a broad chest. Sophie woke up fast, very fast.

'What's going on?'

The purser nuzzled her neck. 'You know you want it, baby.'

'I think –' Sophie gathered up her covers around her, and wished that she could drown in them '– you had better get the fuck out of here.'

'I've got a message for you actually, Ms Hemingway.'

'It had better be good!'

The purser savoured a rare moment of superior knowledge. And then he had to say something before she thumped him one.

'What've you been up to? Breaking rule seventeen again?'

'Eh?'

'The Captain wants you, at his place, now.' He winked at her. 'Naughty, naughty, can't keep a lid on it, can you? Anytime you want some hot loving, I'm ready. I still want another hand at strip poker.'

Sophie grimaced. What could the Captain want with her now? They were due to disembark soon. The fat lady was on her last chorus.

This time when she took in the Captain's quarters, the glamour, the coolness of it all, she felt nothing. This was the life she had so wanted to be part of, and now she didn't really give a sod.

'I want you to stand there.'

'And good morning to you too,' she said sarcastically. Who the hell did he think he was?

'Get over there,' he barked.

She snapped out of her apathy. The Captain didn't look at her with the adoring eyes as he had yesterday.

229

Even the way he licked his lips was different. Yesterday, he had beamed at her with admiration; today, if she was not mistaken, he gazed at her with contempt.

'There, by the window.'

'What?'

'Get over there.'

She moved. She didn't know why she did, but she was by the window like he told her too. He was so commanding, so austere; it was as if there was no alternative. So this was how he got to be Captain.

'I want you to strip!'

'I beg your pardon!'

'I said strip.'

He was not in the mood for messing around. There were no flies on him. The silly bitch, the silly bitch had taken him for a ride – and now he was going to take her for one.

'What's all this about?'

He was up at her. His face inches from hers.

'I know what you've been up to.'

She knew playing the innocent wasn't working. It hadn't worked with Tom and Moira before; it certainly wasn't going to work now. Nevertheless, what else could she do?

'I don't know what you mean.'

'Yes, you do. Where's the money? Where did you hide it?'

He pulled at her handbag. The make-up bag crashed open, hairbrush, comb, mascara tumbled on to the floor.

He paused and picked up a lipstick contemplatively. He remembered an aunt who wore a lipstick. She spent hours in front of the hall mirror applying the thing laboriously. Sometimes, it seemed to him that she dabbed it on, only to blot it off on to tissues. And then she would reapply it all the more vigorously, her lips puckered into a pout. Every time she came back, the lipstick that she had applied so painstakingly was smeared all over her face. It was everywhere, on her cheeks, her chin, even down to the soft collar of the blouse, and one day, her husband had seen her before she got to the mirror to clean herself up and he was yelling like a madman. Have you been with someone else? And the Captain remembered feeling surprised at first – he thought it was a sign of having a fight with make-up and the idea that she had been with someone else, that the lipstick had travelled because she was kissing, simply hadn't occurred to him – until much later. There was nothing sexier than lipstick in the wrong place. He started to keep the discarded lipstick tissues, watching the shapes her lips made, wondering how it would feel to be covered in Strawberry Sizzle, Ice Maiden or whatever was her flavour of the month.

'Put it on.'

'What?'

'The lipstick.'

'I . . .'

'I said, put it on.' His tone was quieter now, but if anything that was even more frightening.

Sophie stood in front of the mirror. Her reflection stared back at her but, inexplicably, her expression was unfamiliar – her eyes looked pleading. She unscrewed the top. The lipstick came out of the tube like a flamboyant erection. It was soft at the peak, melting just slightly. Thick red slices.

It did look good. She looked like one of those girls in sixth form college who tried to have affairs with the lecturers. The rest of them called them slags, slappers, but secretly they admired their cheek. The Captain was delighted with what he saw. Now he understood what they say about the mouth mirroring the female genitalia. Sophie's lips were plump and generous. He imagined that mouth wrapped around his cock . . . no, wait, slowly, slowly. She was staring at him slightly aghast, her lower lip dropped, so there was a wonderful suggestion of the tight wetness inside. Hmm.

'Where is the money?' he repeated.

'I don't know.'

'You tried to con me.'

231

'I didn't.'

'I know what's been going on.'

How much does he know? thought Sophie. Does he know who else was involved?

'You and that friend of yours.'

Yes. He did.

As Sophie trembled, awaiting her fate, it seemed to her that this was the worse blow. The idea that Mick would never be free was even worse than having no money.

'Now strip,' he said, before adding, 'Go on, take off your clothes.' She began with her sweater. It was tight and she had to wriggle to get her wrists free. And then she began on her blouse. She unbuttoned top down and the buttons seemed to sigh in defeat as she popped each one through its hold. She slid the blouse off her shoulders and went towards the chair, but he said no, he wanted it. He laid it over his crotch, where his erection was mounting.

'Your skirt next,' he said. The order had to be right. (Some women just have no idea.)

She looked up pleadingly at him. She wanted to stop. She felt ugly, foolish. There is nothing worse than being undressed in front of the dressed. She felt forlorn and lost, but at the same time, expectant. Something was going to happen.

'Go on,' he said. His voice was quieter now. He had wielded his power; now came the authority. He sat back and lit up a cigar. The smoke filled the room and her eyes reddened.

'Knickers down.'

She pulled her knickers lower, but he told her to hesitate at her knees, wait. She was to turn round and put her hands on the glass.

'I prefer the blue ones.'

Oh, Jesus, how did he know? Her face heated up when she realised the answer. Him, he had been stealing her lingerie, it was him. What had he been doing with her clothes? It made her shudder to think.

He pulled the material tight. Oh God, it felt wonderful.

232

The string dug deep into her. Her fingers were pressed cold on the pane, her pussy on fire. He pulled it this way and that, and she felt it cut into her, and it made each part of her come to life. Oh God, even now, even here, she felt so horny.

Then he relented. After a few seconds, but what felt like forever, he told her to step out of them. So now she was bare, in her birthday suit, as God, or the Captain, intended – and she had never felt so vulnerable in her life. It was as if, with her clothes, she had shed her skin; she had no defences left, nothing. And still her mouth was artificial red, red like some gash of blood.

She had no tricks up her sleeve, no last-minute resources to save her. She was at his mercy – and he seemed to have run out of that rare commodity.

'Turn round.'

She turned, giddily, a merry-go-round. Oh God, he wanted to look at her from every quarter, examine her from every angle. And, what's more, she wanted him to.

He couldn't believe how quickly she acquiesced, how keenly she complied. She was pretending to be angry with him, but she wasn't. It was clear – she was delighted.

'Show me everything.'

Sophie did as she was told. Perhaps that was all he wanted – to watch her. She could see the purple vein beating at his forehead.

She used to fantasise that she would go to the doctors and he would make her do that. She would go and see him about something totally non-sexual, totally non-glamorous, a bunion for example, and he would insist that she raised her top. He would come to her, stethoscope in hand, and press the cold metal against her tits, and she would stand there obediently, dumbly obsequious: What do you think of my breasts, doctor? Is everything OK? And the doctor would fall to her, fall on her, breaking all the rules about getting it on with the patients, because she was the most beautiful patient in the world. But in her fantasy there was none of the awkwardness, none of this burning heat that she felt now.

The whip was taken off the wall, and she bent over his knee. She squirmed over his broad thighs. With Tom she had acted the naughty schoolgirl; with the Captain she was that naughty girl all over again. He smacked her with his hands first, and her buttocks grew hot and stung like crazy. When his palms were sore, he used his very special equipment that he reserved for very special misdemeanours. As Sophie received her punishment, she couldn't help thinking that Jennifer would love this – and then she wasn't thinking about Jennifer any more, only that she wanted now to be fucked and fucked deeply. With each crack of the whip, her pussy contracted, and it took all the willpower she had to stop herself from crying out, 'Please do me now, for God's sake, screw me!'

He made her suck him. She fingered his balls, teasing them. As she did so, he muttered, 'Yes, it's wonderful to see them so up close,' but when she raised her eyes quizzically, he barked, 'Don't stop; suck me, suck me.' She could have bitten him if she wanted. But she didn't. Maybe he would let her off, if she let him get off. When he was near to coming, he told her to stop, and she knew that this wasn't going to be over quickly. The Captain was in no rush.

He gave her a dildo, said he wanted her to use it. God knows where he got it. It was bigger than both of hers. About double the size, and it had a little bit that stuck out, to fit against her clit. The machine hummed and she flicked the switch on and off with amazement. She felt the thing vibrate against her inner thigh. She thought of a time she had gone to stay with a friend with one and the friend's brother had found it. She waited for her commands. She was surprised how calm she was. She was perfectly in control. It was one of those rare times like when you drink a lot and feel distant from yourself, but not drunk, no not drunk.

'Fuck yourself with it, go on, you know you want to.'
'I will not.'

'I haven't got all day.'

She did want to – but she didn't.

She put it near, and then took it away. It shook too much, too frantically. She tried again, but the sensation seemed abrupt, too violent. She preferred the sensitive pads of her fingers. She could tell he was growing impatient.

'One minute,' she begged, but he strode over to her and told her to lie back.

She lay with her legs firmly together. He struggled to part them and then she felt the unmistakable touch of vibrator on her inner skin.

'You like?' the Captain breathed, hotly.

It felt weird at first – too cold, too mechanical – but then, as she felt it thudding out its little rhythm on her clit, vibrating her sex perfectly, she began to welcome the intrusion. It was so big, but she was letting it in, letting it up. Oh God, it began to feel very good indeed. He let go and the dildo flopped, so she picked it up. He sat at the foot of her and watched. He swiped his foreskin up and down. What a head he had, what a head.

She looked up at him, begging with her lips, those lipstick-kissed lips of hers.

'Say please.'

'Please!'

'Say you want me.'

'I want you.'

'What do you want me to do?'

'Fuck me.'

He took the dildo out of her but, before she could be disappointed, he inserted his thumb, and then he was flickering his tongue over her taut nipples. Her cries grew louder and louder and, instead of waiting for the touch, she was crying out between touches – not only at the pleasure itself, but in anticipation of the pleasure. And the more frequently she groaned and thrashed, the more he slurped and tended to those hot little points, the hottest points.

'You like this?'

'Yes.'

It was while this was going on that the purser walked in. Sophie didn't hear him at first. She was studying the Captain's face. He had such a rabid face, full of absorption, and then, suddenly, it was filled with surprise and glee.

'Don't mind me,' the purser said. 'I'll watch.' And the worse thing was that she couldn't stop, she really couldn't, and, regardless of who was there, she was coming faster than a steam train. She was tumbling, furious, like a fucking avalanche, wet and sticky all over the Captain's hot and thrusting cock.

As soon as he was out of her, Sophie jumped up, but he kicked her clothes out of her reach.

'You're our prisoner,' the Captain said to her. And she could see in him the small boy he once was – a small boy who had been bullied at school and had ever since plotted revenge.

'Did you take care of . . . the passenger?'

The purser nodded.

'We've taken the money off him. The police will pick him up – and her – tomorrow morning. They will be here at six a.m.'

'Good work,' the Captain said.

Still the purser hovered. 'You said I would get my reward.'

'Very well,' said the Captain.

'May I?'

The Captain reconsidered. 'Actually, I haven't finished with her yet. We'll have to share.'

The purser liked that idea a lot. He was out of his clothes faster than Sophie could take in the turn of events.

'At the same time, you mean?' she asked incredulously. This was sheer fucking folly.

'What a good idea,' said the Captain. 'I hadn't thought of that, but then, you are quite the little inventor, aren't you? What do you propose we do?'

Sophie shook her head mutely.

'How about him up one hole and me up the other? Is that the kind of scam that appeals to you, little missy?'

'No, no, that's impossible,' she insisted. But when she said that, the Captain was challenged. He wanted to show her that it was perfectly possible.

'How shall we do this?' he said contemplatively, and the slimy purser licked his lips in glee. They had to hold her down, both of them gripping her at once, to stop her squirming out of their hold like a wriggling fish. The purser, bless, took the more conventional route. Sophie was plunged on top of him but, before she caught her breath, the Captain was knocking at the tradesman's entrance. His fingers were prying and then in came his thumb. She could have handled that, of course, she could have put up with that; it was only when he tried to stuff in his cock that the problems began to arise. Sophie screamed as that immense dick (did she once think that it was cute?) and its decoration was inserted into her.

The Captain had torn up all his love poems. No more was she Cathy to his Heathcliff. Romance was dead – long live the fucking! She was a tiger that he had to tame, a wet sticky hole that he had to get inside. For him, for her, for everyone. He wanted to feel her clench around him, clench and slurp, and chew up his cock. He wanted to bury his cock in her arse and never come out again.

He was inside her, they both were inside her. Her body shook with each thrust, her white breasts quivered, and the nipples stood out in shock. Her body was a fucking wonder, and it was amazing what it could do.

Sophie didn't know where each sensation was coming from, but she was electrified. It was like being hit by a truck, but a fantastic rejuvenating truck, one that built her up as well as knocked her down. Two cocks! Two for the price of one. One making music in her cunt and the other setting her arse on fire. Couldn't breathe, couldn't even sigh, couldn't even tell them how much she was loving it.

'Give me more,' she managed to muster. 'I need this.' It may have been a kangaroo court, but its punishments

237

were the best. She would get caught any time, every time, if this was the result.

'Screw me, screw me harder,' she groaned, and it was a huge and wonderful accomplishment to simply spit out those words, to be able to speak while being shafted at all angles.

She felt the thin membrane – so thin – separate them. They were thrusting and she was dissolving into her own cunt, into her arse. She was made up of cracks that were filled with other people; they made her complete. They worked and crusaded up their respective holes and Sophie knew she had never felt so thoroughly fucked. Oh God, they were moaning, so heavily, so obscenely, and she was moaning as well. She thought she might snap in two. But soon she was past caring.

# Chapter Thirty-Five

When the Captain and the purser had done with her, the Captain ordered that she be tied to the mast. It was midnight and she had little hope of being discovered until the morning. And then, the humiliation would be untenable.

Where are you, Mick? was all she could think, over and over again. She wanted him more than anyone else in the world; she wanted Mick to come and rescue her.

She waited and then they came. Three sailors, three big boys, came to her. They pulled down the gag and she felt the muscles of her mouth collapse. If her cheeks hadn't hurt so much she could have kissed them all with gratitude. At long fucking last.

'Are you Sophie?' the shortest one asked.

As if she could be anyone else!

'Yes, why?'

'The Captain sent us here to see to you.'

'Oh God, thank God. Look, untie my hands first, and then my ankles – they're killing me.'

'No, I think you misunderstood . . .'

Another one completed the sentence.

'The Captain sent us here to give you a seeing to.'

Even as she protested that she didn't understand, she realised that she did. She understood well, and the crazy thing was that she was growing wetter and wetter at the prospect. But she had to pretend that she didn't want it. She had to put up at least some semblance of resistance. For goodness' sake, if they only knew how the prospect of having all three of them delighted her.

They were all young, eighteen or nineteen perhaps. One was very big, with a sturdy over-developed neck. Sophie remembered having seen him at the gym. One was bald, a complete egghead. Sophie had absolutely no recollection of seeing him at all, which was weird when you considered the size of the ship and the distinctiveness of his pate. The third, the youngest, had that I've-barely-started-shaving skin, and she remembered seeing him twice before: once, admiring the dolphins and, a second time, when the Captain had gone off on one about the drugs and he (and the rest of them) had been quaking in his little black boots.

'Hey, don't you work in the casino?' The egghead recognised her.

Sophie hung her head.

'I've seen you. You're a croupier, aren't you? I've seen you at the roulette table. Arrogant cow,' he added venomously.

'Not so arrogant now, are you?' sneered the biggest one. They were like three plotting witches. And she was the frog about to be baked.

'I'm not arrogant,' Sophie protested, somewhat arrogantly. 'At least, I don't mean to give that impression.'

'You think you are better than us, don't you? All the entertainment staff do, don't they? Keeping away from the sailors, the real workers.'

'That's not true,' she insisted. It wasn't true. On previous cruises, she had screwed sailors willy-nilly. It was only on this trip that she had been slightly more discriminating.

'What did you do wrong then?' the littlest one asked.

'Don't you know?'

Baldy walked round the side, eyeing her up. She wondered what he thought of her hips, her legs. She

240

almost felt sorry for him for not being able to see the flesh of her thighs, her buttocks (imagine that – she felt sorry for him for not seeing her everything!).

'Which rule did you break? Number seventeen, I bet. Have you been screwing the passengers? Naughty, naughty.'

Don't be daft, she thought. I've been breaking rule seventeen since before you were born. 'It wasn't that.'

'Weren't you the girl who was spying on the passengers?' piped the littlest.

'I wasn't spying. I just stumbled across them. How did you hear about that, anyway?'

'Walls have ears, darling,' the biggest said, happily.

'She's been fucking the cashier. I know that much.'

The other two men looked at the bald one in amazement.

'So, you are a lesbian? I'd love to see that . . .'

The idea evidently appealed to all three.

'I am not,' she said. 'I just happen to get on Moira. Get on *with* her, I mean. Anyway, that's not against the rules.'

'Yeah,' squeaked the little one, 'it must be much worse than that. The Captain usually lets people off with a reprimand for that.'

'What then? Tell us.'

Sophie couldn't resist. 'I cheated the house.'

'How much?'

'A lot. Enough to retire on. And more.'

He whistled admiration, raising his eyebrows. 'And then you got caught? That's fucking harsh.'

'We nearly got away.' Sophie couldn't resist boasting. 'But then ... well, the Captain recorded it, and so ... here I am.'

'Well, gambler, looks like your cards have come tumbling down.'

'Maybe,' she said. Admittedly, it did look that way, but any player knows that changes of fortune happen more often than is logical. She wondered what was going to happen. If not her life, then her body was in their hands.

241

'Let's have ourselves a game.'

He produced a deck of cards.

'Highest card wins. You win and you decide what happens next. All right? Pick a card.'

'You'll have to untie me first,' Sophie said. They looked at her suspiciously, as though, with that, she had come up with an escape plan, and that made her feel like she should. But she had no plans left. There was only one hope – the appearance of Mick on his white charger.

She saw that the youngest one had a semi-hard-on. And a very nice hard-on it was too.

'OK, let's get the rules clear first. I pick a card and then you pick a card. If I get lower then I am ... then you can decide what to do. If I get higher then I decide.'

'No, no! Each person goes separately for his turn. You have to play each of us.'

'All right. Ace is high,' she reminded him. 'And if it's a draw, we go again.'

'Who goes first?'

'Me,' she said.

She pulled a jack. A good card.

Waiting: what would he produce? He pulled out a card from the spread deck and paused before turning it over ceremoniously. It was a king. The boys cheered and clapped each other's hands; howzat.

'Best of three?' she proposed. *Shit, she should have made that part of the rules.*

The guy shook his head. He started to take off his clothes. But he didn't just take them off, he danced them off and draped them over the floor. Bloody hell, she thought, he was doing a striptease, right here, right now. Then, when he was down to his underpants, he came towards her, and the expression on his face was like, hey – who's the lucky lady? Sophie turned her head away so that he couldn't kiss her lips, but she liked the way he kissed her cheeks anyway. Then he was snuggling down, down her chin, her neck, and he was kissing her breasts over her clothes, then pulling her shirt up to get at them.

'Fucking hell,' he said, when her breasts were freed

from their casing. He turned to his mates, who were now staring open-mouthed. 'You won't believe these!' He rubbed his face in her tits and tweaked the rosy nipples.

'The Captain knows a good thing when he sees one,' he said, more to himself than anyone else, but the littlest one said 'Fuck yeah' anyway.

He slathered over her tits. He was playing up, performing for his friends.

'You just wait, guys, these are fantastic.'

'They may not get the chance.' Sophie grimaced. *Mick, where are you?* She remembered something Tom had said when she showed him the photos. He said, 'We are just your little pawns,' and she had joked and said, 'Yes, you are my little porns.' All that wasn't so funny any more. It was the Captain who was conducting this ship – any thoughts that she was in control were mistaken. She was as much a foot soldier as the rest of them. How could she have thought she would get away with it?

The guy took down his pants. He was a fair size. Long and thin, but with an alarming curve in the middle. Honest, his prick stood up like an S – S for Sophie. She was still stuck, weighed back, locked on the pole. There was no escape. He parted her legs, wedged them either side of the pole. She didn't know how he would approach her, fingers, tongue or straight in there. She didn't know what she wanted, but she knew she wanted him. His prick. His prick was first. He didn't want to look sentimental in front of his mates, and so he decided to plunge off, without checking, like a lemming off a cliff.

He entered her. He was curved but heavy too, his prick was enthusiastically pointing up her. She felt it slide through her, slide in her; she felt the shudders begin. He filled her up. He slid up and down her and she was relieved; so he wasn't such a brute after all, his bark was worse than his bite, and he wanted to give her some pleasure – no he wanted to show off to his mates that he could. Sophie resolved she wouldn't give him the satisfaction ... but, as the thrusting grew more and more insistent, and more and more spot on, she couldn't resist appreciating him.

'Oh yes, that's it, just like that,' she guided, and he heeded everything she said, because for him this was a competition, this was war, and he wanted to be the best. He too started to breathe faster, groans of pleasure, little bits of spit falling over her face, and he enjoyed that too, dribbling on her, and, truth to tell, she didn't mind it at all. And he was getting faster, and when she opened her eyes again, the other two men were closer to them than before, and they were mighty pleased with the spectacle.

'Go, Johnny, go, Johnny.'

The men were still watching, applauding, and she thought her eyes were going to pop out. She felt these tremors. And she was almost exploding at the friction. He moved very slowly, gently at first, but his cock was like a battering ram. Then he did something else. He got his hand and put it there, in front of her pelvis, like he really knew what he was doing, and he started vibrating her there, up and down on her clit, up and down, making the whole of her shake. And she picked her legs around him, like she was going up and down the pole at the fire station, and that's how it was. She felt like he was a flame and she was fighting, fighting to hose him down; and they sawed at each other until, until she couldn't stop herself from coming.

'It's my turn,' said the bald one.

They started arguing over it. So then the biggest one, still flushed and proud of himself after such a tremendous denouement, tossed a coin. Sophie watched as they clamoured. Heads or tails. You could, she thought to herself, go to it at the same time, one of you at my head and one of you at my tail. Would that not be a fairer way of resolving the situation? No? She said nothing.

It was decided. The youngest one would go next. The game began again. She picked a nine of hearts. A fair card. Waiting for him to uncover his, she shivered, half cold, half pleasure.

'Well?'

He had pulled a jack. A damn jack. The picture cards were all out tonight. He was looking decidedly sheepish.

'I don't know. I . . .'

'Come on,' said baldy. 'Time's running out.'

'I've got a girlfriend.'

The other one groaned. 'I'll go if you don't want to.'

'I do want.' He looked beseechingly at Sophie. 'Will you just touch me?'

'I – I don't know . . .'

'She always asks me if I've been with any other women. If I could say to her that I haven't, I honestly haven't been with a woman, I would appreciate it.'

What a sweetie!

'Well,' she said diplomatically, 'the whole point of this was that the winner decides what to do, and you are the winner, and if that is your decision then . . .'

He looked as pleased as Punch. Sophie stroked him up and down. She wanted to have sex with him, although she knew it was lunacy. What is it about human nature that wants what it shouldn't have?

She told him to untie her further, and again they looked worried, but then the biggest gave a what-the-hell shrug and freed her wrists and waist and she crumpled down. It took a few minutes to regain her composure, but they were patient now; they knew there was no hurry.

She gave him the best blow job she had in her. Truth was, it was the blow job she had been meaning to give Mick. It was the one she had been saving up. Sophie savoured the control, the power she had over him. His precious cock was in her mouth and she was the source of all his pleasure. This act, this very basic simple act, was the one he longed for. To have his cock there, suckled and nurtured and gulped down. However much male fantasies are dictated by society, this is a fundamental dream.

What man alive doesn't want his cock licked and nuzzled and taken complete and utter, warm and soothing, hot and sticky care of? Yet, thought Sophie, as she aimed to be the greatest, the best, the one he would talk about for as long as he lived, there was one such man who didn't want it.

He came, warm and creamy, in her mouth, in a series of ecstatic jolts. (She would have loved to have enjoyed that in her cunt. Oh well, maybe another time.)

'Thank you, thank you,' he sighed. And he thought it was the greatest, the best, and he knew he would talk about it for as long as he lived.

'My turn,' leaped up number three, the egghead. The sailor's tender display had clearly bored him rigid. Well, he was rigid at least.

The cards were splayed in front of her, for the final selection. Sophie's heart fell when she picked the seven. There was no card more mediocre than that.

She waited. He hovered around the pack with such seriousness, such careful deliberation, that it was as though he were defusing a bomb. Then, finally, he chose his card. They waited while he turned it over. It was also a seven.

'Hey,' they yelled.

'Play again,' he barked, and he was relieved when she didn't contest it. The next time, she pulled a queen and this time, he didn't mess, in he went, straight in there with his sticky fingers. He got a six.

The disappointment was so painful. He looked like a schoolboy who has just been told that Christmas is cancelled. The biggest one evidently thought it was quite funny that his mate was missing out. He started to undo the remaining ropes that held Sophie in place.

'What are you doing?' she asked.

'You've got off.'

'I win . . . that means I get to decide, doesn't it?'

'Yes. But . . .'

'Well then, we haven't finished,' she said. Egghead gazed at her incredulously.

'As the winner, I get to decide what I want. And I have a special request.' (She couldn't help thinking she was thirteen again and hanging around the DJs, requesting a

246

slow song so that she could have a smooch with one of the boys.)

'What do you mean?'

'It's my turn. And I want to see some male-on-male action.'

The three gazed back at her. Less the three witches, more the three stooges.

'What do you mean?'

'You promised me. And I've got nothing to lose. The police will be here soon. I've got no money, nothing.' (And the man I happen to love is hung like a butterfly, but that's beside the point.)

So the young one couldn't go with another woman? Well, he could go with a man. Sophie wanted to see him suck the biggest guy. She wanted to see his lips working, his jaws working. After all, he had such a pretty face, it would be a shame to waste it. The biggest one protested vehemently at first, but when he saw his mates were ambivalent about the whole project, he stopped making such a fuss. He wasn't homosexual, but he was a sailor, after all. And while he couldn't countenance being on the giving end, who was to say that he couldn't receive a bit of 'the other'?

Poor egghead looked beseechingly at Sophie. 'What about me?' he said. 'What do you want me to do? It was my turn, wasn't it?'

'You,' said Sophie, now thoroughly warmed up, 'will service me as I watch and enjoy.'

His kissing was slow and hesitant at first. It was kind of long and winding, like a car riding over a bumpy road. He took the lead as though he were born to do it.

In front of her, the youngest got down on his knees and leaned towards the biggest. And his cock was hard, and the youngest one took it in his mouth and worked it like he was born to do it. The biggest one started moaning and groaning – he couldn't help himself. Baldy stared in amazement but then worked again on Sophie, kissing, caressing and kneading her. Truth was, it was nice background noise. The little one's mouth was so busy, and his cheeks were full like squirrels storing nuts, and the biggest one pressed him down on the shoulders. And all the while the egghead was climbing his way into Sophie's space, between her legs, splitting her in two with his very fine cock. For such a bald gentleman, he was certainly hirsute down below, and his copious pubic hair astounded Sophie. She pulled him to her there, by the short and curlies, and felt him soar up her. She was sailing again. And she couldn't refrain from letting them know how good it felt.

The biggest let out this cry and then, before Sophie could give any more instructions, he pushed the littlest one to the ground and was tearing at his pants. And the littlest one buried his face in Sophie's feet and slobbered all over her toes. He was loving it. The biggest one opened him out and stuck in his erection, pressed it in, rammed it in, and the littlest one was such a good boy that he didn't shout or wail, although the pain must have been considerable; instead he let out this august moan of pleasure. Soon, he was pushing his arse back right into the biggest one's groans and they moved together like that, back and forward, in and out, as Sophie got on with her bald man.

She loved the feel of his head. She stroked and caressed his scalp and it felt incredibly rude, incredibly sexy. He was so entirely naked, and it was the same texture as his balls, yet less wrinkled, but the same softness, the same naughtiness.

The biggest one was speeding up, ramming the youngest. He couldn't help himself; it was wonderful there, tighter than a woman, narrower than anything he'd ever dreamed of. He was watching the vision in front of him, too, the view of his mate fucking Sophie, or rather Sophie fucking his mate, and she was an amazing sexy woman, a bitch yes, but amazing. As he drove harder and harder up his mate, he couldn't stop shooting her little grimaces of reproach – why was she enjoying it with his friend? Why was she making him do this? But he couldn't stop,

248

no he couldn't stop, and he didn't even want to even if he could.

Sophie writhed in ecstasy – see, she knew it! Risks pay off. Sometimes, you can't lose – and she hadn't lost this one. She was coming again. You would have done too.

The egghead fucked like a mule. And he was hung like one too. He took a long, long time, but his mates were encouraging him all the way, and she was bursting with orgasms, not for him, but for it. And she knew then for sure that size is not everything; it is the size of the emotions that count.

But where the hell was Mick?

# Chapter Thirty-Six

Mick was wandering around the maze of the ship. He felt like the ball-bearing in one of those games where you have to tilt the board to try to get the ball into the hole. He had fallen in love with Sophie. She seemed to have chained herself to the core of his brain and he had endeavoured to rescue her. And all the time, stuck in his head, like a comic book character, her clothes kept falling off.

He found her, tied to the mast. The purser was raising her skirt triumphantly, like you would a flag, and helping himself to dessert.

'What . . . what's going on?'

Mick slammed the purser in the chest. Much to his relief and satisfaction, for it had been ten years since he had been involved in a fight, the purser hit the deck. The punch hadn't hurt, but the shock factor had toppled him over. Sophie watched and she wanted to fuck him. It was regrettable but true; the display of violence had excited her. She wanted him to drag her by the hair into a cave (although the cave should be lit with aromatherapy candles and have a jacuzzi). He untied her, hugging her close as she flopped into him. She was numb between the legs. Comfortably.

'Jesus, what have they done to you?'

'I'm all right, I'm OK. What about you?'

'I'm all right. But they took all the money; it's gone.'

So now they were left with nothing. But she didn't care. She didn't care if they couldn't have the money, even if they couldn't have sex. Who cared about anything when he was next to her? A sea change had come over her. She had him; and it gave her a strange sense of satisfaction that she had chosen, out of everyone, to be with a poor man with a small cock – no one could accuse her of being a gold digger!

They started kissing, really firm, thank-God kissing, out there on the deck where they had first met. They were sucking each other's faces with the relief of finally getting there. He had a wonderful thick mouth, big firm lips, and he responded to her every move. Mick smelled of tobacco and maturity – not her dad, that's for sure, but safety and serenity. She wanted to alleviate his suffering. She wanted to be his angel.

'Mick, the police are coming. They will be here at six o'clock. That's in two hours.'

'One hour,' he corrected. 'It's already five.'

'What are we going to do?'

'We're going to do something we should have done ages ago. Come on.'

The Captain wasn't discovered until many hours later. The sailor, who had so long ago discovered the previous croupier nobbing a newly-wed groom, heard knocking in a cupboard near the Captain's quarters. There, he found the Captain bound and naked. He told his friends that the Captain's penis had shrivelled to the size of a peanut (and a small peanut at that). Delirious, the Captain was rambling with this huge beam on his face, like a baby been at the milk, drunken although he was sober, satisfied, sated, bewildered yet understanding. 'She's gone,' he murmured as they took him to the sanitorium. 'They tied me up and now she's gone. I love her, and now she's gone.'

* * *

Mick took Sophie back to his cabin. She was protesting all the way, but what was the point? Once they got there, he wrapped her in his muscular arms and then, when he was sure she was happy, he was all over her again. His kisses rained on her lips, her cheeks and her nose, even her eyelids.

'You're the best,' he said. 'I'm crazy about you. We should have done this ages ago.'

He ripped her clothes off. He tore them off, as though they were made of tissue paper. Like strongmen rip telephone directories – if she'd been wearing one that night, he would have gotten through it. She felt like all her other senses had closed down and she only had one sense, her great throbbing clit, and it was like a goddess she had to obey. It was that powerful, that masterful, she would have done anything to appease it.

He had this amazing intensity, this light in his eyes, in his face. She didn't have to do anything but lie back and be sucked and fondled. She just succumbed to the feelings, the throbbing passion. It was fantastic, mega-great. From the waist down she was on fire; she was occupied completely. She had had her doubts that, after having the two men, maybe one man wouldn't be enough for her, but Mick was everywhere at all times. Jesus, it felt as if he had more tentacles than an octopus.

After she had come three, no, four times that way, she begged him to fuck her. Please. For his sake, as well as hers. He said he couldn't. And even as she pleaded, she could see the light go out from him, and the return of the darkness.

'What if it were the other way round? What if I had really small boobs? Would you hate me?' she tried reasoning.

'No, because men are grateful for any kind of boobs they get.'

'And I'm grateful for any kind of cock,' she said and then corrected herself – 'At least I would be grateful for your cock.'

'I just want to give you pleasure.' He winced. 'And I

know I can't. Not with my cock. With my fingers, with my tongue, yes, but not with my cock.'

'I don't care what it's like – I just want to be close to you. I need to feel close to you. I love the oral and the touching but . . . it's not enough.'

'It is enough. It is.'

'Just let me suck you, how about that?'

Mick was racked with his inadequacy. What woman would look at a man with a small cock? Well, they might look, but what woman would want a man with a small cock?

'Please, Mick,' Sophie pursued. She knew about sympathy shags. She had done her fair share of them. What woman hasn't? The ugliest man in the disco who wept with gratitude and told all his friends. The old friend who was upset after his dog died and needed to snuggle up to someone on the sofa. She had done it for them without even loving them; she would do anything for him.

'Why don't you do me up the arse. It's a very tight space and I . . .'

'No. I can't. You'll hate me!'

'I promise it will be fine.'

'I . . .'

She was swaying him – she would try some more.

'You can trust me,' she said. He smiled again. He didn't need to say it – she said it for him: 'Yes, I know you never usually trust people who say that, but this time you know you can.'

'I know,' he said pensively, 'I know.'

'We've still got –' she consulted her watch '– thirteen minutes.'

'That's not long enough.'

'I am,' she said proudly, 'a fifteen-minute girl – twelve on a good night, and this is a good night,' she added. 'I swear to God, I won't look.'

'You don't have to swear to God.'

'I would like to. Listen. I, Sophie of unsound mind and body, do sodomy swear.'

Finally, he let himself laugh. 'Solemnly.'

'Sorry ... do solemnly swear not to look at Michael Salem's penis.'

'Not now,' he joined in.

'Not now, not ever.'

'From this day forward, Amen,' he said, and she noticed how wonderful his smile lines were.

'Ah men!'

'All right. Let's do it.'

He turned off the light. The room was in pitch-blackness, quite unlike anything that you get on land. Her senses acclimatised and compensated. Her hearing was thrust on to the centre stage, and everything rushed to fill the void left by the absence of sight.

Then she heard him undo his pants, and the swish as the material hit the floor. She held her breath and waited. She had never waited for anything like she waited for that. It wasn't even like waiting to see the next card: would it bring them to 21 or over? That seemed like nothing, trivial crap now.

He spread her legs with his fingers and then held her against the wall. She couldn't have got away if she had wanted to, and she didn't want to. Then he moved against her. Fuck. She thought he would crack her in two. His cock was so wide, so extensive that, rather than worry that she wouldn't feel it, she was petrified that she couldn't contain it. It won't go in there, she wanted to cry out. You can't park an aeroplane in a garage. But he was going to. Oh, yes, he was. He moved up her arsehole and played with her pussy, her clit, with his perfect fingers. She felt like a nut about to be cracked between his enormous thighs, impaled on his massive prick. He was so deep; it was like being excavated. She couldn't move. And then she could.

Some of the passengers later reported hearing a mad-crazy howling around that time. They came up with explanations about the seagulls, or even the pool cleaners, but some remained certain that a beast had been uncovered. Which was true in a way.

After that, Mick and Sophie shared a cigarette, and

looked at each other in amazement. It was like a dormant volcano had erupted. They both knew it, and they both were still a little afraid of it. And then he touched her breasts and she knew, forget the situation, forget the time, they had to do it again.

This time she saw it. He finally realised he had nothing to hide. And she couldn't really miss it; fuck, it was like a chopper. There was no extra skin. It was bare, like a frame, and she could really see every bit of it. She knew that once his dick was submerged in her, she would melt into his entire being. She was so lubricated, he didn't need to touch her. He kissed her fervently, yes, but it was her that took control. It was she – pushing his head from side to side, shoving up her T-shirt so that he could nurse there too. He was no spectator, he was a participator. And when he drove his dick inside her, she couldn't stop.

They fucked on the floor and she was screaming her orgasm from the moment he entered her. She buckled under him. He took her, he was on top, and she was spreadeagled under him, like a slave. She couldn't stop her pelvis from jerking.

She was straddling him and there was no room, but she worked up and down on him, so hot, so fucking burning with, not lust, but greed for him, for these sensations, to consume him in every fucking way. This was the only way she knew how to have him. If she could have turned herself inside out and let him fly into her, launch a submarine up her cunt, she would have.

Her buttocks heaved up and down on his thighs. He was waiting for her, waiting, and she didn't disappoint him. She felt the streaks of orgasm pass through her, the force mounting, the tension growing, surging, rising, and then, oh yes, the gorgeous release as he exploded inside her – the very moment she lost herself in him. It only took a minute at the most.

When she was younger, she used to be proud to see that she had fucked for over forty or fifty minutes – it seemed a sign of their prowess – but with Mick, she was amazed to see that everything had taken place in under a minute. Forget twelve minutes; it only took less than sixty seconds to feel that incredible. Not that she was counting, but time was of the essence just then.

Then they heard the alarm. The police were coming. Mick grabbed his bag, she grabbed her clothes, and they ran up to the top deck. Her heart was pounding.

From there they could see the flashing blue lights of the approaching police boat. It sped through the water towards them. She held Mick's hand. She wasn't going to tell him how frightened she felt. He probably knew.

'They are going to lock us up, and what about Josh? And . . . Oh Christ, I don't ever want to leave you.'

'We have to go now,' he said. He was tying his bag securely on to his back.

'How?'

'We'll swim for it.'

'I can't!' She was exhausted. Every orifice, every part of her had had him in, had been newly touched and brought to life again.

'I'll take care of you now. You did all the work before; now it's my turn. I'm the best swimmer on this ship, remember? Trust me.'

'But we've got nothing, no clothes, no passports, nothing.' She didn't have to say 'And all that money is gone'. He must have been as disappointed as she was. It was nearly over for them. There were passengers coming up the stairs, wondering at the noise. Some of them expected to see dolphins again, but instead saw the police-woman and her fat-boy sidekick on a motorboat coming towards them. It was not as pretty a sight, but still something to take photos of – for the folks back home.

Sophie trembled. She never thought it would end like this. All that hope about being the Bonnie and Clyde of the high seas, well it was all nonsense. They were failed criminals. Mick was rummaging through his rucksack. As she stared impatiently, he produced a large water-tight container, stuffed with small transparent bags. They were full of white powder.

'How much do you reckon we'll get for this?'

Sophie gazed at Mick in amazement.

'So it was you! They came aboard looking for that.'

'Who did?'

'The police. They searched –' she blushed '– all our rooms. They thought a member of staff had it!'

'Ah yes!' This time it was his turn to blush. 'The guy I got it from knew you. And I told him that I worked with you. He must have been caught.'

'Or it could have been a trap.'

'Whatever. It's worth thousands.'

'We'll go halves?'

'Honey,' he said, 'I'm not in it for the money. Not anymore.'

'You're taking the mick aren't you?'

'No, you're taking the mick, I'm in it for you.'

He picked her up and they went to the side of the ship, pressed against the bars, where they had first met. She looked him in the eyes and thought that they were too dark for his hair colour, but they were so very beautiful. She could stare into them for ever. But there wasn't time. The policeman was shouting through the loud speaker.

'Stop. You are under arrest.'

Everyone was looking at them. Sophie could see Moira in a skimpy nightdress and Jennifer and Tom holding hands in matching Noel Coward dressing gowns. They were waving at her. She could just make out their voices: 'Go, girl, go, girl.'

'Put down the bag. Put your hands over your head. Walk slowly away from the side,' the policeman ordered.

Mick helped her climb up the railings. One, two, three, jump. She didn't have time to think of anything. Pure reactions. And they went down, down, down, deep into the Caribbean Sea. It was warmer than she expected, but they plummeted so deep. He kept hold of her hand as they went down, and as they fought their way up. As she spluttered up to the surface, he was still alongside her, and she thought she heard him say, 'Actually, I've heard Florida's nice this time of year.'

BLACK LACE NEW BOOKS

*Published in July*

## SYMPHONY X
### Jasmine Stone
### £6.99

Katie is a viola player running away from her cheating husband. The tour of Symphony Xevertes not only takes her to Europe but also to the realm of deep sexual satisfaction. She is joined by a dominatrix diva and a bass singer whose voice is so low he's known as the Human Vibrator. After distractions like these, how will Katie be able to maintain her serious music career *and* allow herself to fall in love again?

**Immensely funny journal of a sassy woman's sexual adventures.**

ISBN 0 352 33629 3

## OPENING ACTS
### Suki Cunningham
### £6.99

When London actress Holly Parker arrives in a remote Cornish village to begin rehearsing a new play, everyone there – from her landlord to her theatre director – seems to have an earthier attitude towards sex. Brought to a state of constant sexual arousal and confusion, Holly seeks guidance in the form of local therapist, Joshua Delaney. He is the one man who can't touch her – but he is the only one she truly desires. Will she be able to use her new-found sense of adventure to seduce him?

**Wonderfully horny action in the Cornish countryside. Oooh arrgh!**

ISBN 0 352 33630 7

## THE SEVEN-YEAR LIST
### Zoe le Verdier
£6.99

Julia is an ambitious young photographer who's about to marry her trustworthy but dull fiancé. Then an invitation to a college reunion arrives. Old rivalries, jealousies and flirtations are picked up where they were left off and sexual tensions run high. Soon Julia finds herself caught between two men but neither of them are her fiancé.

How will she explain herself to her friends? And what decisions will she make?

**This is a Black Lace special reprint of a very popular title.**

ISBN 0 352 33254 9

*Published in August*

## MINX
### Megan Blythe
£6.99

Spoilt Amy Pringle arrives at Lancaster Hall to pursue her engagement to Lord Fitzroy, eldest son of the Earl and heir to a fortune. The Earl is not impressed, and sets out to break her spirit. But the trouble for him is that she enjoys every one of his 'punishments' and creates havoc, provoking the stuffy Earl at every opportunity. The young Lord remains aloof, however, and, in order to win his affections, Amy sets about seducing his well-endowed but dim brother, Bubb. When she is discovered in bed with Bubb and a servant girl, how will father and son react?

**Immensely funny and well-written tale of lust among decadent aristocrats.**

ISBN 0 352 33638 2

## FULL STEAM AHEAD
### Tabitha Flyte
£6.99

Sophie wants money, big money. After twelve years working as a croupier on the Caribbean cruise ships, she has devised a scheme that is her ticket to Freedomsville. But she can't do it alone; she has to encourage her colleagues to help her. Persuasion turns to seduction, which turns to blackmail. Then there are prying passengers, tropical storms and an angry, jealous girlfriend to contend with. And what happens when the lascivious Captain decides to stick his oar in, too?

**Full of gold-digging women, well-built men in uniform and Machiavellian antics.**

ISBN 0 352 33637 4

# A SECRET PLACE
## Ella Broussard
### £6.99

Maddie is a busy girl with a dream job: location scout for a film company. When she's double-booked to work on two features at once, she needs to manage her time very carefully. Luckily, there's no shortage of fit young men, in both film crews, who are willing to help. She also makes friends with the locals, including a horny young farmer and a particularly handy mechanic. The only person she's not getting on with is Hugh, the director of one of the movies. Is that because sexual tension between them has reached breaking point?

**This story of lust during a long hot English summer is another Black Lace special reprint.**

ISBN 0 352 33307 3

*To be published in September*

# GAME FOR ANYTHING
## Lyn Wood
### £6.99

Fiona finds herself on a word-games holidays with her best pal. At first it seems like a boring way to spend a week away. Then she realises it's a treasure hunt with a difference. Solving the riddles embroils her in a series of erotic situations as the clues get ever more outrageous.

**Another fun sexy story from the author of Intense Blue.**

ISBN 0 352 33??? ?

# CHEAP TRICK
## Astrid Fox
### £6.99

Tesser Roget is a girl who takes no prisoners. An American slacker, living in London, she dresses in funky charity-shop clothes and wears blue fishnets. She looks hot and she knows it. She likes to have sex, and she frequently does. Life on the fringe is very good indeed, but when she meets artist Jamie Desmond things take a sudden swerve into the weird.

**Hold on for one hot, horny, jet-propelled ride through contemporary London.**

ISBN 0 352 33??? ?

## FORBIDDEN FRUIT
### Susie Raymond
### £6.99

When thirty-something divorcee Beth realises someone is spying on her in the work changing room, she is both shocked and excited. When she finds out it's sixteen-year-old shop assistant Jonathan she cannot believe her eyes. Try as she might, she cannot get the thought of his fit young body out of her mind. Although she knows she shouldn't encourage him, the temptation is irresistible.

**This story of forbidden lusts is a Black Lace special reprint.**

ISBN 0 352 33??? ?

To find out the latest information about Black Lace titles, check out the website: www.blcklace-books.co.uk or send a stamped addressed envelope to:

Black Lace, Thames Wharf Studios,
Rainville Road, London W6 9HA

Please note only British stamps are valid.

# BLACK LACE BOOKLIST

**Information is correct at time of printing. To avoid disappointment check availability before ordering. Go to www.blacklace-books.co.uk**

All books are priced £5.99 unless another price is given.

**Black Lace books with a contemporary setting**

| | | |
|---|---|---|
| THE TOP OF HER GAME | Emma Holly<br>ISBN 0 352 33337 5 | ☐ |
| IN THE FLESH | Emma Holly<br>ISBN 0 352 33498 3 | ☐ |
| SHAMELESS | Stella Black<br>ISBN 0 352 33485 1 | ☐ |
| TONGUE IN CHEEK | Tabitha Flyte<br>ISBN 0 352 33484 3 | ☐ |
| SAUCE FOR THE GOOSE | Mary Rose Maxwell<br>ISBN 0 352 33492 4 | ☐ |
| INTENSE BLUE | Lyn Wood<br>ISBN 0 352 33496 7 | ☐ |
| THE NAKED TRUTH | Natasha Rostova<br>ISBN 0 352 33497 5 | ☐ |
| A SPORTING CHANCE | Susie Raymond<br>ISBN 0 352 33501 7 | ☐ |
| TAKING LIBERTIES | Susie Raymond<br>ISBN 0 352 33357 X | ☐ |
| A SCANDALOUS AFFAIR | Holly Graham<br>ISBN 0 352 33523 8 | ☐ |
| THE NAKED FLAME | Crystalle Valentino<br>ISBN 0 352 33528 9 | ☐ |
| CRASH COURSE | Juliet Hastings<br>ISBN 0 352 33018 X | ☐ |
| ON THE EDGE | Laura Hamilton<br>ISBN 0 352 33534 3 | ☐ |
| LURED BY LUST | Tania Picarda<br>ISBN 0 352 33533 5 | ☐ |
| LEARNING TO LOVE IT | Alison Tyler<br>ISBN 0 352 33535 1 | ☐ |

---------------✂-----------------

Please send me the books I have ticked above.

Name .........................................................................

Address .........................................................................

.........................................................................

.........................................................................

......................... Post Code .........................

Send to: **Cash Sales, Black Lace Books, Thames Wharf Studios, Rainville Road, London W6 9HA.**

US customers: for prices and details of how to order books for delivery by mail, call 1-800-805-1083.

Please enclose a cheque or postal order, made payable to **Virgin Publishing Ltd**, to the value of the books you have ordered plus postage and packing costs as follows:

UK and BFPO – £1.00 for the first book, 50p for each subsequent book.

Overseas (including Republic of Ireland) – £2.00 for the first book, £1.00 for each subsequent book.

If you would prefer to pay by VISA, ACCESS/MASTER-CARD, DINERS CLUB, AMEX or SWITCH, please write your card number and expiry date here:

.........................................................................

Please allow up to 28 days for delivery.

**Signature** .........................................................................

---------------✂-----------------